ONE
Last Breath

Book 2 of the Rescued Series

One Last Breath

Copyright© 2022 by Lyndsay Marie
All rights reserved.
Published by: Lyndsay Marie, April 7, 2022

The characters and events portrayed in this book are entirely fictitious. Any similarity to real persons, living or dead, is coincidental and not intended by the author. That means every bit of it is entirely made up, and any resemblance to real life is purely coincidental.

No part of this book may be reproduced, or stored in a retrieval system, or transmitted in any form or by any means, electronic, mechanical, photocopying, recording, or otherwise, without express written permission of the publisher and author.

Cover re-design by: Staci Hart
Editing: Sandra at One Love Editing
Printed in the United States of America by Amazon™ POD services

Lyndsay Marie

If you want to read my other books, keep up with
new releases, or buy signed paperbacks, check out
my website—

www.AuthorLyndsayMarie.com

Visit me on Amazon —
https://www.amazon.com/author/lyndsaymarie

"I'm pregnant."

"You're what?" I shot off the couch.

"You heard me. I said I'm pregnant! We're having a baby!" Rowan screeched into my ear.

"I know I heard you, but normal people say hey or hi when someone answers the phone."

"Since when have you known me to do anything normal?"

"Valid point. So holy shit, Rowan! You're pregnant? How did that happen?"

She laughed. "Un, I think we both know how it happened."

"You know what I mean. I think we both know *how*." It was a huge surprise—I know it had to be to them too. The last time Rowan had announced she was expecting a baby was at hers and Wes's wedding reception around this time last year. Unfortunately, not a month later, they had to call everyone they knew and tell them that she had unexpectedly lost the baby. She and Wes were devastated. Hell, I think we all were. It was the second time she'd been through that. I didn't think she wanted to try again.

My mom barged into the room, carrying a cardboard box in her arms. "Who's pregnant?" she blurted out.

I covered the phone mouthpiece. "Shh!"

Rowan laughed. "That must be your mom. Tell her I said hi."

I uncovered the phone. "Sorry, Rowe. She walked right in on that one."

"No worries," Rowan said. "It's okay if she knows."

Mom waved me off. "And I'm walking right back out. We'll catch up later. Tell Rowan congratulations." Then she disappeared from the room without so much as another word. Not knowing all the details of the latest gossip, even if it involved my life, would eat at her until she knew.

I put my attention back on my BFF. "Mom says congrats. Ah! I'm so happy for y'all."

"Thank you, thank you. Speaking of your mom, how's the big move going? Y'all getting everything settled?"

I dabbed away a tiny bead of sweat dripping down my temple with the edge of the sleeve of my T-shirt, careful not to wipe away my foundation. Someone could've at least picked a better month than June to force a family to uproot their lives.

"If by move you mean me living with my parents against my free will in my thirties? Then

I'd say it's going swimmingly well. Everything is just fine and freaking dandy."

One of us laughed. Hint: it wasn't me.

"Aw, come on, Sugar. Don't sound so excited. Your parents are amazing people!"

"Indeed they are. Why don't you come live with them, then?"

"Oooh, no, I didn't say I wanted all of that."

"Hmm. Exactly." I gulped down water from my Las Vegas souvenir bottle. "But you're right. They are amazing…from across town. Not across the house."

"They just moved in. It can't be *that* bad."

"Yet," I said, as if to finish off her unspoken words. She held back a giggle. I was just glad someone found humor in all of this because I, for one, was not a fan of having my life unexpectedly turned upside down. Expecting the unexpected at work was one thing—that was part of the job—but having my consistent and organized life in complete disarray was another.

"Don't worry your pretty little head. It won't be for forever."

"Yeah, right. It doesn't feel like it." Even though she couldn't see me, that didn't stop me from sticking my tongue out at her. "That still doesn't mean I want to *live* with them…*again*." Unfortunately, that had been my—hopefully temporary—reality. There was a reason I'd moved out at seventeen, and it hadn't been because I'd been swept off my feet by Prince Charming on a white horse. It was because my mother drove me up a damned wall with all of her demands on me to give one hundred percent, one hundred and ten percent of the time.

Now here we were full circle damned near fifteen years later. Everything happened so fast. Less than four weeks ago, my parents received a certified letter, hand-delivered by a local law enforcement officer. The letter declared domain over all of their land and the house they'd purchased just a few years ago. They'd bought the acreage and farmhouse with the intent of one day turning it all into an actual farm with livestock and gardens. Mom's dreams went up in smoke, Dad lit up a smoke, and the entire process from appraisal to paycheck took one solid month—a whole thirty days. Hiring a lawyer to fight the process would have cost them everything they'd owned, regardless. To them it hadn't been worth the fight.

So, the three of us—Dad, Mom, and myself, with the help of a couple of neighbors—had spent the past few days moving most of their things out of their big house and into a storage unit. Their necessities came with them here.

"True, but hopefully time will fly by, and you'll be out on your own again soon enough, or they'll take that fat check they got and buy another farm somewhere else."

"Who knows. You know how damned picky my mother is. Look how long it took them to find that place."

She sighed. "True. Good luck, I guess."

"Thanks. So, you're gonna have a baby! This is exciting."

"Oh, it is. We're pretty ecstatic. Scared shitless too."

"I bet you are. It'll work out this time."

"We sure hope so."

"Well, give me all the details, I need to know everything."

"There's not much to tell. So far, not very many people know. We've had to keep this one under wraps for a while for obvious reasons."

"I don't blame y'all. Wait. What do you mean for a while? How far along are you?"

"Umm, well—"

"Spit it out, Rowan."

"Like five months?"

"Five months! Are you shitting me right now? You've been pregnant for five months?"

"Yes?"

"And you didn't freaking tell me?"

"I'm so sorry."

Five months? Insane! I could never keep a secret like that for that long.

"So, when are you due?"

"October."

"I can't believe you kept this from me for this long!"

"I know, I know. I'm sorry," she huffed into the phone. I could picture her physically relaxing, glad to get the weight of that secret off her shoulders. "We were just being extra, extra cautious. I hated making all those phone calls last time. We wanted to wait until I was well into my second trimester before telling more people."

"I understand, but still."

"Trust me. I've wanted to tell you since we first found out, but I didn't want to jinx anything, ya know?"

"No, I get it. It's just crazy! So what are you having?"

"Well, we don't know. We're going to let it be a surprise."

"What? Ohmigod! How am I supposed to baby shop if I don't know what you're having?"

"The same way we are. We're just gonna wing it."

"Ugh, Rowan! Fine. Then at least tell me what made you decide to call and tell me now?"

"Well, I mean, I'm pretty far along, so I think it's safe to finally start tellin' people. Plus, we'll have to start planning for a baby shower, and I'm gonna want your help."

"Ah-ha! I knew you had a motive for calling me. When were you thinking about having it?"

"I don't know. Things have been so chaotic here. That's why I want your planning expertise."

"Hmm. Well, you're due in October, so sometime in early September? That way it won't be too cold, yet, and it still gives folks plenty of time to plan to attend."

"Good enough for me. We'll work out an exact date later. I need to check Wes's calendar."

"Aw. I can't wait to help you! I'm so glad you still need me. But hey, at least y'all have your anniversary trip coming up. Now y'all can celebrate and relax a little."

"That's another thing," she huffed. "We can't go."

"What do you mean you can't go? Why not? Y'all have had this planned since your wedding."

"I know. I'm super bummed, but because of how my last pregnancy went, *neither* of my doctors—emphasis on neither since Wesley has proclaimed himself to be one of them—wants me to do any traveling. Not even by car. So that kind of put a damper on our anniversary trip coming up since it requires driving *and* flying."

"Well, shit. Are y'all just gonna reschedule it, then?"

"That's the other thing. We can't. Everything is paid for and insured, but only for up to a year from the time of purchase. Either way, the flights and resort reservations are gonna expire if we don't use them. It'll all go to waste because everything expires soon."

"That's some bullshit. So you're just gonna lose all that money you've already spent, plus miss out on the whole vacation?"

"Not unless someone takes our place."

"Why does it sound like you're trying to hint at something, Rowan?"

"Because I am?" she said in a playful tone. "I'm offering you the trip. All of it—airfare, private resort, bungalow on the water. Yours for the taking."

"*Me*?" I practically yelled at her.

"Yes you."

"Rowan. No way. I can't—"

"Yes you can. Katie, you need it more than anyone else. You're a damned workaholic, and I know you haven't been on vacation since when? Vegas? How long ago has that been now?"

Too long. "Whatever. I'm not taking it, and I'm damned sure not going on a trip like that by myself."

"Oh, come on! You can do it. I have faith in you. Live a little."

"No. Absolutely not." Not only did I rarely take time off from work to do anything fun, but I damned sure had never vacationed alone, and out of the country, no less.

"It'll be fun. An all-inclusive resort with bottomless adult beverages, daily massage at your fingertips, white sandy beaches? Please? You'd be an idiot not to go. Besides, I know you're available for the next two weeks because you took time off to help your parents move."

Shit. "What's your point?"

"My point is it sounds to me like you don't really have any excuses not to go. And I know you could use a little *me* time. Take a damn break. Hell, go and do something wild like have sex with a stranger."

I scoffed at her suggestion. "I do not need to get laid." *Yes I do.* That was beside the point.

"Fine. Don't go get laid. Just go and have some fun then. Jeez. Something, anything. Please, for the love of God. You need a vacation, and I don't want this to all go to waste."

Unbelievable. "Trust me, I know I need a vacation, but this is extreme. What about Wesley's brother, Warren? Did y'all ask him if he wanted it?"

"We did." She cleared her throat. "He won't take it either."

"Why not?" Seriously? I could not be the only person either of them knew who could go.

"Work. What else?" I could practically hear her rolling her eyes.

How sad was it that my best friend had to literally beg me to take her place and go on vacation to the Caribbean?

"Ugh. At least give me time. Let me think about it. I make no promises."

"Seriously?" she squealed into the phone. "Okay, okay, fair enough. But don't think too long. Plane leaves Monday."

"Monday? Rowan! That's like less than two whole days!"

"Yeah? So. What's your point? What else are you going to do with your time off? Work?"

Other than helping my parents get settled, my excuses fell short. "Nothing."

"Exactly. Please?"

Well, shit. Rowan had me backed into a corner. "Fine. Send me the details."

"Eeek. So you'll go?"

"Maybe."

"Fair enough. I'll email everything to you now. If you decide you want it, let me know, and we'll get it all set up for you and send you the confirmation."

We said our goodbyes and hung up the phone. I leaned back and kicked my feet up on the coffee table while I could still get away with it. My mother would have had a shit-fit if she knew I'd been propping my feet up on my great-grandmother's antique handmade table.

I glanced down at my phone that dinged with a new email notification.

Rowan.

She'd wasted no time. Then again, if I were going to do this, I needed to decide fast.

"Wow," I said out loud to myself as I scrolled through and read over the information she'd sent me. This wasn't my first time seeing pictures of the resort because I'd helped Rowan pick it out, but it was the first time I'd really taken the time to comb over the website.

After analyzing all of the details of the inclusivity and the amenities the resort had to offer, a week at a place that resembled my idea of paradise didn't sound so crazy after all. Cold drinks, warm sun, soft sand, sapphire-blue water as far as the eye could see, free food and bottomless drinks around the clock? Not to mention the option for a daily massage on the beach?

Anyone else in their right mind wouldn't have hesitated or even given a second thought to this fantasy vacation. So why me? Because that's just who I'd always been—the overplanning, overthinking, overprotected, straight and narrow, no-risk-taking one. As I considered actually going, I'd never been more convinced that I was going out of my mind.

I scrolled to the bottom of the email and realized Rowan had already filled in the itinerary with my name. The next email that came through from her was my flight information.

Looked like I was going to St. Lucia.

TWO
Katie

"Mom, seriously, you didn't have to do this."

"Oh yes I did. Don't think for one minute that I was going to let some stranger in a random vehicle that I know nothing about take you to the airport."

"No, of course not." She'd insisted on taking me. It was a sweet but kind of a ridiculous gesture. I wanted to take an Uber, but she refused to "allow" me.

"Please be safe. You know your dad read over every statistic about missing persons and sex traffickers at these all-inclusive places—even the fancy ones. He almost didn't want you to go."

I rolled my eyes but only enough for me to feel the muscles strain. 'Cause if she'd actually caught me in the act of rolling my eyes, I'd have risked boarding the plane with a handprint on my cheek. "I'll be in the Caribbean, not Mexico."

"Alone, mind you."

"I'll stay on the resort property. It's not that bad there." *I hope.* It seemed safe enough from what I'd read.

She pulled up to the curb at the drop-off zone and put her car in park, not a minute too soon. "We just worry about you. Plus, I think the reality and stress of all of this mess with the farm is starting to sink in. One of these days, I hope it'll be you dropping me and your father off at the airport for some time off of our own. I can't remember the last time we took a vacation."

At least I knew where I got it from.

I leaned over the middle console and hugged her. "We'll start planning y'all's trip as soon as I get home."

We said our goodbyes as I made my exit. I grabbed my luggage out of the trunk, and when I closed the lid, I signaled to my mom that I was good to go.

Once I checked my suitcase and passed through security, I made my way to the gate and sent Rowan a text with a selfie, reassuring her that I was at the airport and hadn't backed out at the last minute. She replied almost immediately, telling me to enjoy myself and to make sure to take a ton of pictures. Then I tucked my phone away in my purse and sipped on my iced cinnamon vanilla latte as I waited to board flight one of two.

Rowan was right; I needed this. Things had been lonely in Memphis ever since she and Chloe had both moved away.

First, I'd lost Rowan to Wesley. Going from seeing her upward of six days a week to not having her around at all was a major adjustment. But she was so ridiculously happy with him, it was impossible to be mad at her for leaving her life in Memphis behind for a better one.

And Chloe? Good Lord, that girl. She'd run off and left me to be with Daniel, and now they had recently gotten engaged. Though, that was no surprise considering they thought they'd already been married once. *That one weekend in Vegas was an interesting one, to say the least.* Hell, I wouldn't have put it past them to do it again for real this time and sooner rather than later.

Then there was me—last woman standing. Unfortunately, I didn't have the kind of luck those two had. My love life had feast or famine and revolved around the same toxic person for way too many years that I'd never get back.

Justin had been that one guy that, no matter how hard I tried, or how shitty he had treated me, or how many times we had fought and argued, I could never seem to let him go. Over the course of almost five years, we'd spent just as much time together as we did broken up. The last time being right before Rowan's wedding. While we didn't technically get back together as a couple afterward, we did hook up a handful of times over the next few months. What had once taken me months to muster up the courage to end, because I could never seem to find the balls to be the one to end things, took him less than thirty seconds. He had the gall to tell me that hooking up had been a huge mistake, all while still lying naked beside me in my own damned bed. It was then that I'd realized he just had to have the last word. He couldn't handle me breaking up with him.

Now just thinking about him made my stomach sour.

Thankfully, it had been several months since I'd last seen or heard from him. This go round had been the longest we had ever gone without communication. I had no doubt in my mind it was only because I had finally convinced myself to block his number in my phone—out of sight, out of mind. I had always wondered why he'd never shown up unannounced. My hope was that he was done-done with me this time.

Being forever single had never been my life's goal, though it certainly had its perks. I didn't have to check in or keep up with anyone else. I didn't have to worry about where someone was or who they were with, if they were thinking about me, or if they were even alone. I'd always thought I'd be married by now, have a kid or two, my own house with a yard across town. I especially missed having a warm, masculine body to cuddle up to, especially at night.

Maybe Rowan was right. Maybe I did need to get laid. This could be the perfect opportunity— hook up with a local, then leave like nothing had ever happened. That didn't mean I had to jump on the first dick I laid eyes on.

As easy as it was for me to kill time sitting at the terminal wallowing around in self-pity, thinking about my failed love life, I refocused my attention on the fact that I was less than an hour away from being on a plane to what would be the start of the week of my dreams.

♡♡♡

After a missed connecting flight due to my detour through the women's restroom, an unexpected extra security check of my carry-on bag, and two cab rides later—because the first car had broken down—I'd finally arrived at the resort long after the sun had set.

Miss first sunset? Check.

I stood at the counter, gripping my suitcase handle, more than ready to get the key to my room so I could unwind with a much-needed drink and maybe a soak in the tub. Thirty minutes later, the young and incredibly handsome-looking, very tan man at the front desk handed me back my driver's license, along with the key to the bungalow, a welcome packet, and a flirty smile.

He has potential, I thought to myself. Maybe he'd be the one to break my celibacy streak.

"Would you like me to show you and your guest around to your suite, miss?"

"Oh, no, that's not necessary. I'm here alone. Thank you, though." We were off to a great start: single woman comes to vacation in paradise alone. *Lame.*

His smile faded as he raised an eyebrow. "All right, then let me walk you through the grounds and point you in the right direction. The property and all the pathways are lit up, but it's still very dark around here at night."

"Fine. Yeah, okay," I conceded to his request with one of my well-practiced beauty pageant smiles plastered across my face. "That'd be great. Lead the way."

Whether he was being sweet or just doing his job, the least I could do was let him show me where to go so I could finally hide away for the rest of the night and plan out the next five days.

He rounded the desk and grabbed my suitcase from me, wheeling it behind him. "Follow me."

We exited the cool, dry air of the main lobby and stepped out into the warm, balmy night. The smell of salt water in the air made up for the loss of my missing the sunset. It renewed my anticipation of what had yet to come.

The man stopped on the sidewalk just short of a long boardwalk and tilted my suitcase toward me. "If you go right up this walkway, follow it all the way to the end. Your suite is the very last one at the end on the right. I'm more than happy to take you there if you'd like."

I grabbed the handle from him. "Thank you for everything, but I'll take it from here. Maybe next time."

"Yes, miss. If you need anything, ring the desk. Concierge services are available twenty-four hours. All of the information is in your folder." He bowed dramatically, winked, then turned around and strolled off into the night.

The night was eerily quiet, save for the tinging sound of steelpan drums that drifted from somewhere on the mainland and the noise of low-rolling ocean waves gently lapping against the wooden posts that held these tiny villas above water. Who knew a place like this really existed? I'd only ever seen them in the movies or in a magazine. Now here I was making my way to my own.

I walked along the boardwalk over the water, passing by the other bungalows—some were completely darkened, just as black as the night. Others were lit up like Christmas on the inside. Each of them was unbelievably amazing.

"Last one on the right," I reminded myself out loud, not believing that I was here alone. Once I reached the very end, I double-checked the number on the door to the one on my key tag. "Here we go."

I unlocked the door, and crisp, cool air blasted me when I pushed the door open. The wood-planked floors creaked underneath my feet as I stepped inside. The suite was one massive room divided into separate living, sleeping, and dining spaces, each separated by huge area rugs and strategically placed furniture. There were wall-to-wall windows, covered only by sheer white curtains, flanking the back patio door. In the middle was a giant king-sized bed fit for royalty, and closest to me was a small, overstuffed couch and two side chairs. The room smelled faintly of ocean water, freshly washed linen, with a hint of something fruity. The lights were off except for the lamp on one of the bedside tables.

I rolled my luggage over to the beautifully made-up bed and tossed it onto the middle, along with the welcome folder. That's when I'd spotted a fully stocked bar with a built-in wine rack across the room near the back door. "Bingo."

I walked over and picked up a bottle from the rack, flipped it around, and as luck—or Rowan—would have it, it was my favorite brand. I swiped a long-stemmed glass off the shelf, and with bottle and glass in hand, I headed straight for the bathroom.

I pushed through the double doors, and boy, was my intuition right about this place—pictures didn't do it justice. Sitting front and center was a showstopping, freestanding soaker tub. One that could easily fit two people. Next to it was a walk-in shower and a bedroom-sized closet that rivaled my own. Well, what *was* my closet but had since been taken over by my parents.

I turned the water on full blast. As the tub filled, I released my hair from its ponytail and shook it loose. There were very few times in life that I'd let my hair down. This was one of them.

Steam quickly surrounded the entire room. I scanned over an assortment of bath supplies displayed on a small wooden table beside the tub—salts, soaps, bubbles, oils—and settled on a hefty squirt of some fancy-looking iridescent, blue bubble bath.

The tub filled up, and I stripped out of my clothes, leaving them in a pile on the floor. With my bottle of wine in one hand and glass and a corkscrew in the other, I carefully stepped into the tub and slid into the water, sinking up to my neck into a thick layer of foam. I didn't even bother to put my hair up, just let it sink into the water. What was the point? Half-wet, all-frizzy hair had been the last thing I was worried about. Nobody would see me like this anyways.

Popping the cork on the wine, I poured myself a hefty glass, filling it almost to the brim, and debated on just drinking straight from the bottle. It had been way too long since I'd felt this relaxed. For the first time since I could remember, I didn't have this intense pressure to be on the go or impressing someone and doing something. No stress, no worries, no one to answer to. Just me, my wine, and my bath.

I turned the faucet off with my toes and listened to the sound of tiny bubbles popping all around me.

Okay, now it was way too quiet.

The bathroom had at least twelve-foot ceilings with three huge skylights overhead. This one room alone was stunning, and I was about to test out the acoustics. I topped off my glass, then without hesitation, I started singing one of my favorite songs by Adele. After a few notes, I really started belting it out. *Thanks, mom and Dad, for all those years of singing lessons.*

Just as I was getting into my song, the sound of a throat clearing had interrupted my concert for one. The sound caused me to let out a yelp while simultaneously dropping my freshly refilled glass of wine straight into the tub. My arms flew around my chest, not sure what I was trying to cover up or how much of me could even be seen, because let's face it, there wasn't much for me to hide. That was one department where I hadn't been gifted.

"What the—you scared the ever-loving shit out of me!" I practically drowned trying to sit up, slipping in the soapy water. Thank the Lord I didn't have to run, because I was naked and had nowhere to go.

Lyndsay Marie

Gradually, my intense panic subsided as recognition of the person standing just a few feet away hit, and my heart rate almost returned to a rhythm sustainable with life. "Wha—what are *you* doing here?" I asked with a shaky voice.

My empty wineglass bobbed in front of me in the now red-tinged bathwater. I could not believe my eyes as I sat gawking in disbelief at the figure practically filling up half the bathroom doorway. A man who had clearly not been invited.

Warren. *Un-fucking-believable*. Of all the people in the world, it just had to be Warren. There was absolutely no denying it was him—even if I'd only been around him a handful of times, not to mention he'd always been fully dressed. Yet here he was—very real and *very* half-naked.

All I wanted to do was slip beneath the water of my wine bath and not come up until he was gone. But oh my Lord, he was still one of, if not the sexiest, man I had ever seen. A mix between Henry Cavill and Nick Bateman. *So much for not wanting to jump on the first dick I laid my eyes on.*

He wasn't even supposed to be here, yet there stood Warren Miller…tall, hands on his hips like he was going to punish me, wearing only a fluffy white towel wrapped tightly around his waist. Though, judging from how low it hung on his hips, I guess he could have had on swimming trunks, but I couldn't tell. His ensemble left little to the imagination, which, at this point, had mine running wild.

His dark hair was wet and tousled, like he'd just climbed out of a pool and ruffled his hands through it. Tiny drops of water dripped from the ends of his hair, down his neck onto his bare chest, creating a path over every flexed muscle of his stomach, down, down, down along his happy trail, until it disappeared into the front of the towel.

I bit my bottom lip, letting my eyes wander a touch further south, lingering just a little too long, apparently, because Warren cleared his throat again. My eyes snapped back up. *Whoops.*

He shook his head, keeping his posture stoic and his facial expression set in stone, completely unreadable—just like I'd remembered how he'd been when I'd met him for the first time in Chicago last year—all serious and businesslike.

Gah. What a grinch.

He could be pissy all he wanted. Personally, I'd found his dry personality to be silly and unnecessary. I had to chew on the inside of my cheek to keep from smiling. Though the wine helped…or hurt, since he didn't have a sense of humor, and I had a hard time reeling mine in due to my lowered inhibitions.

"Katie," he finally spoke. "It's nice to see you again."

"Is it, though?" I guessed from his perspective it could have been nice to see me in this vulnerable disposition—butt-ass naked, up to my neck in a soaker tub. I'd just started to feel the effects of my merlot when intimidating-as-hell Prince Not-So-Charming killed my buzz and party for one. If he thought it was nice to see me, he sure as hell didn't let it show.

His expression still hadn't changed—not a smile, smirk, or hint of amusement anywhere on his face. Just *blah*.

His jaw ticked. "You want to tell me what's going on here?"

"I'm…taking a bath and drinking wine. Or was." I gestured to the water in front of me.

"It would seem so."

"You want to explain why you're in my bathtub?"

"Your bathtub? This isn't *your* bathtub; it's mine. What are you even doing here, anyway? I'm supposed to be here *alone*."

He stared down on me. I felt like I was shrinking by the millisecond. All I wanted was for that big, beautiful, soaker tub to open up and swallow me whole.

"Interesting. I was under the same impression."

Judging by his flat tone, he was not amused by any of this, either. Our so-called friends had clearly set us up, and I wasn't entirely sure how I felt about it. I mean, it *was* kind of nice knowing I wouldn't be here alone, but on the flip side? I'd be here with *him*. And I'd be damned if his strong and deep voice, or his dominating presence didn't have me squeezing my thighs together, as my body betrayed me.

"To be fair, I thought this was going to be my tub for the next week." I really had no idea what was going on anymore. Not only had Warren walked in on me belting out one of my favorite Adele songs at the top of my lungs, but somehow what was supposed to be a *me* vacation had quickly turned into an *us* getaway. *Note to self: kill Rowan, and anyone else involved.*

He shoved off the doorframe and walked over to the towel hanging across the room. I'd have been lying if I said I hadn't checked out his ass. He pulled it down and offered it to me, all while looking at the floor, as if to avoid seeing me naked.

"Thank you," I said, taking the towel from him, my voice sounding small as he towered over me.

"You're welcome."

"Just so you know, no one had mentioned to me that this trip came with a travel companion. When I left Memphis, I was supposed to be the only one here."

"So was I," he said. "It seems that piece of information was left out of the itinerary, but I have my suspicions."

"Yeah, me too. Are you going to get your own room?"

He cocked his head back and laughed. "Me? Why would I do that? This is my room for the week. If you'd like, we can go in the morning and get *you* a room, but I'm not going anywhere."

What in the? "Well, I'm sure as hell not leaving. Rowan damn near begged me to take this vacation because she couldn't. So—you know what? Never mind. Just forget it. I'll figure something out."

Either way, the next few days were either going to be really interesting or incredibly more uncomfortable than the last few minutes had already been. It would definitely require a hell of a lot more wine.

"Something," he mocked under his breath, as he turned to leave.

"Wait," I called out, stopping him. "I didn't see your luggage. Did you already unpack your stuff somewhere?"

He glanced back down at me over his shoulder. "That's because all of my shit got stuck on the wrong flight and sent to who the hell knows where. All I have, at least until the morning when the shops open, are the clothes I had on my back when I left home this morning, and they're out on the back deck."

"Oh. Okay. That really sucks." Though I was grateful for the mishap if it meant a few stolen moments of him half-naked wearing only a towel.

Try as I might, there was no denying he looked delicious.

He huffed. "Indeed, it does. Anything else?"

"Yeah. Why are you all wet?"

He nodded toward the back door. "I was swimming."

"In the dark?"

"Well, it is nighttime. Plus, I don't have anything to swim in, or I would have done it earlier when I got here. I figured the other guests would appreciate not seeing me naked."

That made one of us. *Damn it*. I needed to get myself together. "Oh, okay then."

"The water's pretty warm, and it's barely chest-deep in most spots. Why don't you put something on and come join me."

An invitation to go swimming with a nude Warren? Tempting, but no, thank you. I didn't think I was ready for that yet. "Umm, I would, but I just got in here, and *this* water is warm too. Not to mention, free of slimy things that I can't see swimming around my legs."

"Suit yourself." He shrugged, then headed toward the back door.

I called out to him again as he disappeared into the suite. "Wait, are you seriously skinny-dipping?"

"Guess you'll have to find that out for yourself," he called out. Even though I couldn't see his face, I'd have sworn there was the teensy tiniest hint of amusement in his voice when he responded.

When I heard the back door close, I draped the towel across the bamboo table beside the tub and sank back under the water. Rather than dwell on my newfound situation—because I couldn't really do anything about it at the moment—I popped the cork on my wine and drank it straight from the bottle as I watched my empty wine glass bob around in the water.

By the time I emptied the bottle, I started to reconsider Warren's invite. What would it hurt? After all, he was the one who'd asked me to join him. Was that an olive branch of some sort? A truce for suggesting I go get my own room? Surely he wasn't serious about that…was he?

I pulled the drain before I changed my mind about joining him, climbed out of the tub, and wrapped myself in the towel Warren had given me. If I didn't know any better, I would have sworn it smelled faintly of him, or what I remembered him smelling like from the night of Rowan's wedding. As long ago as it was, Warren wore cologne that was not easily forgotten.

I peeked out of the bathroom. The coast was clear, so I padded over to the bed and rummaged through my suitcase to find a bikini because, yes, I'd brought more than one. After what felt like way too long trying to just pick out two pieces of clothing, I settled on black bottoms that tied on each side and a strapless, hot pink top.

Since all of the windows faced the ocean, I didn't worry that anyone would see me change. So, I unwrapped my towel and tossed it onto the bed next to my suitcase, then quickly slipped into my bathing suit.

I took a deep, calming breath before heading outside.

My nerves were shot. Everything about Warren made me tense as hell and had me on edge. It could have been his standoffish demeanor or his tense posture, but I hoped that after talking to him some more, my stomach would settle down and stop feeling like someone had turned a full blender on high with the lid off.

If it were one thing I'd learned throughout my adult dating life, it was that a man could be both amazingly hot and a total asshole at the same time. I hadn't known Warren for very long, or been around him much, but unfortunately, Warren Miller, so far, seemed to be that man. The softest I'd ever seen him was the night after Rowan's wedding reception. I'd celebrated just a tad too hard, and he'd somehow ended up being stuck carrying me—literally—to bed. Not his bed—the guest bed. I didn't remember much from that night, just waking up in a strange place with a pounding headache to the smell of coffee and bacon. Even better than that, was the sight of a shirtless Warren standing at the stove, making breakfast. Chloe, Rowan's mom, and Rowan's Grandma sat around his dining room table, eating and gawking. Hell, I didn't blame them one bit. We all exchanged good-morning greetings as I joined them at the table. We stuffed our faces with Warren's cooking, and an hour later, we were all out the door, heading home. He'd said less than twenty words to me the entire time I was there. I knew then that he was the kind of guy I should avoid—only admire from afar—but sometimes, even though I knew better, I still wanted to poke the fire just a little bit.

It was damned near pitch-black out as far as the eye could see, except for the soft glow of light from the bedside lamp shining through the window and the white light from the almost full moon illuminating the back porch and glittering off the tops of the low ocean waves.

I walked down the steps that led straight into the ocean, and the warm water lapped against my feet.

"Warren?" I called out. There was no response, and he was nowhere in sight. "What the hell? Warren?" I whisper-yelled and waited for a response.

Nothing.

"He just came out here," I said out loud to myself. I mean, there were only so many places he could go off the back porch, and surely he hadn't swam out into the ocean at night?

"Where are you?" I called out louder this time.

I leaned over the railing, and just as I was about to turn and head back up the stairs, he popped up out of the water from under the dock, causing me to jump back.

I threw my hand over my heart. "Seriously?" I said, catching my breath. "Do you have to do that?"

Even in the near dark, I could see his blinging white teeth when he smiled. "Maybe you shouldn't be so jumpy. Personally, I don't think I'm that scary."

Says you. "I beg to differ." I folded my arms over my chest. "Where were you?" I asked, watching him swim on his back away from me, further out into the darkness.

"I was under the dock. I heard you come out."

"So you did mean to scare me, then."

"No, that was just an added bonus." He stopped swimming and stood up, the water waist-deep. "Are you coming in?"

"Eventually." I twisted my unruly hair into a loose bun and secured it to the top of my head as I stepped out into water. "For the record, I hate being scared."

"Noted. I'll try not to do that again."

"Thank you." The waves rolled gently against my thighs as I made my way out closer to Warren but still kept as much distance between us as possible. "Are you really naked?"

He smiled again, his teeth barely visible in the moonlight, then submersed himself all of the way under. When he came up, he was much, *much* closer to me than before. He stood, shaking the water from his hair with his hands—exactly as I'd pictured how he'd done earlier. "Of course I am. I told you, I don't have anything here."

Lord have mercy. Instinctively, I glanced down, hoping he didn't notice my trying to sneak another peek at his goods. "Okay then."

"What? Never seen a naked man before?"

"Well, yeah, of course I have." *Just not one that looked like you.*

"So what's the problem?"

I took a step back. "No problem. None at all." *Other than you're a big, damned, unexpected, mean-as-hell, and unnecessarily sexy complication.*

He swam around, keeping his lower half beneath the water. "I thought you were supposed to be a terrible singer?"

"What? Where did that come from, and who told you that?"

"Just a story I heard from Wes and Daniel when they were in Vegas. Something about you guys at karaoke and it being awful. I think his words were something along the lines of it being the worst karaoke he'd ever heard."

I let out an amused laugh. "Wooow. I hadn't heard that story yet."

"Probably for good reason. But I just heard you sing, and it was far from terrible."

I could feel my face flush with heat. "Thanks. I don't do it very often. That night was an exception, and I was feeling pretty good. We all three sang together—Rowan, Chloe, and me. When you team up two not-so-good singers with a decent one, it's easy to drown out the good one, I suppose."

"Interesting. Though, I'd say you're better than decent. You actually sound pretty amazing."

Amazing? That was quite the compliment coming from Mr. Stick-in-the-mud personality. It was enough to make my face flush with heat. "Thanks. Gotta give credit to my parents, who'd strongly encouraged me to take piano lessons as a little kid. That eventually led me to singing. I never did anything with either of those skills, other than perform in school functions, the occasional karaoke, and the bathroom. Then I became a respiratory therapist."

"Maybe I'll get you to sing for me later."

I shot him a *not a chance in hell* look. "Not happening."

"Well, I damned sure don't want you to ever have to use your medical skills on me."

"Touché."

"So, Miss Hidden Talents, tell me more about how you ended up here. You said Rowan practically begged you to take this trip."

"Yeah, she did. She called me a couple of days ago and asked if I would stand in for her. Well, she pretty much told me I was coming here. You probably already know, she's impossible to argue with."

"I can't argue with you about that. She's definitely strong-willed, we'll say."

I giggled. "Strong-willed. That's one way of putting it. How about you?" I asked, curious about his story. "Did Rowan

"Actually, no. It was Wes. Though I'm fairly certain Rowan was in on it. Wes doesn't have it in him to conjure up something like this by himself."

"Now that wouldn't surprise me one bit, if they were in on this together."

"Wes was oddly persistent that I take this trip, even knowing how against going I was from the beginning."

"Why would you be against coming here?"

"Busy, work, no time, name it."

"Then what convinced you to cave in.

He was quiet for a minute, and then his dark eyes stared directly into mine when he finally answered. "A picture of you."

Katie. Out of every human I'd ever known or had been acquainted with, my kid brother had to choose Katie to set me up with. That wasn't even a question, because I'd no doubt in my mind that's what this was, and his every intention.

Now I could see crystal clear why he'd practically begged me to take a week off from work at the very last minute. Not that I couldn't easily get the time off—because he knew damned well I could but that I didn't need a vacation—but Wes had a motive, and it wasn't out of concern for my well-being.

What I hadn't known when I signed up for this was that I'd be sharing a very close and intimate space—one massive bedroom on a semi-private island—with *her*. She was not supposed to be here; nobody except for me. This was supposed to be a week alone consisting of only golf, booze, and the occasional dip in the ocean. At least that's what some of the ideas Wes had tossed out there to lure me into this when he pitched the idea.

That asshole.

And while I had zero intentions of getting laid anytime soon, that didn't mean I didn't want to or that Katie wasn't sexy as fucking sin with her mouth hung partially open in shock—a mouth I could picture sliding my dick into—when I answered her question about what it was that had changed my mind about accepting this trip. Already it had taken every internal thought I could conjure up about sports, medical research, and other mundane bullshit to overcome all the dirty images of what I really wanted to do to her. Even more so now with her at the sight of her in that tiny string bikini—starting with untying the top with my teeth.

Fuck. I needed to shake the image ASAP, or she was going to know exactly what I thought about her as soon as I emerged from the water.

"Me?" she squealed. "What did I have to do with this? Did you *know* I was going to be here?" Her voice practically hit a higher octave than it did when I'd busted in on her naked in the tub, singing at the top of her lungs. She had a set of pipes on her, that was certain. I wondered what else her talented, sexy little mouth could do.

"Relax, Katie. I didn't know you—or anyone else, for that matter—were going to be here," I reassured her. "I wouldn't lie to you about that. If I'd wanted you, I would have just gotten your phone number from Rowan, or some shit. So, when Wes called and offered this," I said, with a wave of my hand, "I was told I'd be here alone. He'd never mentioned otherwise."

She wiped her face, probably relieved that she hadn't been the only one who'd been set up, even though for some fucked-up reason, she actually thought I had something to do with this.

Not my style.

Even less my style was tossing back at her that we would go find a room for *her* to stay in while we were here. Now *that* was an asshole move on my part. Did I mean it? Kind of, but not really. I really didn't have a problem staying with her, the problem was did she really want *me* to leave?

"Well," she said with a huff, "nothing we can really do about it now. Except one of us is going to have to find somewhere else to stay."

"I wasn't trying to be an asshole earlier. Seeing you here just caught me off guard."

"So, you didn't mean it then? You aren't going to kick me out?"

"Of course not. But do you want your own space? If so, we can work something out, but it'll have to wait until tomorrow. It's too late to do anything about it tonight."

She rubbed her hands down her face, seemingly conflicted on how to answer. "There is no wrong answer here, Katie. It's okay with me, either way."

She sucked in a deep breath. "You can stay, but no funny business."

I threw my hands in the air and laughed. "No funny business. Got it. Thanks for granting me permission to stay in my suite."

"*My* suite," she corrected me. "I'm curious about something. When did Wes call you about this vacation?"

"Hmm, maybe a month ago."

Her mouth fell open. "A whole month?"

"Yeah, he called to tell me that he and Rowan are expecting. I'm assuming you've known."

"I do now, but I just found out. That was Rowan's whole reasoning for me taking her place. She said neither of her doctors would let her travel."

"She's not lying. Wes has been pretty firm on her travel restrictions since her real OB told her to stay put. He's pretty protective of her." Though, I didn't blame him. God knew he loved that woman relentlessly, and they'd been through a lot. "But wait, you just found out she was pregnant? I would have guessed she would have told you from the beginning?"

She shrugged. "You'd think. She said they wanted to wait until she was further along before they started telling everyone, myself included."

"Interesting. So, when did you get swindled into all of this?"

"Saturday, actually."

"Saturday? As in two days ago?" Holy shit. That meant Rowan must have waited to extend this vacation offer to Katie until *after* I'd given Wes my answer.

"Yup. I was in the middle of helping my parents move back in with me when she called," she let out a sigh and shook her head. "Don't even ask about my parents. That's a whole other story for another time, but Rowan used my situation as leverage to get me to come here because she knew how much I needed the break, and I never would have otherwise taken a vacation—especially by myself."

"I see." I'd turned him down the first few times he'd asked me, but then, something—or rather, someone—had changed my mind.

I couldn't help but smile at the thought of the picture of Katie and me together—the one taken by the wedding photographer at my brother's wedding last year. Both of us dressed up in our formal attire. I could see us clear as day— me in a slate-gray custom-fitted tux, Katie with her long, platinum-blonde hair braided down to the side, her body draped in that bright, jewel-toned, blue satin dress that hugged every one of her subtle curves from head to toe.

"What's so funny over there?"

"Nothing. Nothing at all. I was just thinking."

She shook her head. "You're an odd man, Warren."

"Odd? I think that's the first time anyone has ever referred to me as odd."

"What else have you been called?"

"Oh, let's see. I've been called a wiseass, cynical, harsh, terse. Those I'm familiar with."

"Wow. That's pretty harsh. Do people really think that of you?"

"Sometimes, though I prefer to think of myself as misunderstood." They didn't grasp that about me—not that I'd ever needed to explain myself to anyone—that my being constant and routine was often mistaken for my being an uptight asshole, along with all the other aforementioned adjectives. You bury yourself up to your eyeballs in work for fifteen-plus years, habitual solitude tends to become your way of life.

"Well, I'd hate to hear all the good things they have to say about you," she said in a sarcastic tone.

"I don't know what you think of me, but I'm not a terrible guy, Katie."

"Sounds kind of like you are to me."

Ouch. Apparently, I was going to have to work a lot harder if I wanted her to warm up to me. "But is that what you think?"

She shrugged. "I'm not entirely sure, yet."

"Great." She was going to be a tough cookie to crack. Granted, we hadn't gotten off to the best start possible, but I thought we were finally getting somewhere. "So, moving on from me," I said, steering us away from me as the topic of conversation, because from the tone of her voice, I didn't even want to know what opinion she had already formulated about me—first impression or now. "Did you have any big plans for the next couple of days?"

"Nothing much, really. I just figured I'd explore the property, see what all's around here, probably spend most of my time on the beach, hopefully not find somewhere else to stay," she said with a smirk as she waved her hands lazily back and forth in the water. "What about you, Mr. Personality? Did you make any plans?"

"Nothing in particular. I haven't set anything in stone. Thought about playing a few rounds of golf, do a little day drinking…probably spend too much time at the resort bar."

I hadn't come here with the expectations of remotely trying to get laid, as my brother had so graciously ordered me I'd needed to do. When I boarded my plane to St. Lucia, I had no motives, no intentions, no expectations.

Katie wasn't supposed to be here. No one was.

She and I were here together, alone, and there was no changing that now.

Quite frankly, I didn't want to.

The more time I spent with her, even if she seemed put off by me and my *personality*, the more I'd found myself wanting to be around her.

I swam around, closing the space that she had put between us. I wanted to be near her but figured it was best to still keep my distance. She didn't back away from me, so that was nice.

"Well, it looks like I'm here now," she sighed. "Surprise!" Her tone sounded almost somber, like she thought her presence was a hindrance on my unplanned vacation. "Sorry if I ruined any of your plans."

What the hell? She really did think her being here was a problem? "Katie, are you serious? I, for one, am glad that you're here. So put that out of your mind."

"Oh! Really?" Her tone perked up. "You're not mad that I'm here?"

"Mad? Why would I be mad? There are certainly worse people I could be stuck here with for an entire week." I internally cringed at my response. Now she was going to think that I thought I was stuck with her. *Smooth move, dumbass.*

She shrugged. "True, I guess. You just haven't seemed very…overjoyed since realizing I'd be around. And if we're going to share a suite for the next few days, I don't want to feel like I'm intruding."

I knew I'd come across like an asshole, but it wasn't intentional. That's just me. The last thing I wanted was for her to feel unwelcomed or that I didn't like her—quite the opposite.

"You're not a bother to me at all, Katie," I reassured her. "Just very unexpected."

"So, is that a good thing or a bad thing?"

"I have no idea yet." Because being in a forced-proximity scenario with this incredibly beautiful and apparently very talented woman was going to put every limit I had to the test. Only time would tell just how this would end. "In the meantime, I think I'm going to head in and fix myself a drink. Would you like one?"

"Umm, I'm okay for now. Thank you, though."

"Let me know if you change your mind. Are you staying out here by yourself?"

She glanced around the darkness. "Yeah. I think I'm gonna stay *in* the water for a while." Her voice had a slightly innocent and playful undertone.

"Is that some sort of a hint?"

"A hint? At what?"

"Uh huh." I knew exactly what she'd been referring to. "You emphasized that you're going to stay *in* the water as opposed to getting *out*. Are you worried that you're going to see something you might like?" Because there was no way in hell she wasn't not going to look. She'd damn near devoured me with her eyes at least twice. And fuck, I couldn't deny what the sight of her half-submerged under wine-stained water, covered in soap bubbles, did to me. I needed to block that image out before I really gave her something to drop her jaw to the floor.

"Pretty sure I already have." This time her words were barely audible, but I'd heard the message loud and clear.

Well, well, well. Maybe she didn't entirely hate *Mr. Personality* after all.

"Interesting. Well, that makes two of us, then."

We held each other's gaze for a moment until I finally broke whatever moment we had and waded through the water, heading toward the suite. I'd almost reached the steps but was still in waist-deep water, keeping my bottom half submerged.

I could feel her eyes on me the entire time.

I glanced back at her over my shoulder as I approached the steps. "Are you waiting for something?"

"Nope. Not at all." Hell, if it had been me, I would have watched her the entire time.

"I'll be back in a bit." Finally, I stood up all of the way out of the water and climbed the steps. "Just call out if you change your mind about that drink."

Then I heard what sounded like a gasp. "I thought you said you were naked?"

I smiled to myself. "I thought you said you weren't looking?" All I heard was a grunt. That made me laugh out loud. "Don't stay out there too long," I said to her as I made my way up the back steps.

I towel-dried off and went inside. Instead of pouring myself a drink as I'd originally planned, I decided I'd had enough of the ocean for one night and opted to take a quick shower. After the day I'd had, my body felt like it needed a good cleansing, even if it meant wearing dirty clothes, more than a glass of scotch at that point.

I quickly washed up and threw on the only pair of jeans I had with me—sans boxers, because those were dripping wet—hanging over the edge of the bathtub. What Katie didn't need to know was that I had in fact been swimming naked before she showed up. I'd made a last-minute decision to put my boxers on after I'd left her alone in the tub earlier.

When I finally emerged from the bathroom, Katie was still outside. So I headed over to the bar and poured myself a crystal tumbler of Johnnie Walker Blue Label, then popped the cork on a fresh bottle of wine. I laughed to myself at the thought of Katie submerged in her spilled wine. I filled up a new glass for her. One thing I'd learned from my brief time with Katie back in Chicago that she preferred her glass a little more than half-full.

Carrying our drinks, I made my way out back and found Katie stretched out on one of the lounge chairs, her long, slender body barely covered by that tiny-ass string bikini. No towel.

"All done?" she asked as I handed her the wine.

"Yeah. It's kind of weird not having a clean change of clothes to put on or dry underwear."

"I bet. You were taking too long, so I went in to check on you and heard the shower running."

"Thanks. Sorry I didn't let you know. I figured you were safe out here."

She looked me up and down with a smirk. "You're a big boy—you don't have to tell me anything. As long as you don't stink, I think you'll be fine."

"I'm relying on you to tell me if I do."

"Maybe." She took a long, slow sip of wine, eyeing me over the edge of the glass. "Thank you, by the way…for this."

"You're welcome." I sat down on the lounge chair beside her. "I plan on going off the property in the morning and see what I can find in terms of clothing and other necessities. I just need enough to get me through the next few days, and hopefully take a real shower and put on fresh, clean clothes."

"I understand that. Do you want me to go shopping with you?" "No, not necessarily. Unless you want to. I was letting you know as a courtesy in case you need anything or if you wake up and I'm not here."

"Sounds good. But I get up pretty early, though."

"Me too." I tipped my glass of scotch toward her wine. "Cheers."

We clinked glasses. "Cheers," she said, taking another sip.

"How is it?"

She held up her glass as if to inspect the contents, giving it a gentle swirl. "It's my favorite, actually, but tastes much better than it would if I were drinking it at home alone."

"I'll drink to that." Because if not for being here, that was exactly what I'd be doing. I lay back in my chair, taking in the moment. We sat there in silence, enjoying the sound of the waves rolling by.

"Speaking of alone, can I ask you a personal question?"

She turned her head to face me. "Sure. Shoot."

"And tell me if I'm crossing a line, but I'm going to assume it's safe to say you're single and not still talking to your ex?"

Her jaw practically hit her chest. "My ex? What do you know about my ex?"

"Let's just say I've heard things. The last thing I need is for my being here with you to come back and bite me in the ass."

"No. I'm not still talking to my ex. I don't care what you've heard, that's none of your business, and enough about me."

"Ouch. Fair enough." *Note to self, Katie's ex strikes a nerve.* "Moving on."

"Okay then. My turn."

"Go for it."

"I want to know about this picture, the one that you said was the reason you changed your mind about coming here."

I took a long, slow sip of my scotch, savoring that warm, familiar burn, hoping she would have forgotten I'd ever said anything. I knew if I didn't tell her now, she'd likely never let it go, and I might never hear the end of it.

"It's a picture of us together at the wedding. One of the ones the photographer took."

"Oh. The group picture?"

"No, Katie. Just us."

I stared out into the darkness. There was no longer a definitive line between water and sky. Everything beyond the porch railing was solid black. It was peaceful and terrifying all the same, not being able to see more than a few feet out into the unknown.

She was quiet for a moment before she spoke again. "Just us?"

"Yup. Just us." I wished like hell I could have seen the look on her face a little better. She had to have known which picture I was referring to; it was the only one she and I had taken together. We'd taken several group photos, and then the photographer had us take couple pictures.

This one, though? *God damn*. This one in particular had felt different. I would never forget the way Katie's body felt pressed firmly against my side during the shoot. She had her elbow propped up on my shoulder, the other dropped down her side holding her bouquet of white calla lilies, standing in some sassy, possessive pose like she owned me, while I had my arm wrapped tightly around her waist with my hand splayed low across her hip. And *fuck me*. I knew she hadn't been wearing any panties because I could feel every smooth inch of her searing hot skin beneath my palm through that thin silk dress.

What she also didn't need to know about that particular picture was that it had been framed and was sitting on top of my dresser ever since the weekend after the wedding when Rowan shared the link to their photos.

I held her gaze as she eyed me suspiciously. "Why do you have a picture of only the two of us, and what about that picture in particular had anything to do with this trip? Since you're steadfast on not having known that I would be here, because now I'm finding that really hard to believe anymore."

"Katie, please believe me. I have no reason whatsoever to be dishonest with you, and I'm not about to make myself out to be a liar now. I swear to you I did not know you were going to be here."

She took a long sip of her wine. "I'm listening."

I let out a sigh, not quite ready to give up all my secrets just yet. I at least owed her this much. "After Wes's initial offer, I contemplated for damn near a month about what I wanted to do; whether or not I was willing to give up a week of work, and risk missing a deadline, just to come here. But this past Friday night I was lying in bed, still undecided. Then that picture of us caught my attention, more specifically that blue dress you were wearing. It reminded me of the ocean. I knew then that this is where I wanted to be, whether I came alone or not."

Her mouth fell open. *Close your goddamned mouth, Katie.* She had no fucking clue what seeing her like that did to me.

"Shocked, eh?"

"I—I don't believe—"

"Believe it. I've got nothing to hide." *Except for this hard-on.*

Maybe now she'd quit worrying whether or not I was mad or disappointed that she was here. I sure as hell wouldn't want anyone else with me.

"I think I need a refill," she said, standing up, her empty glass in hand. "I'll be back."

After a few minutes of absence, she returned to the porch. I thought for sure she had gone inside to hide away for the night. Surprisingly, she'd come back out. It didn't take me long to notice that she'd let her hair down. Not pulled back tight or twisted in some bun on the top of her head. I had only ever seen it down and out of place twice before now. Once just a while ago, when she was in the tub, and then the day after Wes's wedding when she'd spent the night at my place. She'd slept with her hair in a braid but had taken it loose the next morning.

Now, here she stood barely ten feet in front of me, her long blonde hair falling in wind-blown waves down her back, almost to the top of her ass, as she casually leaned forward against the railing, fresh drink in hand, staring out into the night.

I sucked in a deep breath and slowly released it as I fought off the urge to walk up behind her, wrap my arm around her waist, and pull her ass back into me, letting her know just how *not* disappointed I was by having her around. The thought had me adjusting my hard-on through my jeans.

Try as I might, there was no denying just how really fucking attracted I was to her, here now and since the first time I ever laid eyes on her. Clearly, the physical attraction I'd felt for her since day one was damned sure not going to go away anytime soon. Especially not with her this close. As much as I had tried to convince myself that I didn't want or need to give in to my desire for her, I didn't *not* want to even less.

This could go one of two ways—she'd either eventually kiss me or kill me. Either way, she was worth the risk.

Fuck it.

I set my glass down as I stood up and stalked forward in three long strides, stopping just a few inches short of reaching out and putting my hands on her. Whatever perfume she had been wearing drifted off her skin, assaulting my senses.

She glanced back at me over her shoulder as I approached, and before she could speak, I pulled her glass from her grip and gave the burgundy liquid a few swirls and a whiff. Then I drank down what was left of its contents in two gulps.

"Hmm. That *is* good." I handed the empty glass back to her—all while looking her straight in her eyes.

She gawked at the empty glass, then back up at me. "What the fu—"

"Kit-Kat," I said, cutting her off. "I've seen the way you look at me, and I know what that look means. So correct me if I'm wrong in what I'm about to tell you." I brushed my knuckles lightly down her arm from her shoulder to her elbow, causing her skin to prickle with tiny goose bumps where my fingers had trailed, even in the one-hundred-degree heat of the night. She glanced down at my hand, then back up at me.

I continued before she could process what to say in response, because I could tell from the look on her face, lit only by moonlight, that she wanted to say something. "The way I see our situation is we can go about this one of two ways." Her head tilted to the side as she raised an eyebrow. "We can accept the fact that we're here together, like it or not. We can give in to whatever it is sparking between us—one week, no strings. Then, when all is said and done, we each go back to living our routine lives as though none of it had ever happened. Or we can just spend the rest of our time pretending as if the other one isn't here, and we'll cross paths wherever, whenever. Though, I find the latter to be the bigger challenge."

Not giving her a chance to respond, I bent forward and kissed her cheek. "Good night, Katie," I whispered in her ear, right before I walked away, leaving her standing alone on the back porch, empty wineglass in hand.

Warren had balls of steel, I had to give him that much. First, downing my entire drink and then taking off like he didn't just what? Proposition me to "give in to whatever was sparking between us" and screw like rabbits for the rest of our trip? Mind you, he was the one who was going to help me find my own room!

Ugh! The man had me wanting to rip my hair out! *Hot, cold, hot, cold.* And as much as I'd hated to admit to myself, screwing him for a week without strings didn't sound like such a terrible idea.

Before I'd boarded the plane in Memphis, I'd minutely talked myself into at least being open to the idea of getting laid while here. Lord knew how bad I'd needed to be thoroughly fucked, but of all the men out there, by Warren? If you'd have asked me an hour ago, I would have sworn he loathed my presence. Now? Hell if I really knew anymore.

There was one thing I did know for sure: he was easy on the eyes. The sight of Warren wearing only a pair of dark denim jeans slung low on his bare hips—no shoes, no shirt, definitely no underwear—was damned sure no problem. I mean, a girl could look, right? Just because I'd gotten caught admiring and appreciating his nicely toned body with perfectly placed patches of dark hair, a dazzling white smile, and a deep, commanding voice that sent chills down my spine did not mean I wanted to throw myself into bed with him.

Okay, maybe that was a tiny bit of a lie.

Because that was the first thing that had crossed my mind that night we met. But that didn't mean it had to happen. A girl was allowed to dream, right? I never expected him to actually proposition me with it. Not here, not now…or ever.

I had half a mind and just enough buzz to march up to him, shove my finger in his chest and tell him he was out of his fucking mind, and ask him who did he think he was? Just because he'd caught me ogling him a few times did not mean I was willing to throw my clothes on the floor, or myself at him.

Then again, maybe I could take him up on his offer and get a few days of some good dick out of it. I could hear Chloe's words in my mind loud and clear. *"The only way to get over a man is to get underneath another one."* Warren had all but handed me the opportunity to do just that with him seven ways to Sunday on a golden plater.

Convenient? Yes…for now. But with *him*? I could think of a million reasons why crossing that line with Warren would be a bad idea—strings or not—starting with him only wanting me for a week. I'd never been the no-strings type, hadn't even thought about it until now. One week was different than a wild one night with a stranger. Not to mention, I hadn't been with anyone except for Justin for the past almost five years.

I stood on the back deck overlooking the dark water for a little while longer, letting the events of the day and Warren's words sink in. Between exhaustion from travel, the wine in my system, and Warren's whispered words in my ear, I'd found it hard to clear my head. Everything about him screamed *run*. Run far and run fast.

I held my empty wineglass in one hand and touched my arm where Warren's fingers had grazed my bare skin with the other. Chills ran down my spine, sending a jolt straight between my legs when he'd done it. Then the longer I stood there and thought about everything, the more I began to think I was the one out of *my* mind for even considering any of what he'd offered.

But almost an entire week with Warren, no strings, just straight fucking? Could that be something I could do? What if one of us caught feelings? Though doubtful, it was still a possibility. What if he had a small dick or the sex really sucked? I could see either of those happening before one of us fell in love.

Shit.

Trying to decide right now was all too much.

By the time I conceded to the day's events and forced myself to go inside, Warren had made himself a bed with the extra blankets and pillows from the linen cabinet and had fallen asleep on the couch—even if the sofa were at least six inches too short for his height.

The poor guy did not look comfortable, though him sleeping there was probably our safest bet. Lord, what I would have done had I found him asleep in the bed? I didn't know what I would have said to him or if I would have even found the words to speak coherently had I come face-to-face with him again that soon.

I reeeally wanted to text Rowan or Chloe, but there was no internet service this far out on the water, only at the main resort, and it was way too late to go inland alone.

Warren had left the bedside lamp on, so I quietly tiptoed around the room, dug my pj's—a pair of cotton shorts and a tank top—out of my suitcase and locked myself in the bathroom and changed. Under any other circumstances, I would have slept in the nude. *Not this time.*

Warren's black silk boxers were draped over the edge of the bathtub. I stilled and listened for any sign of movement beyond the bathroom door. All was silent except for my erratic heartbeat that whooshed in my ears with every beat. Once I'd assured myself it was safe, I sucked in a deep breath and did what any completely sane and perfectly normal female would do—I picked up his underwear and examined them front to back. Even covered in wet salt water, they still looked and felt like high-quality material.

I let out a sigh and hung his shorts back up.

Honestly, I hadn't been the slightest bit disappointed at all to see his body dripping wet from head to toe, covered only by a pair of boxers that clung to his ass like wet tissue paper when he stood up out of the water. Or the way the muscles on his back and shoulders flexed without him even trying. If we had been in a movie, "Dream Weaver" would have played in the background as he stepped out of the water…you know when I wasn't supposed to look? How could I not? This was Warren we were talking about here. Hell, I half expected the man to be naked, which was the whole reason why I watched him out to begin with. The only disappointing part was I couldn't see his front. If only he'd turned around.

Hmm. Forget it. *Just go to bed*.

I turned off the bathroom and bedside light and tucked myself in between the cool, velvety cotton sheets. Even still, as luxuriously cozy as it all was, I could not get myself to relax. I flipped back and forth from my back to stomach, tossed and turned side to side a few times, and finally settled onto my back, staring up at the shadowy, palm leaf ceiling fan as it spun around in circles.

My mind played back over the days' events like a movie on loop that wouldn't turn off. What if I hadn't missed my connecting flight? Would we have gotten here at the same time? Or been on the same plane? *Holy shit*! I wondered how *that* interaction would have gone if we'd met thirty thousand feet in the air.

I pulled the covers up to my neck and turned on to my side with my back to Warren. That position didn't work for me, so I flipped over and faced him. It was dark, but there was just enough moonlight beaming through the windows to see across the room. I quietly giggled to myself at the sight of his tall body stretched out on the too-small couch. Poor guy. He still looked peacefully comfortable, even with his feet hanging off the end.

I closed my eyes and finally dozed off while watching Warren sleep.

♡♡♡

"Good morning, princess."

I stretched my arms over my head and rolled from my side onto my back. Every muscle from my neck to my shoulder and down my arm had some serious cramping going on, and my entire right hand tingled. It felt like my body hadn't moved all night from the same position I'd fallen asleep in. Hell, I probably hadn't. When I finally did doze off, I slept like the dead.

Cautiously, I cracked my eyes open, shielding them from the bright sunlight that lit up the entire room, silently cursing the sheer curtains because they did absolutely nothing to block out any light whatsoever.

"Good morning. What time is it?" I didn't know what time the sun rose in St. Lucia, but it had to have been early.

Warren sat on one of the overstuffed chairs beside the bed as he tied the laces on his tennis shoes. "It's almost eleven thirty."

"No way!" I jolted, sitting straight up.

He grinned. "Yes way."

"Ohmigod. You're kidding?"

"Nope." He sat back in the chair, his arms resting casually on the armrest.

"Wow. I must have needed it. I *never* sleep this late. Ever. Eight, maybe, but even then, that's after a really, *really* bad shift at work."

"No worries. You're on vacation. You're supposed to sleep in."

"True." I massaged my head, then hastily combed my half-numb fingers through my tangled hair in an attempt to do…something—I didn't know what—to it, because without even seeing it, I knew it was awful. Between traveling, extreme tropical humidity, the steamy bubble bath, and salt water, my hair felt dry, stringy, and gross. The last time I'd seen my hot mess of a mop was right before I'd gone to bed. It was seriously unruly then.

"Your hair looks fine. Leave it."

I shot him a *yeah, right* look. There was no way he thought that *any* of this looked *fine*.

"If you say so." I finger-combed my hair some more and flung it into a sloppy ponytail with the band I kept around my wrist. "So what time did you get up?"

He shrugged. "Around four, I think."

"Oh good Lord. Four? I was going to say next time wake me up, but even I don't get up *that* early."

"What can I say? I'm a dedicated early riser, not just self-proclaimed." He glanced over at the couch, then back at me. "Plus, that wasn't the most comfortable place I've ever had to sleep."

I bit into my bottom lip. "Oh, yeah. Sorry about that."

He gripped the arms of the chair and pushed himself to stand, hands on his hips.

As he did, I eyed him from his laced-up shoes to his thighs, the slight swell at his zipper, all of the way up his body to his chest pressing through his stretched-out tight tee, drinking in every inch of him along the way to finally meet his eyes. Fully clothed, the man had me practicing my Kegel exercises.

"You have nothing to be sorry about. I could have just as easily slept in the bed with you if I wanted to."

"I'll trade places with you tonight," I quickly offered, knowing damned well I didn't want to.

"No you won't. That's not necessary."

"If you say so."

"I'm about to run up to the main resort and see if the concierge can point me in the direction of someplace I can go and get a few things. I was going to grab something to eat. You want to get ready and meet me for lunch, or would you rather me bring something back here instead?"

My stomach growled at his offer. "Here would be better. I'd really like to take a shower and clean up a little," I said, gesturing to myself.

He closed his eyes as if to collect his thoughts, but when he opened them, I could have sworn there was something else there—a shift. His heated gaze sent a wave of warmth through me, like I hadn't been the only one who was starving. Except it wasn't food that he wanted.

He took a small step forward and stood right beside the bed, just inches from me—his *dick* was inches away from my face.

I looked up at him and swallowed hard.

He started reaching his hand out toward me, then dropped it and stepped away. "I—fuck. Do you have any specific tastes or preferences?"

"Depends. Food or bedroom?" I threw my hand over my mouth as fast as the words had left my lips. *Shit. Katie!*

"Food, Katie. I was talking about food. Christ, I—never mind."

My face flushed with embarrassment. *No shit he was talking about food.* Clearly, I was the only pervert thinking about more than lunch at the moment.

"Sorry. I just figured…and after what you said last night…I—"

"Do you really think that low of me that I'd approach you about what I said to you with a question like that?"

"Well, no—I don't guess so."

"If so, then I need to work on my strategy."

"Sorry, but in my defense, I didn't expect you to come at me like that last night either. Let's just start over. You're going for food. It's almost lunch, so bring me whatever you can find. I'm not picky. How's that?"

"Perfect. I'll be back in a while." He strode across the room without so much as a glance back at me and left.

"Shit!" I yelled out loud as soon as the door closed. I threw myself back against my pillow and kicked the tangled covers off me. I could not make heads or tails of what in the hell was going on between us.

I lay there for a few more minutes, contemplating on getting myself off really fast, knowing it wouldn't take long. I could probably get two out before he made it back. Or I could walk around all day, maxed out with sexual frustration.

I blew out a heavy sigh.

The latter won. Instead, I opted to get up and get ready for the day. Prepare myself for whatever other embarrassing moments were in store for me, because clearly with my big mouth, guaranteed there would be more to come.

After a long, hot shower, hard scrubbing and shaving from head to toe, I dried off, oiled up my skin, and threw on a stretchy, formfitting, coral-colored sundress with a hem that landed midthigh. I ran through my usual routine, pulled my wet hair into a sleek ponytail, braided the end, then twisted it into a bun on top of my head.

I slapped on a full face of makeup, then topped it all off with a few extra swipes of black, waterproof mascara and sparkly pink lip gloss.

Warren had been gone for nearly two hours. My stomach rolled to the point of physical pain from hunger.

Just as I came out of the bathroom, the front door opened. Warren's hands were full, one loaded down with what looked like shopping bags, the other holding what I'd hoped were paper bags full of food.

"It's just me. I'm—" He looked up, stopping dead in his tracks.

I walked over to him and held my hand out for him to give me something to carry. "You're…?"

He handed over the bags with what smelled like lunch drifting out of them. "Starving," he finally said, clearing his throat. "And sorry that took me so long. I did my best at shopping with what resources are offered here. Then I went ahead and called the airline while I had service to check and see if they've found my luggage."

"Any luck with that?" I took our food over to the small dinette table and started unboxing everything and setting it all up.

"No, and at this rate, they may as well send it back to Chicago when and if they ever do find it." He dropped the rest of his stuff on the bed next to my suitcase before making his way over and standing close, noticeably too close behind me. He leaned over my shoulder and inhaled slow and deep. "Smells amazing."

I glanced up at him. Something about the look on his face had me questioning whether he'd been talking about lunch or something else—*like me*.

Right now wasn't the time to ask. I needed to eat.

"Yes. It does. Now, let's eat before I get any more hangry than I'm already feeling. I'd hate to take my starvation out on you."

He reached around me, pulled a chair out for me to sit down, tucked me in, then sat himself at the one directly across from me.

"Fair enough. I wasn't sure what your *food preferences* were, so I grabbed a little bit of everything. You said you weren't picky."

"Not at all. I'm pretty open with my *preferences*." My emphasis on "preferences" should have been a dead giveaway that I was not talking about food this time. Not that I'd ever been a super-freak or that I'd ever do anything kinky with him, but there wasn't much I wouldn't consider trying with the right person. Right now, I just enjoyed flirting.

"Is that so?" he asked, stabbing into some scrambled eggs. "Care to elaborate?"

"Nope." I poured some orange juice in a glass and handed him the champagne. "Pop that for me, please."

Taking the bottle from me, he twisted the top off with a quick flick of his wrist. He handed it back with a grin. "Twist top."

"Figures." I scanned over the spread of food in front of us, rubbing my hands together, ready to dive in. "It looks like you brought half the restaurant back with you."

We had a bottle of champagne, a small container of orange juice, two glass bottles of sparkling water, cut-up fresh fruit that had probably been grown here on the island, eggs, wheat toast with butter, oatmeal, some kind of smoked fish, and a handful of assorted condiments. "All of this looks incredible."

"So far, the food here hasn't let me down."

"If I were alone, I might try to eat all of it."

He took a bite of melon, then washed it down with a swig of water. "Don't let me stop you. We're going to need all the energy we can get today."

I arched an eyebrow at him. "What exactly did you have in mind to do today that we'll need all this energy?"

"Probably not what your dirty mind is thinking."

Whaaa? Whaaa—who? Me?

"It's hot as hell out there," he continued. "Anything we do outside of this room is going to be draining. Well, for me, specifically. I'm not used to this type of heat."

Being from Memphis, I was used to the scorching, muggy heat. We had days during the summer with one hundred percent humidity and a heat index of 110 plus. This weather was nothing for me.

"Well, we could always just stay in all day?"

"Maybe, but I don't think that's such a good idea."

I stabbed a piece of strawberry with my fork and pulled it between my lips. "How come?"

"Because of shit like that right there." He pointed to me with his own fork. "I don't trust myself not to lose grip of my self-control around you."

"If all it's going to take for you to lose any restraint with me is my eating a piece of fruit, then I'd say you're already fighting a losing battle, and you've got a long road ahead of you, buddy."

He folded his arms over his chest, tipping his head to the side, curiosity written all over his face. "And why is that?"

"Well, for starters, I never would have pegged you as the giving-in type. I've barely been here half a day and you've already propositioned me." His jaw ticked with the faintest movement, but I didn't miss the ever so slight tug at the corner of his mouth, like he was trying to hide a grin. "Second, in your defense on that, I was planning on inviting you to have dinner with me tonight so we could finish the conversation you started last night."

SIX
Warren

I never should have propositioned Katie like that. I knew better, and she deserved better.

Now here she sat a few feet across from me, inviting me to have dinner with her to further discuss my invitation. No sooner had I talked myself into approaching her last night than regret kicked in as soon as I'd left her alone. Katie was not a wham bam thank you, ma'am, kind of woman. She deserved so much more than just a few sleazy nights tangled in between the sheets with me, *or anyone else*, for that matter.

More than that, I knew damned well from the beginning that I would not be able to spend any amount of uninhibited time with her, no strings attached, just to go back to life as though she had never happened.

Yet I took the risk and pursued her anyway. *God damn.*

Katie had proven not to be an easy woman to resist, which had been easy for me to do up until now, because I'd not been around her except for my brother's wedding. Little did she know, she'd already had me, hook, line, and sinker, from the first moment we'd met. There was something about the way she spoke, the way she presented herself to the world, that had me second-guessing my disposition to remain single and married to my career until what I had considered to be *the* absolute perfect woman came along. I was sure no such woman existed, then we met.

She was polite, poised, well put together, and almost too perfectly beautiful—like some real-life Barbie mixed with a down-to-earth, small-town beauty queen. She had a light sense of humor without overdoing it and a contagious laugh that could elevate the mood of anyone in the room. Everything about her seemed too good to be true.

Now I had to tell her I was revoking my offer, that I hadn't been thinking straight when I'd said it.

Then watching her do something as simple as pulling a fork between her lips had the image of replacing that fork with my dick stuck in my head. Who knew eating a piece of fruit could be so damned seductive?

First on the agenda was redirect my thoughts back to neutral ground because I was not ready to go there, and she'd all but told me she was adventurous in the bedroom, or at least willing to try. That was the last thing I needed to hear, now that I had to somehow tell her that I'd changed my mind and was revoking my initial offer.

"Let's discuss my offer later." Way to go, dumbass, put off the inevitable.

"Okay then." She pulled her bottom lip between her teeth. "So, what would you like to do today? Did you have anything in mind for where to start?"

I shoved some food around on my plate and picked at my eggs. "I'm not entirely sure yet. I wasn't expecting to do anything that required me to consider someone else's interests or plans."

"Ah. I guess I shouldn't have assumed you'd want to spend your time with me. I apologize."

"No need to apologize, Katie. I didn't mean it like that. I just meant—" Christ, I needed to get my shit together. "—I thought I was going to have to do everything solo. What about you? Anything you'd like to do?"

She shrugged. "Not really, but I don't think you want to spend half the day lying on the beach, tanning, drinking, and listening to true crime podcasts."

"Is that what you want to do? If so, I'm willing to sacrifice my personal comfortability for a few hours, anyway."

She threw her head back and laughed.

Everything about her lit up when she was seemingly genuinely happy. Watching her also stirred something inside me, a feeling that made me uncomfortable.

"No, no," she said, still smiling. "It's fine. You do not have to do that. I will not be held responsible for your death by boredom. Besides, like you said, it's probably way too hot out, maybe even for me." She shoved her plate away to the middle of the table and leaned back. "I am so full. Thank you again for bringing back breakfast, or lunch. I haven't had a real meal since before I left Memphis yesterday."

"Glad I could help, though I can't say the same. I had dinner at the resort last night about an hour before you got here. It was nice. We'll plan on going sometime in the next few days."

She smirked. "Are you accepting my offer to have another meal with me? Are you sure that's safe?"

"Of course it is." *Probably not.* "I just won't watch you eat." I leaned back, matching her posture. "The difference is your motive is to discuss my offer, which, before we go any further, needs to come off the table." I was half-joking, half-serious. I'm sorry." Better to just rip that Band-Aid off now. No sense in dragging it out longer than necessary.

Her smile faded as she looked at me almost in shock. That bright sparkle she had in her eyes fizzled out fast. "What? Why?"

I sighed. "Because, Katie, I just—I can't do that to you."

"What do you mean? Do what to me?"

Fuck. The disappointed look she had on her face pained me. "Tell you what. Let's start this over. Let me take you out on an actual date tonight, then we'll go from there." I was such a pussy. But God knew I wanted to fuck her seven ways to Sunday, and maybe she wanted that too. It was the potential complication for wanting *more* that came with something like that.

I wanted her bad. Every cell in my body came to life at the mere thought of Katie. I also didn't want to use her. If we were going to possibly subject ourselves to God only knew what outcome, then I needed her to want me just as much as I wanted her.

"Oh. Well, okay then. We can do that too."

I breathed a sigh of relief, tossed my cloth napkin down on my empty plate, and stood up. "Good. Until then, I'm not going to do anything out of line. Also, think about what you'd like to do between now and dinner. I'm going to go jump in the shower."

Without looking back, I grabbed my shopping bags and carried them into the bathroom before I changed my mind again and did something really fucking stupid. Like toss her down on the bed right then and there and see how far she was willing to go.

Steam filled the bathroom as water poured from the rainwater showerhead. I stripped out of the T-shirt and jeans and stepped into the water. There were no words to describe the relief I felt as the sting of scorching hot water blasted almost two days' worth of grime off my skin. Between traveling across the country on three different flights, swimming in the ocean, and not having showered since the night before I'd left home, I could have only hoped I didn't smell like a New Orleans back-alley dumpster. If I did, Katie didn't tell me. Thankfully, after today, that would be a nonissue going forward.

As I scrubbed soapy lather all over my body, my mind instantly went to Katie. Most recently the sight of her in a string bikini, and that dress she had on now did absolutely nothing to prevent my wandering mind. Just like always, any and every thought I had of her made my dick stir and in mere seconds had it standing stand on end.

"Shit," I said quietly to myself while looking down at my dick, now looking back up at me. "Not fucking now."

I continued washing up, avoiding the one part of my body that continued to beg for attention. Even though I knew better, I eventually said to hell with it. Katie would never have to know that I'd gotten myself off to her in the shower—now or ever.

With a handful of conditioner, I grabbed my dick and gave myself a few long, slow, appreciative strokes. Then, because I knew time had been limited, I squeezed firmly, picking up the pace, and *fuck* did it feel good—way too good. Every muscle in my body tensed, and my toes curled as I propped myself up against the wall with my forearm for support.

I closed my eyes, and there she was. Her tall, slender, bikini-clad figure bent forward over the railing on the back porch. Her long, soft blonde hair gently brushing against her lower back in the breeze. Me standing behind her, dragging my knuckles across her skin from her shoulder, down her back, over her hip, finally landing on the tie that held her bottoms together. Teasingly, I twisted the string around my finger before giving it a tug, causing the bottoms to fall open. I traced my finger from her hip to under the curve of her ass cheek and slipped it to the slit between her legs. She was wet. *So fucking wet*. I slid my finger between her folds, then pushed it inside of her. She let out a moan in response to my touch.

My breath caught in my chest as I prepared to unload myself down the drain as my orgasm quickly built, threatening to explode.

There was a soft knock at the door. "Hey, Warren?"

"You've got to be shitting me," I mumbled to myself. I cleared my throat of any sign of my looming ejaculation. "Ye—yeah, what is it?"

"Sorry to bother you, but someone from the front desk just dropped off an envelope for you."

Fucking Christ—*really*? Katie interrupted my jerk-off session to tell me I had a letter? *Hello, blue balls*. "Fine. Just leave it. I'll get it in a minute." I tried my best to hide my frustration with the whole damned situation.

If only I had squeezed a little bit harder and pumped a little faster, I could have finished, but no. Clearly not happening.

I looked down at my sad, semi-hard dick. "Next time," I whispered, making an empty promise to myself, because I knew at this rate that I'd never catch a fucking break.

I quickly rinsed myself clean, dried off, then threw on the first outfit I grabbed. The trip into town hadn't been a total loss, because I'd managed to find enough to get me through the next few days, but my wardrobe options were slim to almost nothing. I was just thankful I'd at least found clean underwear.

Shaving was out of the question when I realized I'd forgotten to buy a razor. I hoped Katie liked a beard because mine had grown in fast.

When I finally came out of the bathroom, the suite was empty. I worried that my gruff tone had scared Katie off. I grabbed the letter she'd left on the end of the bed and headed straight out to the back porch. I actually breathed a sigh of relief at the sight of her sitting on the next-to-last step with her feet submerged in the water.

"Well, do I look like a tourist now?" I had on a button-down cotton shirt with an array of brightly colored tropical flowers plastered all over it, white linen shorts, and a pair of leather flip-flops. This would be the first and last time I would ever wear or own anything like this.

She shielded the sun from her eyes, scanning me up and down, then smiled. "You do. You'll fit right in."

"Great. I didn't have much of a choice. Options were slim."

"You look fine. Did you see your letter? I left it on the bed for you."

"I did." I held it up.

"Well, did you open it?"

I gave her my best arrogant smile. "Curious, are we?"

"Cocky, are we? Don't you at least want to know what it is?"

"No. Not really." Of course I wanted to know, but the mail wasn't nearly as important to me as what I had sitting in front of me.

"Suit yourself," she said, turning back around to face the ocean.

I ripped the envelope open and headed back inside. Just like I'd predicted, Katie came springing up the steps. I felt her presence close behind me and smiled to myself.

"Well? What is it?"

I glanced over my shoulder at her. "Nosey."

"Very. But you're right. It's none of my business."

I handed her the letter. "It's just a welcome letter from the front desk."

"Oh. Well, that was uneventful."

"Indeed it was." *But oh so much fun watching you squirm a little bit.* "So, have you thought about what you'd like to do today? I'm hoping it'll have cooled down a little by the time we make it out of here." I checked my watch. "It's just after two. We still have plenty of time before dinner."

She sat down on the edge of the bed, slipping her feet into her wedge sandals, buckling the straps around her ankles. "I'm up for anything as long I get a chance to do a little exploring and take pictures at some point. That was one of Rowan's requests—take lots of pics."

"Well, we could start with a walk around the property? See what else is around here. I saw they have tour-guided horseback riding on the beach if you wanted."

She casually leaned back, supporting herself on her elbows. The hem of her already too-fucking-short dress rode even higher up her thighs, leaving very little to my imagination. *Down, boy.*

"Normally that sort of thing would sound fun and romantic, but I'm kinda terrified of horses."

"Really? That's a thing? How come?"

"For me, it is. I was tossed off of one when I was twelve, and it almost killed me. So I never got back on one."

"I guess I can't say I blame you there." I gave some more thought as to what I wanted to do, and as it turned out, I didn't really want to *do* anything. All I really wanted was to spend what time I had with her. At this point, I didn't care what the hell we did, as long as it meant getting her far away from a bed and out of that position. One wrong move and I'd know whether or not if she had on panties.

Then, it hit me. I knew exactly what we were going to do. Without a word, I reached for her hand.

She eyed me suspiciously. "Yes?"

"Let's go."

"Where are we going?"

"Come with me. You'll see."

She thought for a moment, eventually putting her hand in mine. I pulled her up to her feet. When she was upright, I could have just as easily let her go, walked away. But no, of course, I didn't. That would have been the smart thing to do.

Instead, I hooked my arm around her waist and yanked her flush into me. She squealed, caught off guard by my move, gripping onto my biceps for support.

"Warren, what are you doing?"

I knew deep down holding in my arms her like this was a terrible idea. Especially if my only intent was to ever go our separate ways. No reward comes without risk, right?

"You know, for someone as uptight as you make yourself out to be, you sure know how to make a girl blush."

"First, let me make one thing clear. Nothing about you is *girl*. You are all woman. Second, just because you find me uptight doesn't mean I can't still be charming too."

She licked her lips, and *fuck*, I wanted more than anything to take her bottom lip between my teeth, then kiss her senseless.

"True," she said, her voice low. "Why are you single?"

"Choice." I released her from my hold before she got a feel of a lot more than she'd bargained for. I turned and headed for the door with my dick leading the way. "Coming?"

"Yup. Right behind ya."

SEVEN

The late-afternoon sun blazed down on us as we stepped outside into the oppressive heat. I double-checked the door to make sure it had locked, and then we made our way toward the shore.

"You haven't seen this place in the daylight yet, have you?"

"Not really. It was well after dark when I got here." We slowed our pace as we reached the end of the boardwalk, and she looked around, taking it all in. "It's stunning."

I glanced down at Katie beside me. "Yes it is. Where to first?"

"I have an idea. Follow me."

We started to make our way, walking shoulder to shoulder down the sidewalk that wound around behind the main clubhouse, before disappearing into the densely wooded tropical forest. The concrete under our feet transitioned into tightly placed stone pavers that eventually faded into a well-worn, well-maintained dirt trail lined with tall grass. Lush greenery flanked up either side of the path and hung overhead from the trees like a living canopy.

"Do you know where you're going?"

If not for the wood sign staked in the ground with a hand-carved waterfall and an arrow pointing toward the trail, I didn't know that I would have thought to venture back here. Thankfully, it didn't seem like Katie had seen it, which worked out in my favor because I wanted our final destination to be a surprise.

"Maybe. Are you nervous?"

She bumped into my shoulder. "My mama did warn me not to go off alone with strange men I didn't know."

"Lucky me, I'm not a stranger to you." I heard the faint sound of rushing water as the trail curved. "Almost there."

The trees opened at the end of the trail, and the hidden oasis came into view. A waterfall cascaded over the edge of a rocky cliff and collected into a sparkling blue pool-like area surrounded by sand and large, smoothed rocks for resting.

Katie stopped and stared in awe. "Oh my— this is—this is amazing, Warren." She quickly ran over and sat down on a huge, flat rock near the edge of the pooling water and removed her shoes. "I can't believe you found this."

I shrugged. "It was nothing. Honestly, I had no idea what we were going to find. I just followed the sign."

She stepped into the edge of the water. "It's so warm."

I watched her as she danced along the water's edge, following the shore around the perimeter, then making her way back up to the trail before she disappeared behind the waterfall.

"Warren," she called out. "You have to come back here. This is unreal!"

I picked up her shoes that she'd left behind and followed along the same trail, making my way to Katie.

She was standing directly behind the waterfall, letting it splash off her hand with the biggest smile on her face. "Is this not the coolest thing you've ever seen?"

I walked up beside her and briefly stuck my hand under the cool water. "Yeah, it is pretty awesome."

What was even better was the fact that we were completely secluded by a curtain of cascading water. Everything beyond it was a blur, which meant if we couldn't see out, no one could see in. Not that we needed the privacy.

"You know what?" she asked, dipping her hand through the fall.

"What's that?"

"You need to lighten up. You always look so serious." She waved her hand under the water, causing it to splash in my face.

I raised an eyebrow, wiping away the droplets. "Maybe I was just lost in thought."

"What exactly are you thinking about Mr. I'm So Serious?" She threw more water at me.

"This." I set her shoes down as I reached out, angling my hand under the water. It spilled off my fingertips into a long stream that sprayed her square in the neck and chest. It wasn't what I'd been aiming for, but lucky me, anyway.

She screamed, then laughed, shielding herself from my attack. "Oh, now you asked for it."

From there it became an all-out battle of splashing each other, ducking away from the other's attack, and trying not to get drenched in the process. We were like two kids playing in the sprinkler on a hot summer day. It was the first time in a long time I could remember feeling so free.

This went on for I don't know how long, splashing, laughing, ducking, and diving. Just the two of us.

"Okay, okay," Katie eventually conceded. "You win. You've proven you're a way better water splasher." We were both practically soaked from head to toe, everything drenched and dripping wet.

"I'd say you're not too bad yourself," I said as I shook out my hair. "Thank you for that."

She scrubbed away water from her face and eyes. "For what?"

"Everything." Then without thinking, I unbuttoned and shrugged out of my shirt.

Her eyebrows shot up to her hairline. "*What* are you doing?"

"Helping you out." Judging by the way she scanned me over, you'd have thought I dropped my pants too.

She pointed at my bare torso. "Um, not like that you aren't."

"Trust me, it's not what you think." I found a dry spot on the back of my shirt and folded it, then gently dabbed the water off her face. "See? That's all I wanted to do. I wasn't trying to get you all worked up." *Or myself* for that matter.

She reached up. I thought she was going to take my shirt from me. Instead, she placed her hand over mine.

I held still, not wanting to lose contact with her.

She closed her eyes for a brief second before looking up at me. "Thank you," she whispered.

"You're welcome," I told her as I brushed a few rogue strands of hair out of her face. I told myself we needed to leave, that we'd had our fun and it was time to go. If we stayed like that any longer, things could get out of hand. I'd told her, and myself, that I wouldn't do anything out of line. Instead of getting us out of there, I placed my other hand on her cheek and held her face between my hands.

We stood face-to-face but still had some space between us. Too much if you asked me.

I pulled her closer, our lips just a few inches apart now. "Katie."

"Hmm?"

"I really, *really* want to kiss you."

Her eyes fluttered closed, and when she bit into her bottom lip, ever so subtly, my dick jumped. "I really want you to," she whispered.

I knew I'd said I wouldn't, but if she were willing, at least this one time, then so was I. Without hesitation, I made my move. Except our lips never had the chance to touch.

"Woah, sorry. We didn't know anyone was back here," a guy's voice sounded, breaking us apart.

"Fuck," I said under my breath. Then, "No problem," I called over my shoulder. "We were just about to leave. It's all yours."

Katie dropped her head forward into my chest. "Damn it," she mumbled.

"I'm so sorry," I whispered in her ear. "I'll make it up to you." I gave her a kiss on the top of her head, then reluctantly pulled away. I handed her shoes in exchange for my shirt, then grabbed her hand and led us out from behind the waterfall. We needed a cooldown anyway. I know I sure as hell did.

Warren tried to kiss me.

Holy shit.

We'd almost kissed, and I was pretty sure I almost peed my pants.

Okay, maybe not quite, but damned close.

I felt like I was in middle school all over again, about to be kissed for the first time ever. The possessiveness Warren emitted from the way he looked at me and the way he held me in his hands? His touch was like fire that melted me to the core, and at that point, I was ready to go all in, right then and there without hesitation. I sighed at the thought of what his soft, full lips would have felt like pressed to mine, or how our tongues would have felt gliding across one another, or how the stubble of his beard would have felt as it brushed against my skin.

Only it would figure we'd be interrupted. Though it was probably for the best for both of us. Granted, we probably could have just as easily gone back to our suite and picked up right where we'd left off, but it seemed the moment had passed. He didn't offer; I didn't ask.

We made our way out of the hidden oasis, taking our time, making light conversation as we retraced our steps back to the main resort. I stopped a few times here and there for pictures of the wildlife and exotic plants and flowers. I even snapped a few selfies with the beach in the background. I wanted to document every little detail as much as possible so when it was back to reality, I had proof that this all hadn't been one amazing dream.

When we finally reached the room, I went out onto the back porch. The day was slowly coming to an end, and I was not going to miss the sunset this time. I snapped a few more pics of the low-hung sun hovering above the horizon as it painted the sky different hues of red, yellow, orange, pink, and deep purple. When I went back inside, Warren had lain down on the too-small couch. He had his arm thrown over his face.

"Well, Mr. Adventure, what now?"

"You sure have a lot of nicknames for me. Mr. Personality, Mr. I'm So serious, now Mr. Adventure."

"Hey, I can think of a few more."

"I have no doubt."

"At least I haven't referred to you as Mr. Uptight Asshole."

He glared at me from under his forearm. "But you've thought it?"

"Not out loud."

"Lovely." He covered his face back up. "I'm up for whatever you want to do."

I plopped down onto my stomach on the bed and scrolled through all the new pictures on my phone. Damn it. I wished Warren and I had taken at least *one* together. I didn't even have any of him in the background.

"You look like you're up for a nap."

"I'm getting there."

"Why don't you come lay down in the bed? It's probably more comfortable than the couch."

"I'm sure it is. This is a safer bet right now."

"Suit yourself." He was probably right. If he did come lie over here, I'd have to get up and go to the couch. I didn't think lying next to him in a bed was a smart move at this point. Not until we talked more, laid down some ground rules. Hell, I didn't even know if we needed them at this point. It didn't seem like we were getting any further than just admiring and frustrating the hell out of each other.

"I am kind of starting to get hungry," he said. "What time do you want to go for dinner?"

I rolled over onto my back, loosened the straps on my shoes, and kicked them off the foot of the bed. "Whenever. It's still a little bit too early for me, and I'd like to take a shower or at least clean up before we go." I checked the time on my phone. "It's just after five now, so maybe another hour or so? That good for you?"

"Works for me. It's not like I have anywhere else to be."

I was grateful for that. Plus, having had Warren here with me so far had been the highlight of this trip, despite our bumpy start. His presence had been surprisingly refreshing and welcoming, and he did seem to be loosening up a little bit around me. Someone like Chloe around would have been fun too, but I wasn't interested in kissing her.

I set my phone down on the table and worked my way underneath the blanket, snuggling into the pillow. Thinking about spending time with Warren was the last thing I remembered right before I closed my eyes. The next time I opened them, the room was pitch-black.

"Holy shit." I shot straight up in bed. The only light in the room came from the ajar bathroom door.

"Warren?" I called out. There was no answer. I checked the time on my phone. "Holy shit!" *Seven fifteen*?

I scrambled out of bed and ran straight for the bathroom to get ready. In my haste, I'd almost missed the note stuck to the mirror. I plucked it off.

Lyndsay Marie

Sleeping Beauty, meet me at the outdoor lounge whenever you get this. It's six thirty. —W.

Whew. That was a huge relief knowing he hadn't been too far ahead of me, which meant I still had a little time to make myself presentable. I was already late. A few more minutes wouldn't make a difference.

I jumped in the shower for a quick wash-up, sans hair, and a fresh shave. When I got out, I threw on a black, flowy, spaghetti-strap maxi dress and a pair of flat, strappy sandals. To complete my ensemble, I applied a fresh, light coat of makeup. Then I unbraided and gave my hair a fresh, loosely twisted bun, smoothing out any flyaway hairs.

"Good enough," I said to myself in the mirror.

I grabbed my room key and headed out.

As I made my way toward shore, the same reggae music and tings from a steelpan drum drifted in the breeze.

When I finally found the lounge, I spotted Warren through the trees, sitting at the bar with his back to me. He had a drink in hand, talking and laughing with the bartender.

The place was at probably less than half capacity. People, mostly couples, eating, drinking, all lost in conversation. Warren's distinguished, booming laugh was easily heard over all the chatter through the glassless windows.

As I approached him from behind, my stomach did flips and twisted.

I sucked in a deep breath and tapped him on the shoulder. "Is this seat taken?" I asked, pointing to the empty barstool beside him.

He shifted in his seat and didn't even try to hide the fact that he was the one now eyeing me from head to toe. "Well, I'm waiting on this beautiful woman to eventually join me, but if she doesn't show up soon, you're more than welcome to take her place."

My face flushed with heat. I just shook my head and smiled, then propped up on the seat beside him. "You're such a flirt."

"Only with the right person." He took a long pull of his drink. "You look exceptionally beautiful, Katie. Not that you don't always. You just look…different."

"Different, huh? But not in a bad way? Because I really didn't do—"

He stopped me. "Never in a bad way, so get that idea out of your head." He gave me one more head-to-toe glance, then faced forward. "Now," he said as he reached for the drink menu and slid it over to me, "would you like a drink?"

I scanned over the two-page menu. "I'm not entirely sure yet. They have a lot of options." I looked at his almost empty glass. "What are you drinking?"

"Same thing I always drink. Scotch."

"Ah. Same as what's back at the room?"

"That would be the one."

"I see you're really branching out here." I, on the other hand, had decided to order the most tropical, frozen fruity drink I could find. I gave the bartender my order based off a picture without reading the description. "I prefer to indulge something I can't easily make for myself at home."

"Maybe I'll branch out next time." He finished off his scotch, then set his glass down. "Turn around. Let me see the back of your hair."

"My hair?"

"Yes, your hair." He reached for my seat and spun it around before I had the chance to contest. "Don't move."

"What are you—"

"Shh. Just trust me." I felt his hands moving around my hair, gently feeling around until I realized that he'd pulled out the long pin that had held my twisted bun in its place. Every hair on my head fell loose as he used his fingers to gently shake it out of place. "There," he said, handing me my hairpin over my shoulder. "Much better."

I combed my fingers through my hair, trying to give it some order, as I turned back around to face him. "What was that for?" I started to pull it back, but he moved my hands away.

"Leave it, please. I want to see it down. You always keep your hair so neat and uptight."

"Habit, I guess." That wasn't entirely a lie. Having spent more of my life than not always fussed at about upholding certain beauty standards, old habits tended to die hard.

"Well, you're on vacation. Have a little fun."

I looked at him like he'd lost his mind. "You're one to talk. I only ever see you in serious mode, except for that one time today."

The waiter returned before Warren could defend himself and placed my drink down in front of me. I laughed at the size of the glass. "Holy shit. That is not a glass. *That* is a fishbowl."

"Wow. You are not kidding. Good luck with that."

"Um, looks like we're sharing, 'cause I'm going to need a drinking partner, not luck to finish this off. I can't drink all of this by myself."

He smiled. "No?"

"Absolutely not."

"Eh, It'll sure be fun watching you try."

Using the straw, I stirred it up, mixing the frozen part with the liquid that floated to the top. The glass itself was topped with slices of pineapple and orange and a bright pink hibiscus, then rimmed with blue sugar. The colors reminded me of the sunset I'd caught earlier today—a rainbow of yellow, orange, and red. It was almost too pretty to drink.

Almost.

I took a long, slow pull through the straw. "Wowza. That is good…and really strong."

Warren raised his freshly refilled glass and clinked it against mine. "Cheers."

"Cheers."

We sat for a while, talking about everything and nothing. He touched briefly on his childhood, the baby brother he and Wes had lost, his career research, and love of all things routine. I told him about my pageant and cheerleading days and my mother's need to live vicariously through me.

Eventually, we decided to order food before the kitchen closed for the night. When it finally arrived, we ate in silence for the first few minutes, just savoring each delicious bite.

Then out of nowhere, he steered our conversation in a whole different direction. One I hadn't been prepared for.

"So," he said, taking a bite of his food, "did I hear you correctly, you live with your parents?"

I guess there are worse things we could talk about.

"Correction," I said, washing down a bite of food with my half-full, mostly melted drink. "They moved in with me—well, technically I live in and rent their old house from them. Their land recently got taken over via eminent domain, so now they're back living with me for now, I guess." The last thing I needed was for Warren to think I was some grown woman in my midthirties still living at home with Mom and Dad.

"Eminent domain? That's interesting."

"It's something, all right."

"So what happened? The Men in Black just showed up, knocked on their door one day, and told them to move out?"

"More or less. That's what happens when you own a shit-ton of prime acreage and the government can get better use out of it with interstate access and a medical research park." I finished telling him their story and how it all came to fruition from beginning to end. "So now, here I am."

"That's a shame—about them, not you being here. I really like that part of your story."

I smiled. "I'm really glad I'm here too."

"Do you have any idea what you're going to do once you get back home?"

"I guess once I return from fantasy island, I'll sit down with them and see what they want to do. If they want to try to buy another farm or if I'm going to have to start apartment hunting. They talked about buying an RV and traveling at one point."

Just then, the tiniest green lizard skittered past us, running across the tiled countertop. Warren flinched.

"Did you just jump?"

"Absolutely not."

"Sure looked like it to me. Wait, are you—" I leaned back, trying not to laugh at him or fall off my barstool. "Are you scared of a baby lizard?"

"I wouldn't call it scared," he said as he lifted his plate, checking for more critters. "Let's just say I'm not particularly fond of them. We don't see many in Chicago."

This time, I laughed and did not hold back. "A big, strong man like you is afraid of a tiny reptile."

He shook his head and lifted up his glass, checking the bottom of it. "You're learning way too much about me."

"Don't worry, your secret's safe with me." I sucked down the last of the drink in the bottom of my fishbowl.

Warren pointed to my glass. "You want another one?"

Oh, hell no. That was the last thing I'd needed. My head was already swimming. "Nope. I'm beyond done. Thanks for helping me drink that."

He smiled and raised an eyebrow. "As much as I'd love to take credit, that's all you."

"What?" *Oh, shit*. "Are you serious?"

"I only had one sip; the rest is on you."

I glanced down at my glass, then back at Warren. "Oops."

"No worries. We're on vacation. You're supposed to be having a good time, letting your hair down. Remember?"

"I hope you're right. I'm sure once that drink hits, it'll be over for me."

"There's one way to find out." He stood up and held his hand out. "Dance with me?"

"Seriously?"

"Of course I am."

"Right now?" I listened for a few seconds and noticed that the music had changed from the lively reggae music to something slower and instrumental that was actually perfect for a slow waltz.

"Yes, right now."

Warren and I had only ever danced together once before at Rowan's wedding. So to say I was terrified was an understatement. The butterflies I'd felt when I first saw him tonight were back, though that could have been the strawberry mango mai tai marga-whatever-it's-called that I'd apparently smashed on my own.

"Okay, but just one. I make no promises on my coordination right now." Guess I'd soon find out the effects of my drink once I stood up. I offered him my hand, and he pulled me into him.

"No worries," he whispered in my ear. "I've got you."

We drifted away from our seats and out into the middle of the empty concrete floor. The bar was void of almost all patrons, with the exception of a handful of people scattered throughout, still eating and drinking. We were the only two dancing.

I let Warren take the lead as he held me in his arms. His moves hadn't been awkward, and the alcohol didn't seem to have any effect on his ability to dance. I didn't seem to fumble or step on his feet.

I had one hand on his shoulder for support and the other one in his while he kept one arm wrapped around my back. I thought it had been all in my head how smooth he'd danced at Rowan's wedding, but as it turned out, my intuition was correct—the man could move with surprising grace and ease. Even in my altered state, I could just feel it.

Maybe it helped that I had taken ballroom dancing classes when I was a teenager, but it took at least some skill from both dancers to move as effortlessly together as we did.

"You're a really good dancer," he said. The sound of his voice vibrated against my chest as it pressed against his.

"Yeah, you're not so bad yourself."

He stepped back, spun me around, then pulled me back into him even closer. "Dance lessons."

"Really? Me too."

"I had a feeling," he said as we swayed back and forth. "Don't tell anyone. I'll never admit to it."

"No worries. I'll keep that tidbit of info in my back pocket, along with the lizard, just in case."

"Fair enough," he said. He wrapped his arm all of the way around my waist and gripped my hip. Even in my liquored-up state, I felt hyperaware of his every move and touch. The contact of his hand felt scorching hot, even through the fabric of my cotton dress.

For no reason at all, I smiled against his cheek. "How did you know I could dance?"

"Just a hunch. That and I could tell when we danced at my brother's wedding. You moved differently than someone who doesn't have professional experience."

"Interesting observation. I had no clue such an intuition existed."

"It's my job to pay attention to detail."

The song eventually came to an end, and Warren led us back to our seats.

"Oh! That was so much fun," I said as I fanned myself with my hand. I practically dripped with sweat from head to toe, completely out of breath. "I haven't danced like that in forever."

"Indeed it was, Kit-Kat. We'll have to do that again before we head home. Not tonight, though." He shifted in his seat to face me and rested his hands on my thighs, right above my knees. Maybe it had all been in my hazy, drunken state of mind, but I'd have sworn his touch felt hotter than it should have.

I looked down at his hands splayed over my thighs, then back up at him. His hazelly-brown eyes had changed to a dangerously darker shade, almost black.

Nope. Definitely not all in my head. He was coming for me, even after he'd said he wouldn't, and I couldn't have been more open to the idea. I didn't know the exact moment when the mood had shifted, but it felt like we had gone from zero to one sixty in five seconds.

Feeding into his advance, I inched myself forward, forcing his grasp to slide further up my legs. He could take his offer off the table and shove it. I wanted the man, and he would know just how much right the fuck now. Whether he took the bait or not, I'd soon find out. We'd either end up in bed together or licking our wounds, and he could take the couch again.

I watched his chest as it rose and fell a little faster with each breath he took. He was fighting an internal battle. Probably similar to one I'd been fighting. Did I make my move or wait for the other person?

I leaned forward, gripping onto his shoulders, and pulled him closer to me. The stubble of his beard brushed against my cheek.

"You wanna know something?" I whispered, my lips against the shell of his ear. His fingers dug into my legs as I spoke.

He let out a low, deep growl, causing every hair on my body to stand on end, sending chills down my spine. "I want to know anything and everything you want to tell me."

"I really, *really* like it when you call me that."

"What's that?"

I licked my lips, wanting to trace my tongue across his ear, but refrained. "Kit-Kat."

"Hmm. Do you now?"

I closed my eyes as he spoke. I nodded. "Umm hmm. Wanna know something else?"

"I'm not sure I'm ready to hear what else you have to say, but yes."

I bit into my bottom lip, debating on my next words. My inhibitions were long gone by this point, so it didn't matter what I said.

Screw it. I went for it, anyway. All in.

"I'm really, really horny right now."

His head shook ever so subtly. "You're fucking killing me," he whispered back. "I hope you know that."

I leaned back up, putting us face-to-face. "How so?" I asked with a smirk.

Okay, I knew damned good and well exactly what I was doing and what was going on between us. He'd already admitted once that he shared the same desire for me as I did for him. But I'd finally allowed myself to accept the fact that I was ready to go all in with him, even though that was never my plan. He was never in the cards, and the sheer thought of getting slightly involved with or being with a man like Warren terrified me.

He broke contact with me as he sat back, turning to face forward, then taking a casual sip of his scotch.

What in the hell? That was *not* at all the response I'd expected from him. Not at all. One minute I thought he was just as hot and ready to go as I was, then the next, he was gone. *Poof.*

"I'll have you know," he said without looking at me, "it has taken every ounce of restraint I have in my soul to not come on to you as much as I've wanted to. To sit here and try to lie to myself that I don't want you."

"Then why are you holding back?" *For the love of God, stop holding back.*

Warren sat quietly as he thought for a second, seemingly choosing his next words carefully. "Because. I don't want to hurt you, Katie. I can't give you any more of me than what I can offer in the short amount of time we have together, and I think you deserve better than that."

Wow. That was an interesting and completely unexpected sentiment. "Wait. So, you're looking out for my best interest? What *you* think I need? Because I'm a big girl. I can—"

"Katie." His tone was laced with warning.

"Don't 'Katie' me, Warren. I can hold my own." I reached for my glass, but it was gone. The bartender had already taken it away. *Shit.*

"I didn't mean it like that."

"Right. Is that what you want to do? Shut me down? Or do you want to do what we've been doing and flirt and come on to me?" I didn't need Warren to protect me. I was used to asshole men with their fuck 'em and leave 'em attitude. Thus far, that had been the story of my love life. Tonight didn't have to be any different.

He set his drink down, the highball glass clanging against the tile countertop. He shifted to completely face me again. "Oh, I want so much. You have no fucking idea."

I reached over and grabbed his hand and pleaded with him. "Then tell me, Warren. What do you want?"

He looked down at my hand on top of his, then worked his fingers to intertwine with mine. "Oh, I want to come on to you, then on you...*inside* of you."

His admission almost threw me off my barstool. I felt my eyes practically bug out of my head. But there it was, exactly as I'd requested, and I couldn't even form a response. He'd actually said the words out loud, and all I could do was stare at him in disbelief.

"I think you heard me loud and clear," he said, knowing I hadn't said a word. He stood up from his seat, wrapped his arm around my waist, and hauled me up to my feet, completely flush against his front.

Oh! He was dead serious.

"And if I'm being totally honest with you right now," he continued, "I don't want to wait any longer than I already have."

Holy shit. This man was a fierce force to be reckoned with. The tone in his voice and the power that he radiated set off every warning bell, alarm, and whistle in my body. I was going to be screwed—in more ways than one.

I swallowed hard. My head was reeling, swimming, still unable to formulate words. I just nodded.

"I won't do anything until you give me the green light, Katie. Everything going forward is entirely your call. There's no rush and no pressure. I won't treat you any differently if you change your mind about any of this."

Here it was, the official offer. One we hadn't really discussed or ironed out the details. If I'd said I was nervous, that would have been an understatement. I was scared shitless.

We held each other's gaze as if trying to read the other person's mind, though he'd already said what was on his, leaving no room for any guesswork. After what felt like forever, I found a semblance of my voice. Whether it was the voice of reason or the one of eternally bad decisions, that would be determined later.

"One time. One night." Those were my terms. Any more than that with Warren and I knew I'd be up shit's creek without a paddle.

He cocked an eyebrow and repeated my words. "One night, one time? That's it?"

"That's it," I said, trying to sound confident in my decision. "So you'd better make it a good one,"

"Is that a green light, Katie?"

I wrapped my arms around his neck, his embrace tightening around my waist. "Green light."

Those were all the words I needed to say. In an instant, he swept me off my feet—literally—as he picked me up in his arms and hauled me out of the bar. He carried me all of the way back to the bungalow and somehow unlocked the door with one hand without dropping me.

As he pushed the door open, he stopped just before stepping inside.

Shit. He was having second thoughts. I just knew it.

"By the way," he said, nuzzling his nose against my neck, "I really like this dress on you."

That was it? He wanted to compliment my dress? Not at all what I'd expected him to say.

"Um, thank you? I think. Is that it? You're not changing your mind about me?"

"What? God no. I just wanted to tell you that before I forgot."

I wrapped my arm tighter around his neck as he lifted and adjusted me in his arms. "I don't care what anyone says about you, you really are a gentleman."

He smirked. "I do try my best, but there is one thing I can assure you."

"What's that?"

"Once we go through this door, I won't be."

NINE
Warren

Holy fuck, what a night.

I had Katie secure in my arms, and it was one of the best feelings in the world. Only second to what it would feel like buried balls-deep inside of her, and I wasn't far off from knowing how that felt too.

As much as I would have liked to have just thrown her down onto the middle of the bed, ripped that dress smooth off her, and ravaged her body—and believe me, I wanted to—she deserved to have every single, solitary ounce of her savored, not wasting a drop. I'd need more than just a week with her to do that. Selfishly, though, I was going to take whatever she was willing to give me with what time we had.

I kicked the door closed behind us, then walked over to the bed, carefully lowering her down onto the edge of it.

"That was so much better than walking," she said, leaning back on her elbows. "'Cause I don't think I would have made it back in one piece if I had to do that on my own. I'm feeling pretty buzzed."

"Are you going to be okay?"

"Oh, yeah. I'm fine. I think."

"If you ever aren't, please let me know. You had a lot to drink." I knelt in front of her, careful not to fall back on my ass. "And for the record, anytime you need to be carried, I'm here. Plus, I'd think by now you'd be used to me carrying you around when you've had too much to drink," I said with a smug grin.

"Ha. Ha. That was one time, twice if you're counting tonight. I could have walked just fine."

"I have no doubt in my mind you would have tried. You're stubborn like that."

As I sat on my knees in front of her, I gently held on to her ankles—for support, and because I needed to have my hands on her—rubbing my thumbs along the inside. The occasional soft moan she let out in between let me know she enjoyed it as much as I did.

"Hey! You only did it the first time because Rowan ordered you to."

"I wouldn't quite go as far as to say she 'ordered' me, but I wasn't about to pass up the opportunity to carry you to bed, albeit my guest bed, but the fact remains."

That night went down as one of my most favorite memories of all time. At the end of the wedding reception, I swooped Katie up into my arms, just as I had tonight, and hauled her back to my condo. Though it was never with the intent of taking advantage of her disadvantaged state. All I had wanted was for her to have a safe place to crash so she could sleep off all of the fun she'd had, and for me to have the opportunity to admire her a little while longer since I didn't think I would see much of her again once she'd gone home. Unbeknownst to me, after we'd made it upstairs, I found Rowan's mom *and* her grandmother both already passed out in my king-sized bed. I knew Wes had set that one up. So I took Katie to my guest room instead and tucked her in. Then, in true gentlemanly fashion, I went and slept on the couch. Though I may or may not have kissed her on her forehead as I covered her up.

Her playful smile faded into something more serious. "Well, thank you for taking care of me."

I massaged my thumbs deeper into her flesh, slightly working my way up. "It's been my pleasure for sure. I wouldn't have let anything happen to you—then or now." Probably forever if it had been an option.

Maybe forever was a bit of a stretch. I needed to wipe any ideas of Katie and me together—beyond the bed tonight and St. Lucia—completely out my mind. That wasn't what any of this was about. We were in the moment—no more, no less.

"Well, I really appreciate you, Warren."

"You're very welcome, Kit-Kat. Just doing what feels right."

At that, I carefully spread her slightly apart, slipping off her shoes one at a time. As I did, I gently massaged each foot one.

"Oh my Lord, that feels so good. You know you don't have to do that."

I worked my thumb into the arch of her foot. "I'm well aware I don't *have* to do it. It's a want, not an obligation."

She softly moaned as I continued to rub her feet, working my way up her calves. Each little sound that escaped her lips caused me to squeeze her tighter and my dick to grow, straining harder against my shorts.

"Remember what I said before? We don't do anything you don't want to do."

She reached out and ran her fingers through my hair. "What about you?"

"What about me?"

"What if you don't want to do this?"

I laughed softly. "Oh, Katie, there isn't much I wouldn't be willing to do to or with you, but everything going forward is on your terms." She dragged her hand down the side of my face and rubbed her thumb across my lips. I kissed her finger.

"Tell me, Katie, what is it that you want right now?"

The light from the bathroom beamed like a beacon on her. I could see each delicate feature of her face as clear as day. Her blue eyes searched mine. I didn't know if she was weighing her options first, to be sure that she made the best decision possible, or if she was feeling the effects of her drink. For a split second, I feared that she might be the one to back down, and I'd land myself another cold shower.

My heart hammered in my chest as I waited for her response.

After what felt like forever in complete silence, she finally answered. "Just you."

That was all I needed to hear. "Say no more."

I lifted her leg and kissed the top of her foot, then the other. I lightly dragged my fingertips up the back of her calves, pushing the hem of her long dress up over her knees. I kissed a trail along the inside of each of her legs, back and forth between each one as I made my way up, until my mouth reached the inside of her midthigh. I gripped her knees and pushed her legs wide open. The only barrier between me and that sweet pussy of hers was a thin layer of black lace fabric.

She eventually lay all of the way back on the bed as I slid my hands underneath her dress to her hips and stopped when I reached the sides of her panties. "Last chance, Kit-Kat."

Her hands reached down and wrapped around the bunched-up skirt of her dress. She arched her back off the bed and wiggled the dress up over her head, dropping it next to her on the bed.

I sucked in a deep breath at the sight of Katie laid back, arms over her head, pert tits on full display with their hard nipples just begging to be sucked.

"Fuck. Me," I hissed through my teeth.

"No, Warren. You fuck me."

"Gladly." I wrapped my fingers around her panties in a death grip and yanked them down to the floor, tossing them somewhere behind me.

She squealed in surprise. "That's so much better," she said as she lay spread out before me— no dress, no panties, no bra, just Katie.

"My God, you are absolute perfection." Every square inch of her exposed skin just begged to be tended to from every hair on her head, all the way down to manicured toes. But tonight, there was only one head on my own body that had been engaged, and it wasn't the one with the voice of reason. And right now, my dick told me to hurry the fuck up before it took care of itself.

I repositioned myself in front of her, ready to dive in, only this time, absolutely nothing stood in my way. I placed my hands just above her knees, inching them upward to the inside her thighs. Slowly, she spread her legs even more until she was completely open, inviting me in.

Casually, I grazed my knuckle down the middle of her wet slit, then back up, lightly rubbing her clit as I did. She moaned and rocked her hips into my hand.

"Warren," she said, my name on her lips a plea, already out of breath. "Please don't make me wait anymore."

"I don't know, I kind of like it when you beg." Who the hell was I kidding? My dick was so hard at this point it physically hurt, and I was completely out of room in my shorts. I damned sure wasn't doing myself any favors by delaying the inevitable.

"Oh, come on—"

Her words cut off when I slid my finger deep inside of her already soaking wet pussy and devoured her with my mouth like this were my last meal and her last orgasm. She let out a long, loud moan as I flicked my tongue against her clit, pumping my finger in and out. Her hands fisted into my hair and pulled while simultaneously pushing my face further between her legs.

When I pushed a second finger inside of her, she clenched down around me. The louder her moans became, the faster I worked my hand and tongue. Within seconds, her hips bucked against my face, and my name echoed off the walls as her orgasm ripped through her in what I considered record time.

I slowed my movements as she came down from her frenzied high with bursts of soft, broken breaths and a small laugh. "Shit. That—that was amazing. And amazingly fast. Holy shit."

Carefully and reluctantly, I dragged my fingers out of her, kissed the inside of each thigh, and stood up tall and proud, my rock-hard dick standing up just the same.

"That was rather impressive, if I do say so myself."

She pushed herself to sit up and scooted to the edge of the bed, her legs still spread apart. "I agree. But that," she said, pointing to my dick, "is even more impressive. Though I do have one problem."

"What's that?"

"You're wearing way too many clothes."

"I can fix that." I yanked my shirt off over my head and threw it across the room. "Better?"

She shook her head, then reached forward, hooking her fingers into the front waistband of my shorts, pulling me forward to stand right between her legs. She popped the button of my shorts loose and pulled the zipper down. As they dropped to the floor, my dick sprung straight out through the hole in the front of my boxers.

I placed my clean hand on the side of her face, then ran my fingers through her hair. "How about now?"

She shook her head again. "Almost." Then she pulled my boxers down, releasing all of me free just inches from her face. "There."

As she wrapped her soft, warm hand around my erection, she grazed the pad of her thumb over the bead of precum on my head. I reached forward and wrapped my hand in her hair, giving it a firm tug that caused her fuckable pink lips to gape open.

She swallowed. "May I?"

"Anything you want, Kit-Kat, anything you want. But you don't have—"

Her mouth wrapped around my dick before I could finish my sentence, practically sucking me all of the way in. It was in that moment I'd have married her if she asked me to.

I couldn't remember the last time I'd had my dick sucked, but it didn't matter. The way Katie worked her mouth on the head of my dick, occasionally taking me so far in that I felt it hit the back of her throat, had me forgetting I'd ever received a blow job from anyone else.

Her hand wrapped around me moved faster, jerking me off while she sucked. My balls tightened as my own orgasm threatened to unload down her throat.

"Kit-Kat. Watch it. I'm really fucking close."

She moaned, and her voice vibrated on my dick. I grabbed the back of her head with both hands, tangling my fingers in her hair, and gently urged her forward as I rocked my hips. I felt her free hand cup my balls as the suction of her mouth intensified. That was it for me. I was done.

"I—I'm coming, Katie. Fuck."

The hand she had wrapped around my dick, now slick with her saliva, pumped just as her mouth pulled me in and out. I let out a low, deep growl as my cum shot out. Katie never once lost control, taking every last drop of me, sucking me dry.

Fucking impressive.

I guided her head back, pulling out from her mouth, and swiped my thumb across her swollen lips. "My God, that was incredible. Thank you."

She smiled up at me. "First time I've ever let anyone do that."

"Do what?" I was terrified of her answer. There was no way that was her first time giving head.

"Come in my mouth."

"Are you serious?"

She shrugged. "Yeah. I'm feeling pretty good, so I figured why not?"

"Christ. Now I feel terrible for doing that."

"Why? Don't feel bad. I wanted to do it."

I let out a sigh. "Don't get me wrong, I'm not complaining. That shit was amazing. I just wish I'd have known first. I hope it was okay? Do you need me to get you something to drink?"

She shook her head. "No, I'm fine. I just feel exceptionally drunk."

"Buzz kicking in?"

"Buzz? I'd say I'm half-tanked right now. How are you feeling?"

"I'm okay, I guess. Maybe a little better than usual, but I don't think it's the alcohol."

"Yeah, I know what you mean. The room is spinning pretty fast. Let me go splash some water on my face and rinse my mouth out. I'll be right back."

"Of course. Take your time." I helped her to her feet and held her steady as she caught her footing.

"I'm good."

"Okay. I'll be right out here. Just call out if you need me."

"Thank you."

I gripped her arms and pressed my lips to hers. Her eyes closed as her mouth opened, letting me in. I didn't even give a shit that I'd just busted a nut in her mouth. I wanted to kiss this woman.

Our mouths moved in a perfectly synchronized motion as she relaxed. My dick perked up again. It dawned on me as our tongues touched, this had been our first real kiss, and it was every-fucking-thing a kiss should be.

She eased back, out of breath, and looked up at me. "I can't believe you just did that."

"What? What'd I do now?"

"Kissed me after I went down on you."

I smiled and shrugged. "So did you."

"True. First time for everything, I guess."

"Go get cleaned up." I spun her toward the bathroom, giving her a smack on the ass as she walked away.

Holy shit.

I, Katherine Michelle McDonald, of mostly sound mind and body, actually swallowed. That wasn't something I had ever done, but how the hell could I not? We—well, mostly me—were so caught up in the moment. It had been entirely too long since I'd put a dick in my mouth and actually enjoyed it. There was a brief moment of what I could only consider clarity when I questioned what in the hell I was about to do. But then that long, drawn-out, low, and rumbling moan that resounded from somewhere deep in Warren's chest reassured me he'd been enjoying it just as much as me. I was more than happy to indulge myself in him. Taking him into my mouth, inch by inch, was worth the challenge. Even the outcome was worth it.

Just seconds before he came, he growled out my name as a warning. As I milked every drop of him with my mouth, my own wetness dripped down my thighs. I was so turned on with how he'd responded to me, I couldn't not give him the pleasure of taking everything he was offering to me. The saltiness, the thick stickiness, while somewhat shocking, wasn't terrible. I'd do it to him again if given the opportunity.

Besides, returning the favor on him was worth my almost gagging on his dick, 'cause Lord have mercy, the man was not small by any standards.

To top it all off, Warren sure as hell could work magic with his tongue. The way he went down on me was nothing short of epic. His tongue spoke a promise of more to come without ever saying a word. Throw in those long, efficient, and talented fingers? I was done. Lord only knew what sex with him would be like. If he could work first through third base the way he did, I could only assume his skills in bed would be a grand slam.

When I finally emerged from the bathroom after washing my face and brushing my teeth—mainly for his benefit—Warren had passed out. Like, dead-to-the-world asleep. Though, I wasn't entirely surprised to find him like that. We'd both indulged in the drinks at dinner.

I tiptoed as quietly and carefully across the room as it spun in circles around me, then crawled across the bed and under the covers beside him. He was in such a deep and peaceful sleep that having sex at that moment was not worth interrupting his rest. Not to mention my doubt that he'd even be able to get it up again. After a few minutes of wondering what being with him would be like, it was my turn to pass out.

♡♡♡

I didn't know how long we'd been lying there, but when I tried to roll over to change positions, I realized we were a tangled mess. The weight of him using me as a human body pillow with his arm across my chest and a leg tossed over mine had me pinned to the bed. I squirmed slightly to readjust. Our skin stuck together. I peeked underneath the covers to confirm my suspicions. Yup, still naked…both of us. I needed to get up, which meant I'd have to physically peel him off me. As I contemplated how to maneuver out from underneath him, he woke up and rolled onto his back. Problem solved.

"Good morning, Kit-Kat," his voice mumbled sleepily out into the pitch-black room.

Wait, it was dark? The sun hadn't even come up yet? I didn't know what time we'd made it back to the suite or crawled into bed, but it had been super late. There was no way in hell it was still nighttime.

"Good morning, but I don't think it's morning yet. It's still dark out."

He hooked one of his strong arms underneath me and flipped me over, pulling me into his side, reversing our original position. Now I had my leg over his and my arm across his chest. That familiar tingling feeling between my legs was back. *Shit*. I hoped he didn't feel it because my bare crotch was pressed right up against his thigh.

He planted a kiss on my forehead. "In here it is. As it turns out, the windows have pull-down shades and blackout curtains. They were just shoved behind the box trim around the windows."

"Well, I'll be damned. When did you figure all this out?"

His thumb gently rubbing back and forth over the back of my arm did not go unnoticed. In fact, I was hyperaware of all his attention to me…last night and now. To be honest, I missed this kind of physical touch. He was gentle, thoughtful, calculated, whether he'd meant it that way or not. *Don't get used to it*, I thought to myself. He'd be gone before I knew it.

"Yesterday afternoon while you were taking your nap. I thought there's no way this place doesn't have a way to cover the windows besides some see-through curtains. Lo and behold."

I snuggled deeper into his side. "I like it. Now I want to know what time it really is."

He moved around and stretched his arm out. The glow from his watch hands came into view.

"Kind of hard to tell, but it looks like four forty-five."

"As in a.m.?"

He softly laughed. "Probably. There's no way in hell I'd ever sleep until almost five in the afternoon."

He set his watch back down and felt around for something else. My phone lit up, almost blinding me. "Yup."

It wasn't even five in the damn morning. Good Lord. You'd think after the night we'd had, between the drinks and energy-depleting orgasms, we would have slept at least until after sunrise. Though, I felt surprisingly clearheaded considering how I had felt when I went to bed.

"How are you feeling this morning?" I asked him.

He wrapped his other arm around me, pulling me into his warm embrace. "After last night? Like I could take on the world. I gotta say, you've got a hell of a mouth on you, if I'm being completely transparent with you."

"I'm glad you think so." I could feel my face flush with heat. I also couldn't help but wonder if I'd get another opportunity to do it again.

"Oh, believe me, I know so." He tipped my chin up and kissed me gently on the lips.

I wish I could have seen his face, his features, the way he seemed to soften when he looked at me now. Rather than seeming like he was annoyed by me or my presence, little by little, it started to feel like he'd meant when he said he was glad to have me around…even if it was only for a few days.

I kissed the corner of his mouth, then his cheek, then the stubble along his jawline, and lightly on his neck before biting into it. His fingers dug into my hip, and I had to keep from humping his thigh.

"Things were just getting good until you passed out on me."

"Boy, did I ever. I'm terribly sorry about that. I assure you, I won't let it happen again."

His hand moved from my hip down my thigh, rubbing back and forth between my knee and hip, softly squeezing and massaging as he went. If he hadn't noticed before, he damned sure would notice the wetness that rapidly built up between my legs.

Instead, he saved his poor leg from my lude behavior by distracting me when he asked, "Any idea what would you like to do today?" And his tone wasn't at all suggestive. *Damn.*

"Hmm. I haven't thought about it yet. What do you want to do?"

His rock-hard dick jumped, brushing against my knee as he tightened his hold around me. Maybe there was hope after all. "We can lay here all day just like this for all I care. I have nowhere to be and all the time in the world to get there."

Except, Houston, we had another problem, and the longer I lay there, the worse it got. "That sounds unbelievably amazing. As much as I would love that, I really need to pee first."

He let out a cross between a grunt and a growl. "You drive a hard bargain, but I won't deny you your basic human needs. Go. I'll be right here."

Reluctantly, I untangled myself from Warren, dragged myself out of the warm bed, and hauled my bare-naked ass to the bathroom. When I came out a few minutes later, the bedside lamp was on, and Warren had gotten up and dressed in a T-shirt and was tying up his swimming trunks.

"Umm. Are you going somewhere?"

He smirked. "We are."

"Oh, are we? This early?" Warren was just full of surprises, apparently. It was barely five in the morning, so nothing was open. I didn't have a clue where he could be taking us.

"Yes, and if we don't hurry, we'll miss our opportunity."

What the— "Okaaay then." Last time he asked me to trust him when he took me out, we'd ended up at one of the most beautiful waterfalls I'd ever seen. Not that I'd seen many in my lifetime, I couldn't even imagine what would possibly top that, especially at this hour.

"I'm going to go freshen up really quick while you get dressed."

"What am I supposed to wear? Hopefully more than I have on." I looked down at my bare skin.

He walked over to me, took my hips in his hands, and backed me up against the wall beside the bathroom. "As much I'd love to keep you just the way you are, you really don't need to do much more than cover up. Because this—" He reached his hands behind me and cupped my ass, giving it a firm squeeze. "—and this," he said, as he traced his hand over my hip, sliding it between my legs, his fingers barely grazing the length of my slit, "is for my eyes only."

Hello, hot, wet, and ready. I knew he could feel it too.

"Hmm." I bit into my lip. "Are you sure we have to leave now?"

He bent down and kissed me sweetly. "Yes."

"Ugh, fine."

He let go of his possessive hold on me and backed away. Naturally, my eyes trailed south, and…*good Lord.* The man had discipline—among other things—made of steel. *Focus, Katie, focus.*

"Shoes? What about shoes?"

"No shoes, no panties. Your choice." He winked, then disappeared into the bathroom and closed the door behind him.

I snatched up the maxi dress I'd worn last night from off the floor and pulled it over my head.

Not a minute later, Warren emerged.

"This dress okay?"

"Perfect," he smirked. "Come. We need to go." He grabbed a towel that had been hanging over the back of a chair, then took my hand and led us out the door.

We made our way onto the beach in almost total darkness, holding hands the entire time. As we casually strolled in the sand along the shoreline, smooth ocean waves lazily rolled in and out, just barely lapping over our feet.

"Warren, where are we going?"

"Not far." He peered back behind us. I let my gaze follow his. The bungalows had all but faded out of sight as we rounded a corner into a more secluded cove away from civilization. As soon as all signs of life had disappeared, he stopped. "Here."

I looked around. "There's nothing here."

"Exactly." He threw the towel down on the sand, far enough away from the tide that we wouldn't get wet, then sat down and gently tugged at my arm. "Have a seat."

"Well, okay then."

I started to sit down beside him. "Not there. Here." He grabbed my hips and pulled me to sit down in between his legs. "Now, lean back." He wrapped his arms around my shoulders, pulling me back to recline into his chest. I gathered up my hair, which I'd left down, and pulled it around in front of me.

We didn't speak for a long time—we just were.

Sitting together listening to the ocean waves, feeling the warm breeze, our toes buried in the sand.

Everything about the moment was perfect. As we sat there in silence, the realization hit me that *this* was what I wanted—*he* was what I wanted. I'd spent so long believing that I wasn't good enough for this—for someone like Warren—it was hard to believe any of this was real. But I also had to remind myself now that none of what was happening mattered in the grand scheme of life. Warren and I were in the moment—an agreement—and that's all this would ever be.

The sun eventually started to barely break over the horizon in a fine line of dark orange. The rest of the sky was still dark blue and faintly blanketed with stars. He kept both of his arms wrapped tightly around me, holding me.

"This is really nice."

"Yeah, you're right. This is really nice." He brushed my hair aside and kissed my neck. Once. Twice. Then worked his way up behind my ear. A wave of heat and anticipation seared through my body, and I'd be damned if he didn't already have me ready to take him right there on the sand.

Was this what he'd wanted? To hook up on the beach? That definitely would have been another first for me. But I'd been more than willing.

I turned my head to face him and offered him my lips. He took them without hesitation. His hand came up and cupped my face, pulling me into him. As our kiss deepened, my need for him intensified. Every sweep of his tongue in my mouth had me wanting to climb into his lap.

Unfortunately, our kiss faded as we slowly pulled away, coming up for air. I pressed my forehead to his. "I am so glad you thought of coming here."

"Me too. It was a last-minute decision."

"Good thing. I was planning on going to go back to sleep."

"Don't worry, I still plan on taking you back to bed when we leave here."

Everything Katie did—every move, every laugh, every touch, hell, even the way she breathed when she slept—all of it added fuel to my fire of lust for her. She was absolutely stunning, a breath of fresh air, a glimmer of promise that not all hope had been lost when it came to women and love in general for me. She'd been the one and only woman who'd remotely piqued my interest in years from the moment I'd laid my eyes on her.

Now, the more time I'd spent with Katie getting to know her, the more I wanted, and at the same time, I'd begun to despise it—for nothing more than the fact that our time together was rapidly coming to an end, and I didn't want it to. Of course, that didn't mean my desire and attraction toward her had to come to a screeching halt; it just meant that I had to prepare myself to let her go. Until then, I was more than eager to take whatever she had been willing to give me.

Now, here Katie and I were, sitting alone on a private beach, watching the sunrise together on the beach in St. Lucia with her wedged between my legs, propped against my chest. So much for trying to psych myself up for letting her go, but this seemed like the perfect place to pick up where we'd left off the night before because I still had to uphold my end and give her that one time I promised her.

"Katie."

"Hmm?"

"Would you be okay if I touched you?"

"You're touching me now, aren't you?" Her tone was playful and sarcastic.

I positioned my mouth faintly against the shell of her ear and spoke in a hushed tone as if there were people around that I didn't want to hear me. "No, Katie. Not like this. I mean, I want to *really* touch you, to feel you…from the inside out."

"*Oh*." She wiggled in my arms. "Then yes, touch me any way you want to."

"Right here."

She bit into her lip and glanced around, then nodded. "Yes. Right here is okay."

Reaching up, I slid one of the straps of her dress to the side and kissed the top of her shoulder, then the base of her neck, working my way up, kissing and licking her neck up to the edge of her ear. I tugged her earlobe into my mouth and sucked it in, scraping it gently between my teeth.

"Right now?"

Her whole body shivered as she nodded again, this time without a word.

The rapid rise and fall of her chest was all the answer I needed. If there was one thing I had learned about Katie in just two short days, it was that it didn't take much to get her wound up.

At all.

I firmly but gently placed my hand over the front of her neck, then slowly lowered it, moving across her collarbone, down, down her chest, until I reached the low-cut collar of her dress. I slid my hand beneath the edge, under the fabric, and palmed her bare breast, squeezing and massaging it. Her head fell lazily back against my shoulder.

"That feel good?"

"Hmm. Yes." Her words were faint and barely audible.

Good. Because, my God, every part of her that I had ever touched felt like heaven beneath my grasp. My dick had become hard as a rock in desperate need of release. There was no way in hell she didn't feel it pressing into her lower back.

I removed my hand away from her lovely tits and slid them together down the sides of her torso, over her hips, finally landing between her dress-covered legs.

I should have told her to wear less.

As I rubbed on her thighs, trying not to lose my shit, the grip she had on my calves intensified as her fingers curled into my flesh.

I pulled at the skirt of the front of her dress, working it up higher until the hem fell over her knees and down her long, lean thighs. I bunched it up in my hands, pulling it back. As I peered down over her shoulder, I instinctively hissed through my clenched teeth.

"Fuck. You really aren't wearing any panties." She had her legs bent and slightly spread apart, resting against the inside of mine for support. All I could see while looking down was the top of her bare pussy, spread slightly apart, nestled between the gap in her thighs.

She shook her head. "Nope. You said I didn't need them."

"You most certainly did not."

With the front of her dress now high around her waist, I gave one last check over my shoulder, making sure the coast was still clear. Assured it was safe, I wrapped one arm firmly around her chest, holding her into me. Then I lightly glided my fingers of my other hand in between her hot, slick, delicate folds.

Her back arched instantly in response as I teased her with my middle finger, sliding it up and down, priming her, even though she didn't need it. Katie had already been dripping wet. Hell, she was soaked before we ever left the room.

As I gently pushed my middle finger inside of her, and then another, she let out a whimper and clamped down on my hand.

Christ, I needed to come. *In due time*, I told myself. Because right now, taking care of Katie and giving her pleasure was my top priority. Plus, I didn't think she would appreciate me humping her back.

"Oh—oh my God, Warren," she whispered. "That feels so—" I hooked my fingers deeper inside of her, pressing my palm to her clit, and rubbed harder. "—fuck."

Her entire body practically melted into me. "That's it, Kit-Kat. Let go."

The faster I worked my hand, the harder she fought to restrain herself.

Her moans and whines grew louder. "I'm so, so close."

"I feel you. Let it go. I've got you."

As I pumped my fingers in and out of her, harder and faster, I used my thumb to rub on her sensitive clit. She let out a moan and dug her nails into my skin as her entire body jerked and writhed against mine. Finally, her orgasm took over, and her already tight pussy clenched tighter around my fingers. Warm liquid dripped into the palm of my hand.

There had never been a single time in my entire life when I had wished my fingers had been my dick. But in this moment, I would have given my left nut to be buried balls-deep inside of her.

I held her steady with one arm wrapped around her as she slowly relaxed and everything loosened up, and carefully slid my fingers out.

"Holy shit. Warren." Her words were breathy and ragged. "You are—my God. You're something else. You know that?"

"What can I say?" I kissed the side of her neck that was slick with salty sweat. "You bring it out of me."

She rolled her head to the side, bringing us face-to-face. She had on the biggest shit-eating grin. "Well, if you're going to bring *that* out of me every time you touch me, then by all means, I'm yours for the taking."

"Is that so?"

"Yes. Yes it is."

I gave her another soft kiss, this time on her lips. "I'd absolutely love to do that again, but not here. Plus, I need to wash off my hand." I held my fingers up for her to see. "Your cum is almost as thick as mine."

Her face flushed warm pink and scrunched up.

"What? Don't be embarrassed. It's fucking perfect." *You're fucking perfect.*

With my clean hand, I flung her dress back down over her knees to cover her up, then carefully stood and stretched. I reached down and offered Katie help to stand.

I walked over to the water, squatted down, washed off my hands, and dried them on my shorts.

Katie stood near the edge of the rising tide, staring out at the sunrise, the water barely washing over her feet, with her long dress blowing in the breeze. The sun had risen sometime amidst Katie's orgasm and bathed her in a soft, warm glow.

She was absolutely stunning. There was no denying that, but going forward, I needed to get all of this *in my feelings* shit out of my head and forget any idea that I might regret letting Katie go after this week. I needed to get my ass back in the game.

One night. One time.

After all, that was what she'd said she wanted too, and that was probably for the best for both of us. So far, I'd failed miserably to even give her that one time, but I was to change that, and soon.

"This is the most amazing sunrise I think I've ever seen."

I was still knelt down in the water, staring at Katie, lost in a daze like some fucking goofball idiot. I didn't even realize she'd been talking to me. "What?"

"The sunrise. It's amazing."

"Oh, yeah. It is." Shit. The last thing I'd been paying attention to was the sun.

"Is that what you brought us here for?"

I walked over and stood beside her. "It is. Everything else just kind of happened."

She leaned into me, and I wrapped my arm around her. "Well, I'm glad it did. Both were amazing."

I kissed the top of her head. "Absolutely."

♡♡♡

On our way back to the suite, we made a detour through the dining hall at the main resort and grabbed a quick bite from the breakfast bar, staying just long enough to eat before heading back to our room.

No sooner had we'd made it back than Katie, in a bold move, lifted her dress over her head and dropped it to the floor beside her. She was barely ten feet through the door, which I'd closed and locked not two seconds prior to her stripping.

I cleared my throat. "What are you doing?" I asked in a tone that I hoped came across more as my being flirtatious than patronizing. I knew exactly what she was doing, and there was no way in hell I was about to stop her. Katie could spend the rest of this trip butt-ass naked, and you wouldn't hear one single objection out of me.

She shrugged. "Nothing. Just getting…comfortable." The full length of the back side of her bare body and ass was on full display.

I reached down and rubbed my dick that pressed painfully against my shorts. "And are you *comfortable*?" Because I sure as fuck wasn't at this point. My dick was going to explode if I didn't do something about it and soon.

She glanced back over her shoulder, a playful expression written all over her face. "Close, but not quite yet."

She finished strutting across the room like she was a model walking the runway. Meanwhile, I hadn't moved an inch. I'd been completely mesmerized and captivated by her every move, wondering what she was up to and what she was going to do next.

She climbed onto the bed on her knees, facing me. Without saying a word, she hooked her finger in a *come here* motion.

You don't have to fucking tell me twice. I yanked my T-shirt off as I practically ran to the bed, stopping just a breath away in front of her. Heat radiated between us. She was so close that every time she inhaled, her pebbled nipples brushed against my bare chest.

I ran the back of my hand down her cheek. "How about now? Are you comfortable?"

She grinned seductively and shook her head. "Nope. Not yet, but almost."

When she pointed down at my ever-growing erection, I knew exactly what she was talking about. So, without further hesitation, I gave the woman what she wanted. I unbuttoned and dropped my shorts to the floor around my ankles. *Guess who didn't wear underwear either?*

"There. How about now?" I asked, knowing I didn't have much left to give her, except for one thing.

"Almost." She spread her knees apart, widening her position, inviting me in. My gaze instantly dropped to between her legs. Sure enough, she was dripping wet.

My primal instincts kicked into high gear, and I all but lost my self-control. I was tired of waiting, and Katie had no idea what I was about to do—she never saw it coming. While she remained in this playful, *come and get me* stance on her knees, legs spread apart, with this teasing demeanor, I was primed to fuck.

I practically lunged forward, covering her mouth with mine. Her squeal was muffled by my mouth over hers, but she didn't resist me. Instead, she gave just as much.

She wrapped her arms tight around the back of my neck at the same time I reached behind her legs and hoisted her up, wrapping her legs around my waist. As I lowered her down to the bed on her back, I slid every rock-solid inch of dick that I had to possibly give deep into her tight, delicious pussy, burying myself to the hilt.

In-tense. The only word I could use to describe my first time with Warren. With a major emphasis on the *tense* part. Hell, what choice did we have? Poor Warren had been on edge—mostly because of me. Not even the blow job I'd given him the night before was enough to tide him over.

My initial plan when I climbed onto the bed had been to tease and play around with him for a while before finally diving in, but he wasn't having any of it. When he flipped me back and wrapped my legs around his waist, then pinned me to the bed with my hands over my head, I thought I'd known what was coming next. A hot kiss? Some nipple foreplay? A tease? Nope. Not even close. He nudged the thick head of his dick between my legs, gliding down, and on his way back up, he rocked forward and slid himself all of the way inside of me in one long, deep thrust.

I sucked in air as my breath caught in my chest at his sudden and filling intrusion.

"Fuck," I let out on an exhale as he moved in and out.

Sweat pooled between our intertwined bodies while Warren pumped his hips hard and fast.

"Fuck is right," he let out on a ragged breath. "I need you there, Kit-Kat. Like, right now. I can't—" He let go of my wrist and reached his hand between us. As soon as his finger found my clit, I immediately came undone. Warren followed right behind me with his own release.

I was just glad that at some point, he'd quickly confirmed that the both of us were clean and I'd been on birth control, because neither one of us had a condom.

He slowly pulled out and dropped to the bed beside me. He hooked his arm underneath me and rolled me on top of him.

"That," I said, still shaking, "was amazing. Amazingly fast but still efficient."

He lazily ran his fingers up and down my back. "You are not kidding."

I sat up and straddled him. Almost instantly, his dick firmed up between my legs. "Well, that didn't take long," I said with a smirk as I leaned down to kiss him.

He moaned into my mouth, gripping my hips, and pushed himself upward, gliding easily between my legs. "Indeed. You have a way with me."

I rocked forward, and as I slid back, he was perfectly positioned for reentry. My breath caught as I pushed back against him, fully prepared to sit all the way down. Then out of nowhere, he pulled me off him and set me to the side.

"What the—" I propped myself up on my elbows, about to protest his move.

"I'll be right back. Don't go anywhere." He got up and disappeared into the bathroom.

Clearly, round two had been out of the question.

The sink turned on, and a few minutes later, he returned with a wet rag. I reached for it. "Thank you," I said, trying to hide my slight disappointment that we weren't already in the throes of round two.

He stuck his hand out, guiding mine away. "I'll take care of this."

That was a first. No one I'd ever been with had remotely volunteered to clean up his own mess. Who was I to stop this one?

As quick as our first time together had been, there was no way we could have lasted longer than we did. Not after everything we'd been through that morning. We were both eager to get it out of our system—especially Warren. The poor man had already sat through giving me one amazing orgasm this morning, not asking for or expecting anything in return. His response to what he did to me was physically obvious as he practically stabbed me in the back with his hard-on.

But what we did in that short amount of time had gotten the job done and done well. Which was a hell of a lot more than I could say about my ex, the last guy I'd had any sexual encounters with. As much as I shouldn't have done it, it was tough not to compare the two. Who didn't compare men to one another from time to time? Seeing as Justin had been my whole world, the guy I'd dedicated my life to for a long-ass time—way too long—I didn't have much else to go on.

While Justin and I had a good run in the beginning, it didn't take long for the fighting to start. It was slow at first, maybe one or two arguments here and there, until it became almost a weekly thing. Then it was at least twice a week, sometimes three. Eventually, it seemed like we couldn't go a day without some form of disagreement, one of which inevitably resulted in a major blowout.

We made up for it, though. We always did…in the bedroom. I'd always thought the makeup sex between us was fiery hot and passionate. But the more hostile our relationship had grown, the worse the sex had become. I'd been lying to myself that what we'd been doing could actually be considered makeup sex. *It wasn't even close*. What was supposed to be the ol' fuck and forgive was really meaningless angry sex. It was a way for him to exude his dominance, and I had just been a place for him to get off.

Stupid me let him do it, which over time left me feeling empty and more broken down than before.

Then there was Warren. Even before we had ever hooked up, I knew he was different inside and outside of the bedroom. He put me first, and that was something I had never truly experienced before from a man. Warren wanted me, and he took. He took, but he also gave. Good Lord, did he ever.

When Warren had finished, he helped me to my feet and wrapped me up in one of the fluffy bathroom towels. "I'll meet you out back," he said with a kiss on my forehead.

"Oh, okay." His demand caught me off guard, but I still made my way out onto the private back deck.

Warren had fixed us each a much-needed glass of ice water. He handed me my glass as he joined me, then sat down in the other lounger with his own drink in hand.

As I sipped on my water, I snuck glances at him from out of the corner of my eye. He didn't even have to *do* anything but exist, and he was drop-dead sexy, even as he lay stretched out, one arm behind his head, the other resting in his lap with his glass of water in hand. If I pretended to look around, I could catch a clear shot of the substantial bulge just below his waist, clearly not easily hidden by a towel.

Shit.

I wanted him.

I wanted him again as soon as we'd finished the first time, and I wanted him again now as we relaxed on the back porch, recovering from our bedroom workout session. I didn't want to think that our first time together would be our last, despite our agreement. I wasn't done with him, not yet.

Not even close.

But I had to accept that even as much as I wanted him, that didn't mean he would go for it again. The way he removed me from him when clearly he could have gone for round two kind of gave that away. He'd already revoked his own offer of one week, no strings, agreeing to my one time. But here we were. Half the day and half the week already gone. We screwed up our one night last night, and our one time had been unexpectedly fast.

So was that it?

It couldn't be. 'Cause once I'd had a real taste of him, I wanted more.

Ugh.

"Were you able to get some good pictures?" His voice cut into my thoughts of him.

"I'm sorry, what?"

"Pictures. Did you get some good ones the other day?"

"Oh! Yeah, I did. I still want some more, though. Just not sure of what yet." Although, the thought of having a few of him—with or without clothing—wouldn't be so bad. "I'll probably go walk around here in a bit. You're welcome to join me."

"Yeah, I'll go with you, if you'd like."

Then I had an idea. "What about one of us?" *Pics or it never happened, right?*

Our chairs were a table width apart, so the moment was more friendly than intimate, never mind the fact that we were both still only wearing a towel.

"Sure." He leaned to the side, making himself more visible to the shot as I held up my camera, and smiled. *Fuck*. He was so handsome.

"That good?" he asked.

"I like it. You want to take another one?"

"If you want to."

"Sure." The more, the better.

I held the camera up in selfie mode. This time, I noticed his gaze was on me, not on the camera. He had a look—*that* look. The one where he studied me like he wanted to devour me.

When I set my phone down, he sat back, straightened himself, and stared out into the water.

"You want me to send these to you when I get service? You could add it to the other one you have of us? Start a collection?" It was only meant to be a joke—kinda. Based on what he said next, I didn't think he'd taken it as one.

"I'd rather you not, actually." His tone had cooled off when he spoke.

Ooooh-kay then. So it was like that now? The man was cold, hot, hot, cold, cold, hot, and back again. *Blah, blah, blah.* So damned frustrating. I just shook my head.

"What kind of music do you like to listen to?" he asked as if he didn't just reject me in some weird way.

"I'm sorry, do what?" So now we're going from Mr. Freeze to wanting to inquire about my taste in music? This man was a piece of work.

He turned his head to face me. "I asked you what kind of music you liked to listen to?"

"Sorry. You just threw me off with the question. You went from smiling in a picture to stone-cold; now you want to know what I listen to? I guess mostly rap, some rock, a little country here and there."

He gave me one of those *you have got to be kidding me* looks. "Rap? And you're overthinking things, Kit-Kat."

"If you say so." I shrugged, taking another sip of water. "And what's wrong with my taste in music? I'm from Memphis. It's what I know."

"Fair enough. I'll give you that."

"What do *you* like to listen to, then?"

"Hmm, let's see. Rock and alternative. Some classical. Depends on my mood and what I'm doing."

"Interesting mix. So why'd you ask?"

"I was going to put on some background music if I can get the app to work. There's no internet, but I should be able to play my downloaded music." He thumbed through his phone. "Country it is. Seems like a safe compromise."

He set his phone facedown on the table.

In all honesty, despite his ever-changing demeanor, everything else about the day was perfect. Midmorning sunlight kissed our skin, a warm, salty breeze kept us cool, soft music played low from Warren's phone, and ocean waves rolled softly in the background, splashing against the pillars of the deck.

The sound of the first few musical notes of Kenny Chesney's "Me and You" carried through the speaker, catching my attention.

"Aw, I haven't heard this song in years. It's one of my favorites." I absentmindedly started humming along with the words.

Warren placed his empty glass on the table, then reached out and took my glass from my hand and set it down next to his. He then stood up and held his hand out for me to take.

I eyed him suspiciously. "I take it you're asking me to dance?"

"No," he said softly, his gaze locked on mine. "I'm telling you because I know it's what you want."

He was so sure of himself, and he wasn't wrong. I did want to dance; I loved to dance—even more so with him. The way he stared me down left me no room to tell him no.

Caving in, I placed my hand in his as he pulled me up to stand in front of him. I readjusted my towel, securing it tighter around my chest.

I wrapped one arm around his waist as I placed my other hand in his and stepped into his hold. Maybe it was the atmosphere or Warren himself, but everything about us together, this close, just felt right. Everything from his height in relation to mine, the way our bodies melded together, how he knew all the appropriate things to say and do at just the right time, to his confident, take-charge personality.

Try as he might to hide it, Warren definitely had a softer side.

We didn't dance carelessly and carefree like we had the other night at the bar. He held us together, strong and swayed steadily to the music.

"So, why is this one of your favorite songs?"

I sucked in a slow, deep breath, taking in the fresh scent of his skin and the salt in the air around us. I slowly exhaled.

"It's just always been one of my favorites."

"Hmm. I see. That's it?"

"Mostly." It was the song I had picked out to dance to with my future husband, a dream that I'd accepted might never come true. He didn't need to know that, though. "This is also the song my parents danced to when they renewed their vows a few years ago."

"And how long have they been married?"

"A blissful thirty-five years."

"Wow. That is a long time."

"Yeah, it is. I mean, they seem happy enough most of the time, anyway. How long were your parents married?"

"Too damned long if you ask me." He subtly shook his head in disbelief. I wanted to pry more but decided to let it go.

"I'm sorry. That's really too bad." I wrapped my arm tighter around his waist.

"It's fine. I think we've all mostly recovered from the messes my dad made over the years." He let me go and slowly spun me around before pulling me back into his arms. He held me close as he sang softly along with the lyrics. The vibrations of his voice carried over from his chest to mine. I didn't know what surprised me more: his mood change or that he'd known the words.

We swayed together as the song eventually ended and another one came on, but he didn't let me go this time. A long, held-in sigh escaped me;

I didn't even realize I'd done it, but Warren must have felt it.

"What's wrong?"

"Hmm? Nothing."

"You know I don't believe you, right?"

I smiled. "It's nothing, really. Just thinking."

"Sounds like that could be dangerous. What's on your mind, Kit-Kat?"

"My mom and dad. That's all."

"What about them?"

"They're perfect for each other. That's my problem. I always thought I would meet someone and have an everlasting love like theirs. They set the relationship standard bar kinda high."

"Hmm. So, what makes you think that you can't have what they have? It's not too late."

Wasn't it, though? I mean, by the time my parents were my age now, they'd already been married for close to fifteen years. "It's not that I *can't* have what they do, but the more time goes by, it feels like my chances of finding the one are less and less."

"Interesting."

He didn't respond; he just kept us moving in a slow sway as we danced.

"Besides that," I continued. I figured I might as well keep the pity party going. "My ex-boyfriend left a bad taste in my mouth for pretty much all men. No offense."

He let out a soft laugh. "None taken." He kissed the top of my head. "Surely not all men, huh? Even me?"

"Okay, maybe not *all* men. This one, he just kinda broke me, ya know? That kind of hurt takes time to heal." Mentally and physically. Justin had really fucked me up in more ways than one.

"I understand. So what happened with him that was so bad? If you don't mind my asking?"

The million-dollar question I was not ready to answer in great detail, or at all if I could help it. Most definitely not with Warren. Not here, not now. "Our situation was…complicated, I guess you could say."

His hand that was splayed low across my back gripped me just a little bit tighter as his fingers dug into me through the towel. If I hadn't been paying attention, I might not have otherwise noticed.

"It's okay if you don't want to talk about it."

"No, not really." That relationship had sailed with the wind for the last time, thankfully, and not soon enough. Besides, I didn't want to ruin the moment Warren and I had been having by focusing on my past.

Even though we talked the entire time we danced, it was worth it to be wrapped in Warren's arms. He felt safe and secure.

The next song ended, and as we stopped dancing, he held on, pulling me firmly against his front. I knew exactly why he hadn't let me go and became more than well aware that the only thing separating us were the plush towels wrapped around our bodies.

I reached behind him and gave his well-constructed, work-of-art, muscular ass a firm squeeze.

"Kit-Kat," he said in a suggestive tone. His words rolled off his lips from somewhere deep inside of his chest.

"Warren," I purred in return.

"What are you doing?"

"Nothing?"

"That doesn't feel like nothing."

"What? You started it."

He grabbed my hand, lifted it up to his mouth, and kissed it. "You're right, I did. And if you're willing to go back on your one-time-only statement, I'd like a do-over from this morning so I can prove to you I can do better than that."

I laughed, probably a little louder than I'd intended. "Sorry. I'm not laughing at you—well, I am, but this morning was pretty damned amazing, considering."

He shook his head. "That was not my finest work, I can assure you that."

"It's okay, really." I stretched up on my tiptoes and kissed the edge of his stubbled jaw. "You still got the job done."

He looked down at me. "I really am sorry—not that I didn't enjoy every minute of it myself, but that was not what I had in mind for what was supposed to be our first and last time together."

"I don't disagree with you, but what the hell happened to you? I was ready for round two then. I thought you were too."

He let out a sigh. "Trust me. It's not that I didn't want to go for round two or three—hell, I'd go all fucking day and night with you—but we'd agreed one time. I needed to be damned sure that any more than that was a good idea for either of us."

Ouch. So he really had been ready to only go at it one time. "Are you okay with it? Because I am if you are."

He grazed his knuckle down my cheek. "You deserve a do-over…better."

"Oh yeah? What would you do differently?" I swallowed down the spit that pooled in my mouth as it watered at the thought of him telling me what he wanted to do to me—and then following through.

He kissed my forehead, my temple, my cheek, then the corner of my mouth, making his way around my face and neck. His hands moved from my back up to my arms, holding me upright.

"I would take my time, tasting you, savoring each and every square inch of your body from head to toe and back up again. I'd get you on the verge of losing your mind, and just as you were about to come, I'd stop." His lips brushed against my ear as he continued. "Then I'd start all over again."

Wetness threatened to drip down the inside of my thighs. "Is that a promise?"

He pulled the towel loose from his waist, letting it drop to the deck around our feet. His impressive and perfectly shaped erection popped free and stood up tall between us. *That answered that.*

"I can…if you let me."

Let him? Was he crazy? I was on the verge of dropping to my knees and begging him to take me back inside and claim me like he was some hot-headed alpha hero in a filthy romance novel, and I was his sex-servant. Since he seemed to have already had the asshole part nailed down, I figured the rest of it would be a breeze for him. Though, I'd been completely taken aback by his unexpected romantic gestures and occasional sweet words. I never would have guessed he had such a soft side. Hell, maybe I had been reading him wrong? Now wasn't the time to try to figure him out, though.

I was horny as hell, and he had exactly what I needed practically stabbing me in the stomach. Whether he wanted to be hot, cold, hot, cold with me, I had only one temperature around him—*hot*. And he was about to do something about it.

I placed my mouth close enough to his to feel his breath on my lips but not touch. "Kiss me," I ordered.

His lips parted, letting me in without hesitation. Warren tasted sweet, like the coconut water he'd been drinking, as his tongue swept into my mouth. He wrapped his arms around me, lifting me off the ground just enough for him to walk forward, moving us back into our room. He kicked the door closed behind him. We stopped moving when the back of my legs hit the edge of the mattress.

"This," I said, grabbing the top of my towel, about to pull it loose, "is in the way."

Warren quickly gripped my wrists and moved my hands aside. "Slow, Kit-Kat. You need to let me take over from here. Please."

"Okay," I reassured him. "But only 'cause you said please." As much as I'd wanted to pout and argue, he was right. He promised to take his time with me, and I was already trying to finish. I needed to let him.

He gave me a quick, sweet kiss on the lips before making his way to the top of my shoulder, kissing down the front of my chest to the small amount of cleavage barely peeking over the top of my poorly secured towel. He loosened the twisted ends and let it fall to the hardwood floor around my feet.

Instinctively, I squeezed my thighs together, well aware of my need to be touched by him. It wouldn't have taken much to send me over the edge right then and there, but Warren had made it very clear that he was going to make me wait.

I ran my fingers through his dark, messy hair as he caressed my body with his mouth, licking and sucking as he moved around. He flicked his tongue over one of my erect nipples, right before pulling into his mouth, sucking hard. Then he let go with a *pop* and repeated the same motion on the other one.

"That feels so damn good." I urged his head into my chest, encouraging him to keep going. "Don't stop."

His soft, warm hands splayed across my bare hips, reaching around to cover my ass. I wanted them on every square inch of me, all over and inside of me at the same damned time. As he dropped to his knees, he pulled me forward, burying his face between my legs. Except he wasn't fast or hurried; he didn't devour me like I'd expected him to—of course not. Warren was in no kind of a hurry. He inhaled deep, right before his tongue plunged out, lunging deep inside my slit, gently but firmly at the same time, stroking across my clit. My grip on his hair tightened as I held on, steadying myself while he licked and sucked and moaned into me.

I raised my leg over his shoulder, giving him better access to eat me out. He had one hand on my ass, holding me steady, while the other reached between my legs. His long, warm fingers glided across my wetness from front to back before he slid one inside of me. As his finger moved in and out of me, his tongue flicked against my clit, I felt myself on the verge of what should have been the beginning of a show-stopping orgasm, and then he pulled his mouth away.

I looked down at him, his head still in my hands. I should have shoved him back into me. "Warren! What the hell? Why—why did you stop?"

He grinned without looking up. "Patience, Kit-Kat."

Fuck. I was running low on patience and high on the need for release. With his hand still between my legs, he started to lick his way up. His finger pressed even deeper inside of me as he ran his tongue over the curve of my hip, across my stomach, between my breasts, until he stood all of the way up.

"Warren." I swallowed hard. "I need you." My heart raced so fast I thought I was going to pass out.

He circled an arm around my waist, holding me flush against him. With his lips brushing against the shell of my ear, he whispered, "How about this?"

Another finger joined the first one, both going deeper than before. This time, the palm of his hand rubbed against my clit.

My eyes fluttered closed as he massaged me from the inside out. "I'm so—Warren, I'm going to—"

Every muscle in my body tightened with his movements. Finally. I reached for his shoulders, holding on as he brought me to the edge.

Then everything stopped. His hand pulled away, leaving the job unfinished yet again. "No you're not. Not yet."

He stood up and lifted me off the ground, then lowered me to the middle of the bed, bracing himself over top of me. He nipped my earlobe. "So tell me, Kit-Kat, what can I do for you? How can I take care of you?"

Oh hell. "What do you mean? You've *been* taking care of me; you just keep stopping. I need you to stop stopping."

He laughed. "I know, but I'm doing what I want to do. What do *you* want me to do to you?"

"I—well." I didn't know how to answer him. "Honestly? I don't really know. No one has ever asked me that before. Things have always just sort of happened."

"Don't think about it. Just tell me the first thing that comes to mind."

I closed my eyes and exhaled. Thinking about Warren and me and what I wanted from him—things that I wanted him to do to me and *with* me. The possibilities were endless, and our time was not.

I squirmed beneath him. "You're the one who said head to toe. Start there."

A devilish grin spread across his face. He pinned my arms above my head while using his knee to spread my legs even further apart. He gripped his rock-hard dick in his hand and agonizingly slowly grazed the head of his dick up and down through the folds of my wet pussy.

I let out a long, held-in breath. "I thought you said head to toe?"

"Changed my mind."

Thank the Lord. I moved my hips, causing him to nudge inward, just ever so slightly breaching my entrance. Already I could feel the pressure from his ample size spreading me open.

"Fuck," I whispered as I closed my eyes. Now that he had me ramped up and ready to go, every touch, every point of contact we had with each other only amplified and felt even better than the last.

I wrapped my arms around his neck and threw my leg over his waist.

He pushed his hips forward, very slowly sliding every thick and solid inch of himself inside of me. Warren was no small man, but I didn't remember him being *that* big. Holy hell. It was like he'd doubled in size since this morning.

He carefully worked himself in and out, little by little, with more ease each time he slowly pushed into me.

"Tell me if I hurt you. I'll stop."

"I will, but I don't think you can—" Before I even finished my sentence, he thrust forward, this time with a lot more force than he had been using, filling and stretching me to the hilt. Okay, so maybe he *hadn't* been all the way in.

Instinctively, I cried out, causing him to stop.

He looked down at me. "Katie? Are you okay?"

"Umm-hmm. I'm fine. Just…adjusting."

"I should probably go a little easier on you. I was kind of rough this morning."

"It's fine. I'm fine. You can keep going." I was used to rough and fast sex. That was the way Justin had liked it, but he paled in comparison to Warren when it came to size. Warren had him— and any other guy I'd ever been with—beat all the way around.

I gripped his taut, bare ass, encouraging him to go deeper. He did, and I let out a whimper.

"I swear, Kit-Kat, if you keep making those kinds of noises, I'll finish long before either of us are ready…again."

"Yeah." I swallowed, regaining my composure, trying to relax as I shifted underneath him. "Don't do that. Not yet. But I'm okay, though. Promise." If I did this once, I could do it again.

He leaned down and kissed my neck. Then he gently bit the spot he'd kissed at the same time he sank all of the way into me. I dug my nails into his ass, raking them up his back as he picked up his pace. Both of our bodies were slick with sweat as his thrusts quickened.

I wanted so badly to tell him to slow down, let me get on top. But I couldn't. He was at the perfect angle, rubbing me inside and out as he ground down against my clit each time he lunged forward. I rolled my hips, matching him thrust for thrust until my orgasm ripped through me, and I called out his name.

He soon followed suit, pulsating deep inside of me.

FOURTEEN

"I can't believe how fast time has gone by," I said to Warren as our waiter set our food down on the dining table in front of us. After round two this morning, we decided to clean ourselves up and head inland for lunch, rather than staying in bed all day. We figured if we were going to go for round three, we needed the fuel, because our one-time agreement had flown right out the window.

Warren thanked our waiter as he walked off.

"Indeed it has."

"I mean, it's barely been a solid two days, but they've slipped by pretty quick. I think they have, anyway." That was an understatement. When I first realized I'd be spending my vacation with *him*, I wanted to slip under my bathwater and not come up for air until the week was over. Now, all I wanted to do was slip into bed with Warren and never come out.

"Tell me about it," he said as he analyzed his food. "I'm only here until Sunday, so, unfortunately, I'll have one less day to enjoy with you."

"Wait, you're only here 'til Sunday? How come?" I was pretty sure I had genuine fear in my voice.

"Work," he stated matter-of-factly. "I've got deadlines to meet this coming week, and I've yet to miss a single one. This won't be an exception."

"Ah, work. I understand." Kind of. If anyone knew anything about being all work, no play, it was me, but even I was willing to sacrifice a few shifts for a dream vacation. I sank back into my chair and poked around the food on my plate with my fork. "Are you having a good time, though? I mean, you said yourself you didn't even want to come here in the first place." Even if his mood had considerably changed since he'd first made his appearance, he still tended to go from hot to cold and back again. *Like now*.

He gave me a puzzled look. "Do you honestly question whether or not I'm having a good time with you?"

"Well, no. I mean, I did at one point, but I just want to make sure." *Hello, insecurity, ya ugly bitch*. It was a feeling I'd been all too familiar with; it had practically consumed me my entire life. Something being around Warren didn't help.

"Katie. There is nowhere else I would rather be or anyone else I would rather be with right now than you. If I weren't, you would know." He pointed to my food. "How's your fish, by the way?"

I took another bite and washed it down with water. "It's not bad, actually. I wasn't sure about ordering raw yellowfin tuna because for one, I've never had it before, but two, it's raw."

Truth be told, I didn't have an adventurous bone in my body—not when it came to food or life or relationships or bedroom—nowhere. I'd always been just as content with boring and consistent patterns and routines. Coming on this trip had given me a bit of a new outlook on the way my life had been going, that maybe I needed to change some things up and make a change. What exactly? I didn't have a clue yet. This would only be the start.

We finished our lunch with a comfortable silence between us, enjoying the sounds of nature and reggae music in the background. Silverware clanged against dishes as people ate; their conversations carried in the air.

"Hey, how's your dad doing, by the way. If you don't mind me asking? I haven't heard much about him in a while." Rowan hadn't mentioned Warren and Wes's dad in months, and I wasn't sure if Wes had been keeping up with him due to their rocky past.

Warren half shrugged. "Worse. We think the end is close, but who knows at this point. He's exhausted all of his treatments—both chemo and radiation. I'm honestly surprised he's made it this long. He's stubborn as a mule, that's for damned sure."

"Oh. I'm really sorry to hear that." My appetite faltered, though I'd known better than to bring it up, but I'd been genuinely concerned for him. "I couldn't imagine going through that."

"It's been harder on us than I thought it would have been, actually. Thank you for asking about him."

"You said 'us.' Are you referring to Wes?"

"Us as in me and Dad, and sometimes his girlfriend slash fiancée—I'm not sure what she is to him anymore; hell, I don't think my dad even knows."

"Ashley?"

"She would be the one."

"Y'all don't speak to each other?"

He looked at me like I'd grown two heads. "Me and Ashley? No. Not a whispered word. She very well may be the mother of my little brother— that sounds even more fucked-up to say out loud, given the huge age difference and circumstances—but she and I are not on speaking terms. Never have been, and never will be. I have no desire."

"Gotcha. Sorry I asked."

"Don't be. It's just not something I speak about very often, or ever, really. No need to."

"Gotcha. How's Wes handling everything?"

"Eh. Wes just kind of sits on the sidelines waiting for the next piece of news, which at this point is certain death."

"Damn." Way to ruin brunch, Kat. *Idiot.* "So I guess they're still on the outs, then?"

"Something like that, I guess. I've been a little more forgiving of our dad after what he did."

"Yeah, I'm sure that's not easy for either of y'all. Maybe he just needs more time. Is he okay with you still talking to your dad?"

"I don't think he holds it against me that I still talk to him on occasion. But even that took some time for him to accept. As far as I know, Wes still doesn't want much to do with him, but his time is running out. Though I can't say I blame him. What our dad did to him was a low blow to the entire family, what few of us are left, anyway."

I listened intently as Warren opened up about him and his brother and all of their family drama. There was no doubt in my mind that he had the ability to love and care for someone deeply. He had way more depth to him than what he let on. Sure, he'd come off as this uptight, certified grade-A asshole, but deep down, I knew there was so much more to him than he had portrayed on the outside. He had shown his softer side more times than I would have thought he could, whether he had intended to or not. Hell, maybe he'd only opened up to me because I was nosey and kept asking questions.

As Warren sat across from me, dishing out the dirty details of his private life, I started to question my agreeing to this no-strings, one week turned one time turned who-knows-what-now offer. About the only thing I knew was that the more time I spent with him, the more I'd come to realize how much I liked him—I mean I *really* liked him, a *lot*. Letting him go in a couple of days was going to be hard.

What the hell did I get into?

"Yeah, I can see both sides of it, I guess. I couldn't imagine having that kind of family turmoil, plus dealing with your dad's cancer and just life in general. What a damned mess." I mean, Wes's own dad had an affair with his fiancée while Wes was in the hospital, *and* he got her pregnant. Ouch.

"It's been disruptive to our lives to say the least. I mostly try to stay out of it. I can only speak for myself because I can't say for sure how I would feel if things were the other way around and our dad had done that to me. Wes still doesn't like talking about it, and quite frankly, I don't blame him. Our dad transgressed over boundaries where he had no business committing, in my opinion, one of the worst offenses imaginable against his own son." He took a swig of his drink. "Enough about me. Tell me more about you. What makes Katie tick?"

I had nothing to offer him on myself compared to any of that. "Well, what would you like to know?"

"I don't know. Tell me anything. You come off as the perfect, all-American-sweetheart daughter. What is your life like outside of here?" He gave a dismissive wave into the air.

Internally, I rolled my eyes. It wasn't the first time I'd been referred to as an all-American sweetheart. *Pssh.* If he only knew the shit I'd been through. How, as perfect as my life growing up had appeared on the outside, it was just as ridiculously out of touch with reality on the inside.

"Well, I work a lot. Beyond that, there isn't much to tell."

He shook his head. "That's not what I meant, Katie. I know that much. Tell me about *you*. Tell me about your upbringing, your parents. I think there's more to you than just a pretty face."

He wasn't entirely wrong. There probably was more dimension to myself than just this prim, proper, and poised façade.

"Eh, maybe. I did ballet when I was little, then gymnastics and piano, which led me into singing. Eventually, I did ballroom dancing. All the while, I attended a prestigious private school for a few years before going public, and I participated in every beauty pageant known to man in the state of Tennessee along the way. There. That about sums up my life in a nutshell.”

“Wow,” he said, raising an eyebrow. “You were a busy girl.”

“Indeed, I was. That’s probably why I work so much now. I can’t sit still.”

“Well, your mom and dad must be proud of you. From what I know about you, you seem to have turned well.”

I smiled. “Thank you. I like to think I’m a decent human being at best.”

Just then, my stomach made a loud groan. He must have heard it—that or he saw the sudden uncomfortable look on my face.

“Kit-Kat. You okay over there?”

“Yeah, fine.” *Nope*. Not fine at all. Something was going on, and I did not like the sound or feel of it. “Just digesting lunch. That’s all.”

I had in fact not been *just digesting lunch*. My stomach gurgled, and it felt like my body was about to revolt against me.

“I’m ready to head back whenever you are,” he said with concern in his tone. “Just let me know.”

“Sounds like a plan. I need to make a quick run to the bathroom first.”

I made it to the bathroom and locked myself in one of the stalls just in time. Whatever it was that didn't agree with me had made its way out faster than I'd taken it in.

Raw fucking fish.

It had to be…and never again. So much for being adventurous.

After spending longer in the bathroom than I had intended, I headed back to the table. I set my hand on Warren's shoulder for balance as I approached him from behind.

He looked up at me. "Jesus, Katie. Are you okay?"

"Not really. I don't feel so great all of a sudden."

"No kidding? You look green."

"I feel every bit of it. Can we go now?"

"Absolutely." He stood up and held on to me as we made our way back to the suite, only letting go just long enough to open the door. "Let's get you inside and relax. No more adventurous food."

"Deal." That was all I managed to say before I practically plowed through him, running straight into the bathroom…again.

Anticipation had been building all morning for what the rest of the day and this trip had in store for us. But no. My body seemed to have other plans. I knew exactly what this was; it wasn't my first rodeo.

I had food poisoning.

Katie had gotten food poisoning.

There was no doubt in my mind that's what this had been. If I had to guess, I'd bet my money on the raw fish—the one she'd been leery about ordering from the beginning but that I had talked her into getting. I felt absolutely terrible for being at least somewhat responsible for this mess.

It absolutely pained me seeing Katie in this disposition when not a few short hours ago, she'd been on cloud nine. The last time I had witnessed or heard anyone be that ill and miserable was my own mother during the last year of her life. Chemo did a number on her, but she fought hard, no doubt. Katie would too.

Thankfully, this would pass, but most definitely not soon enough.

As soon as she emerged from the bathroom the first time, she kicked me out of the suite to the back porch. I didn't blame her. She was sick as dog shit. Every now and again, I stuck my head inside and checked on her. She was either lying in bed half-asleep, or she'd call out to me from the bathroom that she was *fine*.

I knew better. She was not fine.

Despite her vulnerability, I caved in to her persistence to leave her alone for a while and disappeared outside with a glass of scotch and my music playlist—the only thing that I could get to work on my phone with no service. Giving her some privacy was the least I could do for her. She knew where to find me if she needed me.

It was late afternoon, and thankfully, not terribly hot. The porch was angled on the opposite side of where the sun would eventually set, which not only made for an excellent view but kept me out of the direct sunlight.

Regardless of this setback with Katie, our time together had been quality time well spent. I sipped on my scotch, thinking back to the first time we met. I would forever and a day remember that moment.

She had come up to Chicago a few weeks before Wes and Rowan's wedding to help them organize the event. Up until that point, I had virtually no idea she'd existed. My God, though, when I did lay eyes on her, she was the most stunning creature I had ever seen. It was like the world around me disappeared the moment we'd met. It was a shameful moment for me, to say the least, that somehow, the ironclad wall that I'd kept around my tightly bottled-up emotions felt like it had been kicked down in that one small instance with just the feel of her hand in mine. Thankfully, I was able to spend the next few days far away from her, scrambling to pick up the fallen pieces and put them back together before having to see her again. I knew that if I'd spent too much time with her in one sitting, she'd break me altogether.

I'd managed to avoid her by keeping myself occupied with work while she stayed tied up with the wedding. Then, by the grace of God, or the work of the devil himself, she showed up at the club with Chloe. At some point, either Chloe or Daniel or both had sent her over to sit with me so I could entertain her while those two had a moment alone. We hadn't been together for long before I needed to make a quick run to the bathroom.

As I made my way back, my phone buzzed out of control in my pocket. I figured it was either Daniel giving me shit when he should have been sucking face with Chloe, or my brother trying to annoy the fuck out of me. Either way, I reached into my pocket and silenced the vibrations without looking.

I glanced up across the room at Katie and stopped. I'd be damned if Xavier hadn't already moved in on her. I'd left her unattended for less than five solid minutes, and not only had he already taken my seat, but he had her full-on belly laughing.

Suddenly, whatever animalistic instincts that I had buried resurfaced, and I wanted to throw her over my shoulder and carry her out of there.

Two strides in, my phone started again. I cursed under my breath as I jerked my phone out of my pocket. Reading the most recent text from Wes suddenly had me feeling like the world's biggest asshole. He said that he'd taken Rowan to the emergency room and to call him.

That unpleasant feeling of envy I'd felt the night I saw Katie near someone else was just as uncomfortable as the one I felt for her now, except the one I felt now was the one that gave a person butterflies and had them questioning all their life's decisions. I had to remind myself we'd only been together for two days… *Two. Days.*

Beyond this, there was no us.

I tossed back the remnants of my third glass at the thought of it.

Once things had seemed to finally settle down inside, I snuck through the suite and headed inland. I figured I'd take the opportunity during one of Katie's catnaps to go pick her up some Pepto and a few bottles of Gatorade. I also used this time to look through my phone once it reconnected with the internet. I had a text from Daniel asking if I'd gotten lucky yet and another message from a colleague related to an article we were co-authoring asking when I'd be back. A couple of work-related emails came through, some spam mail. Voicemail notifications popped up as my phone regained service, the latest being from Wes.

"Hey, bro. I know you're having the time of your life right now…at least I hope you are, and I hate to be a downer, but da—Van Buren is in the hospital. Not sure what's going on yet. Just think you might wanna cut it short and come home. Call me when you get this."

Fuck. Judging by the tone in his voice, I had to make a quick decision. Dad had already been sick as shit at home on palliative care; now he was in the hospital. Time hadn't seemed to be on his side as of late. Plus, now I had Katie sick as shit too, on top of that. The last thing I wanted to do was leave her alone in her current state. But I knew that if anything happened to my dad before I made it home in time, I'd never forgive myself.

Without another thought, I sent Wes a text that I was on my way. I booked the next available flight off the island, which happened to leave early tomorrow morning instead of Sunday like I had originally planned.

Now I had to go back and break the news to Katie.

After a quick run to the on-site pharmacy, I headed to the room. Katie was awake, sitting up in the bed with her head in her hands.

I crawled up on the bed and sat down beside her. "Hey, Kit-Kat, how are you feeling?"

Lyndsay Marie

"Like I've been hit by a truck."

I brushed her hair back from her face. "Well, you don't look like you have. Hopefully this will all be over soon."

"Ugh. Not soon enough. Warren, I am so sorry. This is so embarrassing. No one besides my parents has ever seen me like this. I feel like I've ruined this whole trip."

"Don't be sorry. You're just as beautiful as ever, and *you* haven't ruined anything. Besides, it's my fault for suggesting the fish. I didn't even think it would be an issue."

She sat back and leaned against the headboard. She faced me and smiled. Even in her current state, she was perfect. "As much as I'd like to lay blame, this is not your fault." She pointed to the bag in my hand. "What's that?"

"Ah. Here." I grabbed a Gatorade first, loosened the lid, and handed it to her. "Electrolytes to start. I wasn't sure what flavor you preferred, if any, so I grabbed you one of each of what they had. Also, this." I pulled out the bottle of Pepto and handed it to her. "It might be too late for this one, but it can't hurt."

"Thank you so much. This is really sweet of you; I really appreciate it."

"You're welcome, but there's more."

"What is it? Chocolate? Please tell me it's chocolate."

"Unfortunately, no, it's not chocolate."

"Damn. I don't need it anyway. What else is there?"

"While I was at the shop, I checked my phone. Wes called sometime last night and left me a message. He said our dad has taken a turn, and he's in the hospital. He thinks I need to get home."

"Shit, Warren. If you need to go, go."

I ran my hands through my hair. "I am. Katie, I'm sorry."

"Don't be. When do you leave?"

"Tomorrow, actually. I hate to leave you, but—"

"Warren, it's fine." She shifted slightly toward me, taking a sip of her drink. "Your family needs you way more than I do right now. I'll be fine. Promise. It's just food poisoning. Thank you for at least staying with me one more night."

The words "I swear I could fall in love with you" threatened to roll off my lips—but I knew better. This was another one of those in-the-moment situations. While I cared for her—more than I wanted to admit to myself—just the mere thought of loving her, much less saying it out loud, would have been serious lapse in judgment on my part.

We lay in bed, talking for a while until Katie eventually snuggled down into my side, tucked deep under the covers and into my arms. I hated knowing this would probably be the last time I'd get to hold her.

"Are you sure you're going to be okay without me?" I asked her while running my hand up and down her back. I didn't know what difference it would have made, if any, if she'd asked me not to leave. Not going home wasn't an option.

"Positive. I'll be fine. I don't get sick very often, but it's nice to be taken care of for a change instead of me always being the one taking care of someone else."

"You're very welcome. You deserve it." I leaned down and kissed the top of her head. "The good thing is you'll still have some time to get out and enjoy your vacation sans unexpected guest."

"I guess. I've really enjoyed being around you, though. If you leaving were under any other circumstances, I'd be begging you not to go."

My heart squeezed deep inside of my chest. *Fuck*. "I know what you mean. Maybe it's for the best that I'm leaving early." Cutting her loose and letting her go now before we got too comfortable together was probably for the best for both of us. I needed to get back to Chicago and regain focus on my life. Katie had done nothing but knock me off my track every time she was around me since the first day we met.

"Yeah, you're probably right. I think everything happens for a reason; we're not always meant to understand it. Just don't forget, I'll be in Chicago in a couple of months for Rowan's baby shower, whenever she decides to have it. We might have to see each other then."

"I'd be okay with that. I see no reason we can't at least be friendly."

Whether I left tomorrow morning or three days from now, the end result would still be the same: Katie and I would go our separate ways. We needed some time and distance to cool down from this whirlwind faux-romance we'd been on these last couple of days.

"True."

Her stomach made a loud rumbling noise. "You okay?"

She sat up and propped herself back up against the headboard. "I'm not sure yet. It comes in waves. There shouldn't be anything left to come out."

I grabbed the bottle of Pepto, opened it, and handed it to her. "Here. Drink this. It should help some."

Katie tipped the pink bottle back and downed probably half of it. Her stomach growled again, and without a word, she shoved the bottle in my direction and bolted for the bathroom.

I screwed the lid back on and set it on the nightstand beside the bottles of Gatorade. Then I poured myself a two-finger shot of scotch and retired out on the back porch.

♡♡♡

Lyndsay Marie

I'd spent most of the night outside in the balmy heat, listening to the soothing sounds of ocean waves rolling by. I stuck my head inside a few times, and once I was absolutely sure Katie had fallen into a deep sleep, I made my bed on the couch and passed out.

My alarm on my phone rang out way too soon.

Thirty minutes.

That was all the time I'd allowed myself to get ready and leave. There was no sense in waking Katie up or hanging around any longer than necessary, dragging out the inevitable.

This was what we had agreed on.

The room was pitch-black, so I used the light from my phone to find my way around. I rolled off the couch, took a quick shower, and dressed for the day. Katie was still sound asleep in the same position. I didn't know if she had gotten up at all during the rest of the night after I'd gone to bed; if she had, I didn't hear her.

I rounded up what few possessions I'd originally brought with me and left everything else stacked neatly on the couch. I grabbed my wallet and phone, shoved them each in a pocket. I put on my watch, then wrote out a quick note to Katie. I carefully kissed her on the forehead so I wouldn't wake her up. I placed the note on the table, then left.

SIXTEEN

Katie

Ruined. That was the only word I could use to describe what had been done to me—and I wasn't talking about my three-day stint with food poisoning either. Though, that had rearranged my insides in a whole different way than I'd ever experienced before. Because that's what Warren Miller had done. He'd officially wrecked me on an entirely new level unlike anything I'd ever experienced before.

After Warren had left, I spent the entire next two and a half days sick as dog shit. I finally started to feel human again on Friday, and on Saturday morning, I was back to normal. I had one solid day left to do anything, so I dragged myself out of bed, showered for the first time in almost three days I'd never admit that to anyone—and decided to walk around the resort and take some more pictures to document my final hours there.

Every step I made reminded me of him. I hated it.

I hated even more that I actually missed him.

Nothing felt the same after he left—not my vacation, not home, and especially not me. It felt like he'd taken a part of me with him when he'd left.

My Uber driver pulled into my parents' driveway. I hadn't told my mom or dad when my return flight was or what time. I wanted to be alone for the drive home, not bombarded with a ton of questions about my trip.

"Thanks again," I told my driver. "Could you go ahead and pop the trunk? I'm going to try to get my stuff out so you can take off before my mom comes running out here."

"Yeah, sure thing. Thanks for the warning," he replied.

I quickly jumped out of his car, ran around to the back, and yanked my suitcase out. No sooner had I shut the trunk and started up the sidewalk than the front door flung open.

"Katie!" my mom called out as she ran out to greet me with Dad hot on her heels. She gave the Uber driver a sideways glance as she pulled me into a hug. "We're so glad you made it home *safe*. You were supposed to tell us when you were comin' home."

I waved to the driver with a smirk as he backed away. I'd warned him about my mom on the ride home, that she might have something crazy to say to him if given the opportunity.

Thankfully, I was able to give him a head start leaving before she could.

"I know, I know. Sorry. I missed y'all."

"Well, we're happy to have you back, Princess," Dad said, pulling me into a hug next.

"So, how was your trip?" Mom asked. "Did you have fun by all by yourself? We were worried to death about you."

Oops. It hadn't yet occurred to me that my parents had no idea that I hadn't gone on that trip alone. I didn't know how in the hell I was going to explain otherwise to my conservative, Southern Christian mother whenever she did find out. My dad would've been a little more forgiving, then probably gotten a kick out of the whole thing.

"It was really nice, actually. Peaceful. You know?"

Dad looked at me like I was full of shit, but he grabbed my suitcase from me without a word and dragged it behind him as he headed toward the house. That was one thing I loved about my dad. Sometimes we could talk to each other without saying a word.

I paused halfway up the sidewalk. "Uh, Mom? What's with the camper parked in the backyard?"

She kept walking, acting as if she didn't hear me. "Oh, it's nothing. We'll get to that later. Come. Let's get you inside. I want to hear all about your trip. Are you thirsty? Hungry?"

"No, I'm okay."

I followed Mom inside, straight into the kitchen. It was where we spent most of our time. If my mom wasn't in the kitchen, you could find her out in one of her gardens.

I pulled up a seat at the island. "How about we talk about it now? I mean, it's kinda hard to hide an entire house on wheels and expect me not to ask about it."

Dad gave Mom a sideways glance. She looked at him, then to me. My eyes darted between the both of them, waiting for someone to tell me what was going on. Seven days ago, there wasn't a camper in our yard.

"Well? Is anyone going to tell me what's going on or what?"

Mom smiled. "We have some news for you. It's no big deal, really. We used some of our settlement money to buy a camper!"

"I see that…but for what? Y'all don't camp or travel."

"Well," Mom said, "we do now! We're going to get all of our things in order, clean this place up again, and hit the road. That way, we can get out of your hair and give you your space back, and you won't have to worry about moving."

Woah. What? Major bomb drop.

"Are you serious? When is all of this happening?"

"Well, we're planning on being in New England by October. So you'll only have to put up with us but for a few more months. Then we'll be out of your hair."

I was shocked. Dead silent. Speechless.

This was so unlike my parents. They were not the adventurous, just get up and go type. I know because they were exactly where I'd gotten it from.

"Exciting, isn't it?" Dad asked.

"I—I mean, I guess. Yeah, that is…just not what I was expecting."

"Us either," Mom said. "It just kind of happened so fast."

"Yeah, I see that. I hope it all works out." Crazy. A week ago, I'd been stressed out to the max having to live with my parents again. Now they were leaving me in a couple of months.

"It was your dad's idea, but I couldn't be happier."

"I'm happy for y'all."

"So, now tell us all the details about your trip! I want to hear everything. Did you have a good time?"

Oh. Shit.

♡♡♡

I barely got out of that conversation by the skin of my teeth. I'd somehow kept a straight face the entire time I sat there telling them about the past week, trying to save face. As far as they were concerned, I went alone. That would forever and a day be my story. At least with them.

My only saving grace was the pictures I had taken on my last day there, because of course, my mom wanted to see all of the pictures I'd taken. Thankfully, I'd already transferred them to their own album—sans Warren—so there wasn't the risk of them seeing the one picture I'd taken of us together.

Mom and Dad spent most of their time out in the camper, messing with this and that. Mom had already started loading it up with necessities and creature comforts and her latest haul from HomeGoods.

I decided to use my alone time to give Rowan a call, seeing as I hadn't talked to her since the day I left town. She and I had a lot of catching up to do, except she had a lot more explaining than anything else.

"How's Wes and Warren's dad doing?" I asked Rowan as I settled back onto the couch, curling my feet up under me.

"He's okay, just took an unexpected turn. You know how that goes."

"Unfortunately, I do. So what's the plan for him now?"

"They've officially got him on hospice. Once he's out of the hospital, he's supposed to go home with that. So, there's really no telling how long he has left."

"That's so sad, Rowan. I'm sorry y'all are going through that."

"Thanks. I think it's for the best, finally. Van Buren's had a rough year, and he's really just been living on borrowed time for a lot longer than any of us expected. I think Wesley has finally come to terms with everything and is ready to move on."

"I bet. You think they'll make amends before it's too late?" My mom drove me batshit crazy, but I didn't think I could ever be completely estranged from her.

"Maybe. I think Wesley will put in the bare minimum to give himself some closure, but that's probably about it. That man can hold a grudge like no one I know."

"You seem to be holding your own with Wes," I laughed.

"Power of the pussy," she said, her tone switching from somber to playful. "And speaking of, tell me all about your vacation. How was it? Did you meet anyone while you were there?"

"Oh, you slick bitch. You already know exactly how it went down! You know I could have killed you."

"Yeah, but you still love me. You can't tell me that wasn't the most amazing time you've spent with anyone in a long time. Hmm. Tell me I'm lying…I'll wait."

I rolled my eyes. I hated that she was right. "You're a liar. It was awful. Terrible. I hope I never have to do it again."

"Yeah, right. Warren came back a whole new man. What did you do to him down there? I think you broke him."

I laughed. More like he was the one who broke me. "It really wasn't that serious, Rowe. I ended up with food poisoning on Wednesday, which damned near took me out for the rest of the trip, anyway. Then he left."

"Jesus Christ. That would happen only to you. I'm sorry you got sick. That really sucks."

"Thanks. Obviously I lived, but I think I left my pride somewhere in the plumbing system at the resort."

We both laughed because that was the truth.

"That's disgusting. Did y'all even get a chance to hook up at all? Please tell me you did."

Did we? That was the best sex I'd probably had ever. "Once."

"Once? What the fuck, Kat?"

"Give me a break. We technically hooked up twice. The first time happened so damned fast it hardly counted. Round two was much longer and insanely intense."

She huffed. "Really? Twice?"

"That was all we had time for before I got sick."

"I guess that's better than nothing."

"You're damned right it was. Trust me, I would have stayed in bed with him for the rest of the trip if I could have. Besides, I barely had *two* days with him. How much fucking do you think we could have possibly gotten done in two days?"

"A lot."

"Right. It's not like he walked in, found me naked in the bathtub, then carted me off to bed and made love to me nonstop for two straight days."

"I mean, that doesn't sound half-bad."

"Rowan!"

"What? Just sayin'. I get it. I guess. That's what me and Wesley did when he came to me that first time."

"You're crazy."

"So I've been told. If I hadn't married his brother, don't think I haven't thought about Warren myself. That's all I'm saying."

"Jesus," I mumbled under my breath.

"Don't Jesus me. So what happens now? Are y'all at least going to keep talking or planning on seeing each other again or anything?"

"Anything." I wished like hell things could have gone differently, but they didn't. We had our fun, he left, and until we were face-to-face again, this was just the way it was.

"Anything? What the hell does that mean?"

"You asked me if we were talking or planning on seeing each other again or *anything*. I'm choosing the latter."

"Spill it already. There's something you're not telling me, and Wesley can't get him to open up either. I bet he's got a little dick, doesn't he? I knew it!"

"I wish. But no, he does *not* have a little dick, not even close. That would have made things a hell of a lot easier, that's for damned sure."

"Then what is it?"

"We agreed to keep things between us casual while we were together, and when vacation was over, we'd go our separate ways and back to our own lives as per usual. That's it. See? No big deal."

The line fell silent as Rowan let my words sink in.

"Rowan?"

"Yeah. I'm here. What the hell is wrong with you?"

"Me? What do you mean the hell is wrong with me?"

"Yes, you! You're gonna sit there and tell me we go through all that trouble, lock you two together in your own private bungalow in the middle of the Caribbean Ocean, and y'all two decide to basically never see or speak to each other ever again?"

I bit my lip. "Well, when you put it like that, it sounds kind of bad."

"Because it is bad, Katie. Damn. You frustrate me."

"What did you expect? For us to get married? I'll leave that for Chloe. I mean, shit, we were only together for two days."

"You're right. I just thought y'all would at least come back as more than friends. Wesley was right—y'all two really are that damn stubborn. But I still love you, though."

"I love you too. But I didn't say we would never talk to each other again, just until we had the chance to see each other *next*. So, probably when I come up for your baby shower. Speaking of, when is that, by the way?"

"September sometime. Chloe is going to help me plan it since she lives here, and since you brought it up, planning it would be so much better if you could come up for a few days and help out."

"You know I will. I wouldn't miss it for the world."

"I know you wouldn't. I'll talk to her, and one of us will get back with you when I decide on a date."

"Sounds good. Keep me updated on their dad."

"You know I will."

We got off the phone, and I started looking over my calendar, checking my availability. The only thing I had coming up anytime soon was a dental appointment, my annual OB, and a full work schedule…starting in two days. Pathetic. I blocked out every weekend in September potentially for Rowan's baby shower and made the decision right then and there to take at least one vacation per year, possibly two.

The doorbell rang, causing me to jump. I shoved off the couch, not exactly in a hurry to get to the door. What was the point? No one was coming to see me; I'd barely been home twenty-four hours. And Lord knew, if it were one of our nosey neighbors asking about the camper, they weren't going anywhere until someone opened up.

"That's probably for me," my dad shouted from somewhere down the hall. "I'm expecting a package."

"Aren't you always?" I opened the door without checking the peephole. I almost never did. Serial killers didn't ring the doorbell or show up midday to a house with three cars in the driveway—at least I hoped they didn't, anyway.

As soon as I swung the door open, I saw his face. My mood did a one-eighty and fell flat on its ass. I should have known that the high I'd been riding wouldn't have lasted forever. *His* expression, however, lit up like the Fourth of July when he saw me. *Fucker*.

"Who is it? Is it Amazon?" Dad called out.

"It's—no, Dad, it's for me." I slunk out of the door, pulling it shut behind me, and stepped out onto the front porch. "What are you doing here?"

He smiled. "You know you used to call me daddy. I miss that."

Eww. He did *not* just say that. I shuddered at the thought, and a wave of nausea crept up from my gut.

"Justin, what do you want? Why are you here?" Jesus Christ. I hadn't seen or heard from him in months, and he shows up *now*?

"I've been trying to reach you."

"Yeah? Well, so have the people about my car's extended warranty, and I'd rather talk to them." I turned to go back inside. No sense in wasting either of our time.

"Katie, wait." His hand grabbed my elbow, trying to pull me back. "Just, just give me a few minutes."

I wanted to give him zero minutes. He'd been given enough of my time over the years. Most all of it wasted.

I looked down at his fingers wrapped around my arm, then gave him a glare that could kill. He must have gotten the hint because he let me go.

"Please?" he begged. "I just want to talk."

I rolled my eyes. Something he would have flipped his shit over when we were together. Now, he couldn't do shit about it.

"Fine." Lord help me. What was I doing? Why now? "Five minutes, Justin. You get five minutes and not one second more."

"Boy, you really meant it when you said you didn't want to talk to me anymore. I don't know whether I should be proud of your willpower, or impressed that you're still this stubborn, or exponentially pissed off that you're ignoring me."

"All of the above." He didn't need to know that the biggest reason he hadn't heard back from me was not because of my sudden strength to resist him—I wish. That had taken a lot of time and practice. It probably helped that I had his number blocked. My hope after all this time was that he would have moved on to someone else by now. Yet here the asshole stood.

"I miss talking to you."

I put my hand up. "Just stop—"

"Only as a friend, Kat. Don't get me wrong. I'm not here to beg you to get back with me. I mean, that would be nice, but I get it, you're done with me. I screwed up a lot." He nudged my foot with the toe of his shoe. "You deserve better."

"Yeah, you're right. I do." So where in the hell was he going with this? My hair was going to frizz if I stood in this hellish humidity any longer.

"I'm sorry."

When aren't you. "Anything else?"

He shrugged. "Nothing, really, I guess. Just thought we could make amends. I, uh, heard about your vacation. Did you have fun?"

I must have looked at him like he'd lost his mind, because that was how I felt in that moment, and I really sucked at hiding my feelings.

"How did you know about my vacation?"

"I came by last week. Your dad told me you were gone."

I had nothing else to say.

He continued standing there, staring at me like a lost, hungry puppy. What was he doing? Waiting for me to divulge all of my personal business to him, tell him all of the dirty details about my trip like he was one of the girls? About how much fun I'd had? Or that I'd spent at least one full day having one seemingly endless orgasm after another that he could never give me? I was surprised he hadn't already asked the whole "who did you go with" question.

What would I have told him if he did ask? No answer was safe with Justin. If he wanted to know the truth, he'd find a way—he always somehow did. Plus, I didn't know how much my dad had already told him…or why he hadn't told me that Justin had stopped by. Either way, it was best to let him lead this conversation. Plus, his time was about to run out.

"Well," he said, "I hope y'all had fun."

Y'all. He said y'all. He was fishing.

"Mighty bold of you to assume there's a y'all involved. For all you need to know, I went alone."

"Sure you did." He grazed his fingertips down my bare upper arm. The same way Warren had. Justin's touch did absolutely nothing for me anymore except make my skin crawl and give me the unwelcoming urge to slap him away. "The tan looks good on you. Always has."

I shifted slightly away from him and out of reach. "Thanks. I think you need to go."

"Yeah, my time's probably up. Unblock my number so I can at least text you, will you?"

What the? How did he know? *Did* he know, or was he just fishing again?

I didn't respond to confirm his accusation or stay to watch him leave. I just turned and disappeared back into the house, locking the door behind me. I leaned against the door, my heart pounding in my chest.

What. The. Fuck?

Dad walked over and pulled the curtains back, peeking out onto the porch. "Who was that?"

"Nobody."

"Musta been somebody. You weren't just standing out there talking to yourself."

"It was Justin. He's gone now, I think."

He kept a watch out through the window as I envisioned Justin getting in his car and leaving for good. "Hmm, he is. You know he was here last week, stopped by."

"Yeah, he mentioned that."

"I was hoping he wouldn't come back." He closed the curtain and pulled me into a hug. "The only thing I told him was that you went on some fancy vacation. Hope that's okay?"

I closed my eyes tight and sucked in a deep breath, fighting off the urge to cry.

Shit. It's fine. Everything is fine. I told myself over and over.

He's gone. He's not my problem anymore. I had no reason to cry. Not one, whatsoever. He was not worth my tears.

"Thanks, Dad." He held his big arms wrapped around me. I looked up at him. Tall as I was, my dad stood over me. He was no small man. "Why didn't you tell me that he came by?"

"I haven't exactly had time. Plus, I was hoping you wouldn't find out and he'd stay gone. He hadn't mentioned to me that he was coming back."

"Does Mom know?" I hoped not because my mom loved him. I mean, she *loved* Justin. She wanted us to get married and couldn't for the life of her figure out why we never did or why we weren't still together. Even with as many times that we'd split up and gotten back together, she defended her stance that we were meant to be together. She also believed that I should be on my third kid by now.

But my dad? Oh, he hated him. He'd never said it out loud, but I knew. Whenever Justin was around, he hardly spoke two words to him and was always watching, listening. Looking back, I could see why. Justin was shady as fuck.

He shook his head. "No, your mom doesn't know. She was at garden club when he stopped by. Y'all aren't still talking, are you?"

"No. We haven't been in a long time."

His hold tightened. "Good. I always had a bad feeling about him, and you know I worry about you."

Me too.

SEVENTEEN
Katie

After Justin left, my dad retreated to his office / temporary storage room to wait on Amazon. I disappeared to my childhood bedroom.

The room had barely changed since I was in middle school. The walls were still the same awful shade of washed-out pink I'd picked out in seventh grade. Shelves were packed full of dance trophies collecting dust, with gobs of ribbons and medals hanging from hooks underneath them. An *NSYNC poster was still tacked to the wall over my headboard. Even the linens were the same— white on top of white with a lot of lace, ruffles, and frills. It was cute twenty years ago. Now, it made my head hurt.

Regardless of my atrocious, headache-inducing décor, I needed to be alone, and this was the only place I had to go.

As I lay back on my squeaky twin bed, I debated on unblocking Justin's number out of curiosity, just to see how long he'd been trying to contact me. Okay, maybe it was more sheer stupidity than curiosity that had me wondering. I

89

knew better, even as my finger hovered over his unnamed number. All of his messages had been sitting in the spam folder in bold black, unread. I knew that as soon as I clicked on his message, he would immediately get a read notification, and he'd know that I'd read his messages.

It all bothered me—him showing up here not once, but twice. Him accusing me of going to St. Lucia with someone—not that any of it was his business, but he made it that way. Him trying to convince me that he wanted to be my friend now? After all this time?

What was his angle?

What did he even care now? I figured he'd have been over me by now by either climbing under someone else, drinking himself stupid, or both.

There was a knock on my bedroom door. "Katie? Can I come in?"

Saved by my Dad, yet again. I sat up and scooted back, leaning against my headboard.

"Yeah, of course." I locked my phone and turned it facedown beside me.

"You're not busy, are you? I can come back if this isn't a good time."

"No. Not at all." I patted the bed in front of me. "Have a seat. What's up?"

He walked in and sat down on the edge of the bed. There was a look of concern written all over his face. One I'd seen a few times before, usually when he'd had something to say but had opted to keep his mouth shut and stay out of it.

He was about to say something to me that would either make him, me, or both of us uncomfortable.

"So," he started, "not to pry into your business, but Justin—"

"Dad, we're not—"

"Katie, I know you're not. Please. Just hear me out."

Justin was the last topic of conversation I'd expected him to approach me about.

"I know the two of y'all haven't had the best relationship—whether you'll ever admit that or not. I'm not stupid. Old, but not stupid." He shook his head. "Your mom, though, God love her, she really liked him, but she doesn't have a clue. I think she's secretly still rooting for y'all. But me? I know a lot more than you think I do, Katie. I really get a bad feeling about him that just gets worse the longer this goes on between the two of y'all."

"There's nothing going on between us anymore."

"I know." He took in a deep breath and blew it out. "I just want you to be careful. Okay?"

"I will. But we aren't talking. I promise. I blocked his number a long time ago. We haven't had any contact since then. That's why I was surprised he even showed up here."

"Twice."

"Yeah, twice."

"If he shows up here again, I'm going to handle it myself." His words came out as a promise more than a threat. Maybe both. My dad had never been known to hurt a fly, but that didn't mean he wouldn't protect his family at all costs if he needed to. His closet full of loaded guns proved that, and he had never been a hunter. "Just stay away from him, okay? No more, please."

"Yes, sir."

Shit.

My dad in all of my life had never once talked to me this deeply about any of the relationships I'd been in, what few I'd had, anyway. His only warning had ever been for the guys to keep their hands to themselves. My parents' philosophy had always been to keep me too busy for boys. Boy, did it worked. So hearing him so adamant about me staying away from Justin had me on edge and gave me an uneasy feeling, like he knew something I didn't.

He stood up to leave, stopping in the doorway. "Oh, by the way, I'm glad you and your friend…what's his name?" He snapped his fingers and smiled, looking back over his shoulder. "Warren? Yeah. I'm glad y'all two had fun on your trip. I'm sorry to hear about his dad."

Warren?

I swallowed so loud he had to have heard it clear across the room. What the hell did my dad know about Warren? And us on that trip together? I felt the blood drain from my face. What the hell could I say to that?

"Don't worry. Rowan called me after you'd left and told me what she and that husband of hers had planned. They knew your mom and I would be worried sick about you there alone but knew better than to tell your mom what she'd done."

"Rowan?" My voice barely reached my lips.

"Yup. She's a good friend, Katie. I've known her a long time. I trusted she would never put you in danger."

Oh. My. God. He knew? He knew!

I cleared my throat. "No, you're right, she wouldn't."

"I really like her."

I suddenly felt like I was fourteen and had just gotten caught climbing back inside through my bedroom window after sneaking out in the middle of the night.

"Thanks, Dad"—*I think*—"I really like her too." And I really liked Warren, but now wasn't the time to even mention my feelings for him. Best just leave well enough alone…because *holy shit*. My dad knew! And how *much* did he know? I wanted to crawl underneath a rock and die.

"No worries, baby. Your secret's safe with me." He winked and left my room, shutting the door behind him.

I fell forward, shoving my face into a throw pillow, and screamed. All my friends growing up had known my dad as the cool parent—overprotective but cool and easygoing. We had rules he expected us to follow, but he also expected us to fuck up because we're human.

That didn't mean I didn't still want to kill Rowan—even if she was looking out for my best interest.

After I had time to process the conversation I'd had with my dad, I picked up my phone and went straight to Justin's unread texts. Without further hesitation or accidentally clicking on the text and opening it, I deleted the entire thread. I'd never know any of what he'd sent to me over the last few months. I didn't even want to know anymore.

He was done. Gone forever. I didn't give a flying fuck if he knew that I had him blocked. I no longer cared or worried about him showing up here again because my dad said he would handle him, and I believed him.

My focus and attention were now on the man whose face I couldn't get out of my mind. Though I'm sure ogling the only picture I had of Warren and me together in St. Lucia every chance I got didn't help.

Memories of our brief time together flooded me as I stared at his face. I couldn't remember the last time I'd had any man show me near as much genuine affection as he had. Hell, maybe he was like that with every woman he'd been with, and I was no different to him. I just wish I'd known that morning he vowed to take his time with me would have been our last. I would have suggested we skip lunch altogether and stay in bed for the rest of the day.

Instead, I'd ended up with food poisoning, and we went our separate ways just as we'd agreed to do. He'd taken the agreement literally when he left without even waking me up to say goodbye.

He'd left behind all of his clothes and things he'd bought when he first got to the islands, along with a note that said I could keep them and take them home with me if I'd wanted to or leave them there. I didn't have room in my suitcase for everything he'd left, so I kept the one article of clothing with the most memory attached to it—his floral-print linen shirt. I would have kept his black silk boxers, but he'd apparently worn them home. *Bummer*.

Then that was that.

We'd laid out the rules and expectations, and then he was gone from my life just as fast as he'd shown up.

EIGHTEEN
Katie

"Mom! I'm heading out to pick up something to eat. You want anything?"

I'd been home from vacation for a few weeks, and things had finally seemed to settle back into a familiar routine—work, home, work, home. This followed by the occasional text or video call from Rowan or Chloe or both, checking in and keeping me updated on the baby shower plans. Every now and then, I checked my text message spam folder—so far, so good. It had stayed empty of any attempts by Justin trying to reach out to me. Thankfully, he hadn't stopped by unannounced anymore either.

"Where are you going?" My mom rounded the corner of the kitchen, causing me to practically jump out of my skin.

"You scared the crap out of me."

"I see that. Why are you so jumpy? And where are you going for food?"

"No reason. Just wasn't expecting you. I think I'm going to get some BBQ; you want me to get you something?" I didn't want to tell her I had an uneasy feeling for no reason whatsoever.

"You know I do. How do you know I don't already have something planned for dinner?"

"It's Friday. You never cook on Fridays. Plus, I already checked, and you didn't take anything out of the freezer."

"Fair enough. Get me the same thing I always get: a number one. Sweet tea. Did you ask your father to see if he wants anything?"

"Not yet. I'll text him now. Where is he, by the way?"

She skirted around me, making her way toward the stove and reaching into the cabinet above the vent hood. "He's off at the RV store. Been there all afternoon trying to find more stuff, accessories, toys, things he thinks we're going to need…or not. He should be home soon."

"Ah. Gotcha." He was gonna spend the other half of their payout if he wasn't careful. Dad liked to shop for trinkets and toys. Mom spent money on other things, like manicures, garden club, home décor, and the occasional high-end bottle of gin.

"I mean, honestly, how much crap does one person, well, two people need? It's not like we're going to be gone forever." *You're one to talk*. She poured herself a glass of vodka and took a long sip, finishing half of what she'd poured in one swig. "Just a few months here and there."

Something told me this whole travel the country in an RV thing was more my dad than my mom.

"I'm not sure. You'll have to ask him when he gets home." I was trying to leave, and she wanted to vent.

"I already did. I told him we don't need all this stuff. Yet the boxes and packages just keep coming. Every day. They just show up at the door, one after the other."

She refilled her glass almost to the top. *Lord have mercy*. It was gonna be one of those nights.

"Sorry, Mom. I'll be back in a bit." I kissed her on the cheek as she took another sip. The closer it had gotten to October and the time for her and Dad to hit the road, the more my mom hit up her stash—the one she thought no one knew about until recent years when I called her out on it.

Marcella McDonald had an image to uphold within her home, community, and amongst her friends. Did they have the occasional cocktail? Absolutely. But pouring yourself a drink into a glass without a mixer and a fancy name or special occasion was damned near a crime against humanity in her circle.

As I got into my car and buckled my seat belt, I texted my dad that I was heading to get BBQ at the Pit and to send me his order. He'd been gone most of the day, so I knew he'd be starving by the time he got home. Mom, on the other hand, would be half-tanked before I left the driveway.

♡♡♡

Ten minutes later, I pulled up the Pit. The front parking lot was jam-packed, as expected. It always was on the weekends, especially Friday and Saturday nights. We'd been eating at this same BBQ restaurant probably since before I was old enough to walk. The owners knew our family, and I'd practically grown up in the kitchen with their grandkids.

Since then, coming here had become a tradition for my family. Anytime someone mentioned getting food, it was a given that this was where we were going.

I parked all the way in the back of the parking lot behind the building, along the fence. Even with the minimal lighting, it never bothered me one bit. This was one of the few places in Memphis I felt safe walking alone. I locked my car up with a beep. Just because I didn't feel in any kind of danger didn't mean my car was safe.

This was still Memphis.

After waiting in line for almost thirty minutes, I finally placed my order and had our food—sans drinks because their machine had quit working—balanced in my arms, along with my purse and keys in hand as I made my way back to my car.

"Katie?"

I heard footsteps on the concrete behind me, picking up their pace as my name was called out. The voice stopped me dead in my tracks. I knew exactly who it was calling my name.

"Katie, wait up." Justin jogged up beside me as I continued walking toward my car.

"Go away." I couldn't believe he'd found me. Though, as often as I frequented this place, I was surprised I hadn't run into him sooner.

"Wait, please. Can we just talk?"

"We already did. You had your time. I have nothing else to say to you."

"Just hear me out, okay?"

"Don't you think you've already said enough?" I hit the button to unlock my car, and as I reached to pull on the door handle, bag of food in hand, he stuck his arm out and blocked me.

"What the—"

"Who is he? Huh? There's someone else, isn't there? Just tell the fucking truth."

"What? No, there's no one else. Why would you—"

"Because you've still got me blocked. You don't read my texts or answer when I call. You've never pushed me away like this before. I know there's someone else."

"What do you care? We're not together anymore."

"I know. Just give me one more night with you. You know I'll be better than any piece of shit you're with now." He brushed his knuckles down my cheek. I jerked away from him.

"One more night? Are you delusional?" So that's what he wanted? One more night with me?

"I'm just crazy about you still. We got a lot of years together, Katie."

"And not very many of them are good ones, *Justin*. I blocked you for a reason. Now go away." He was out of his damned mind if he thought I was going to give him one more night. Him dropping me like a bad habit had always been easy for him to do. Me? Not so much. I'd always felt like I needed him; he was a crutch, my comfort zone, my go-to. He had me feeling like I couldn't be without him. Now? I couldn't get rid of him fast enough.

"Then at least unblock me, please."

He moved to the side, and I thought he was going to let me get into my car. Instead, he circled me. I shifted to stay away from him, but now my back was to the driver's door, trapped.

"Justin, you remember the last time broke things off with me? Hmm? Cause I do and very clearly." I didn't know why I felt like bringing it up, but it was a moment that had stuck with me, and it fucking hurt. I'd never had the chance to tell him. Might as well now since I had his attention, and I was feeling petty. "If not, then let me refresh your memory. Remember that one drunken night when I got back from Chicago, and I stupidly texted you? I thought to give you one more night, one more last chance. Of course, you agreed. But then you didn't even wait two whole seconds after you pulled your little dick out of me to break the news that you'd made a mistake, that you never should have come over. You weren't even limp yet."

His nostrils flared as he scrubbed his hands down his face. "Yeah, I—"

"I'm not finished. You rolled off of me, and as you lay next to me in *my* bed, nonetheless, you told me this wasn't going to work for you. Then you got up, grabbed your shit, and walked out without another word. Now it's my turn to have the final say. We are done here. Got it? This. Doesn't. Work. For. Me."

I tried to turn to get into my car, but he grabbed my arm, spun me back around to face him, and pushed me into the door. "What the fuck?" I squealed.

"I'm sorry. You're right. I never should have done that to you. Let me make it up to you? Please?"

I looked down at his hand gripping my arm. "No." I tried to pull it loose, but his grip tightened. "I walked away from you for a reason. Now get your fucking hands off me, and let me go. My food is getting cold."

He held on tighter. "I—I just miss you. That's all." He lowered his voice. "It's been a really, really long time, you know."

I sucked in a deep, frustrated breath. It had been a long time…*with him*. The thought of ever being with Justin again had me wanting to puke in his face.

He stepped forward, removing all the space between us, and pressed the front of his body against mine. "You feel it too. I know you do, Katie. Let's go back to my place. Let me make it up to you, make you feel good again."

Then he kissed me, or he tried.

But I didn't give in to him. Not this time.

He pushed his lips harder to mine, then tried to slide his tongue into my mouth.

I refused.

Never again.

"Kiss me, Katie," he demanded. His breath hung in a cloud between us in the cool air.

I balled my fists at my side, holding my to-go bag in one hand with my food while squeezing my car keys in my other hand so tight they bit into my palm.

"I said no."

He jerked his head back, and we stared each other down in a standoff, waiting for the other person to make a move. I hated that we were tucked away in the back of the parking lot. Not only were there barely any lights, but there was even less foot traffic. Should any unsuspecting person walk by, they might think we were intentionally standing close together.

I tried to wiggle loose from his hold, but he had my back firmly pinned against the driver's-side door. My lungs barely had room to expand.

"Get the fuck off of me," I hissed at him.

"You sure about that?" he said, pressing his dick into me. "You've never had a problem with me before. You used to like it rough. Remember? Since when did you start telling me no?"

"Since now." I didn't want any part of him or his body or his lips or his breath anywhere on or near me.

I squirmed under his hold, trying to shove him off me, using the car for leverage. He didn't budge.

"Get the fuck off of me, Justin." I was louder this time. "Justin, please. Let me go."

He leaned down, his lips close to my ear. "You know I like it when you beg."

I didn't know where the strength came from, but I somehow maneuvered to put just enough space between us and flung my hand with the keys in it forward, connecting directly with his balls. It hadn't been near as hard of a hit as I would have liked, but it did the job.

He shuffled backward and bent forward, letting out a half cough, half choke, fighting to hold himself upright.

"I told you to get off of me!" This time I was loud enough that someone else heard me.

A man started walking over toward us from between two other cars parked near the back of the restaurant. I didn't know how much he had seen or heard, but thank the Lord he'd been there.

Frantically, I tried to get into my car while Justin was still somewhat subdued, but I had somehow locked the doors, then dropped my keys.

"Fuck."

"I think she told you to get the fuck off of her," the other man called out as he maneuvered between cars to get to us.

Justin glanced back over his shoulder at him, then at me. "The whore doesn't know what she wants," he said with a smug look on his face.

Then the man charged at Justin. I thought for sure he was going to take him down, and he probably would have, but not before Justin stood up, reared his hand back, and clocked me in the side of the face with his closed fist, then took off running.

I dropped my food as I grabbed my cheek. He'd hit me so hard I saw stars; the taste of blood filled my mouth.

"Hey! Motherfucker! Get your ass back here!" This time, the man took off in a sprint after

Justin. But he stopped short as Justin dodged around a car driving by and disappeared across the street between two buildings.

The random guy approached me. He bent down and scooped up my keys and food, then handed them to me. My head throbbed, and I could feel tears burning my skin as they streamed my cheeks.

"Hey, miss, are you okay? Fucking shit. He knocked the hell out of you."

I nodded. "I'll be—I'm fine. I really just need to get home."

"You want me to call the cops for you?"

I swallowed the coppery liquid. "No. Don't."

"Ma'am, I really think you should. At least let me take you back inside and get you checked out."

"I said no. Now, please, just let me go. All I want to do is go home," I said, wiping more tears away. "I'll handle it."

I blinked away more tears to get a better look at the man. He had an unreadable look on his face. Concern, disbelief, empathy. Like he understood but didn't understand at the same time.

"Okay…okay. Get in your car, and lock your doors. I'll stand here until you drive off."

"Thank you."

He opened my door, waited as I got behind the wheel, then gently shut the door tight. He tapped his hand on the roof of my car. That was my cue to leave.

I tossed everything over onto the passenger seat and bailed the fuck out of that parking lot a lot faster than I probably should have. I watched every sidewalk, every intersection, like a hawk all of the way home, looking, waiting, wondering if he was going to pop out and finish whatever the hell war it was that he had just started.

Lyndsay Marie

The lights were on in the camper, so I assumed that's where my parents were when I pulled into the drive. Mom probably drunk on her third or fourth glass of gin, fussing at my dad over all the tools and gadgets he'd bought but didn't actually need. Dad on "yes, dear" mode, because sometimes that's all he could say in hopes that she'd eventually end her rant and just let him be. He'd never said a word to her about her trips to HomeGoods.

I killed the headlights and parked on the side of my dad's's truck, hopefully out of view, then ducked inside the house as quickly as I could. I didn't want them to get a chance to see me before I had the opportunity to see myself first.

Dumping the food on the kitchen counter, I grabbed mine, despite having lost my appetite. I scribbled a quick note on a notepad that said "bad headache"—not entirely a lie—and left it with their food. Then I retreated to my bedroom for the rest of the night.

Eventually, the house fell silent.

I snuck out of my room and tiptoed my way to the bathroom, locking myself inside.

My head pounded, blood whooshing in my ears with every beat of my heart. In all my life on this earth, I had never, ever once been struck like that. Not by anyone, not even Justin on his worst day. Sure, he and I had gone back and forth, fussing and fighting regularly. A candle launched across the room here, a hole punched in the wall there. He'd even gotten a little rough with me in the bedroom from time to time during our makeup sex, only leaving marks where they could be easily covered up. Now I wondered how long he'd been holding back, how long had he wanted to do that but for some reason didn't.

I flipped on the light switch and finally looked at myself in the mirror.

I no longer recognized the woman staring back at me. Not because I'd changed or because of the giant red mark on my cheek or the bruise that had formed under the side of my eye. It was because the person I saw staring back at me was miserable and weak and afraid. I'd become a shell of myself, or at least the person everyone thought I was supposed to be.

Always the strong, confident one. Always the pretty one. The smart one who had her whole life together, had it all figured out.

Perfect hair? Check. Flawless makeup? Check. Tall, thin, athletic? Check, check, and check.

It never ended.

And for years I'd listened to Rowan and Chloe tell me I needed to get away from Justin, needed to leave him alone. They always suspected something was off and not right, just not sure how much. Each time, I'd come to his defense, making excuses for his actions or our decision to get back together. Deep down, I knew they were right about him, yet each and every time we broke up, he came back, and I welcomed him right in.

Everyone has their breaking point, and I'd finally reached mine.

I dried my eyes and face, then covered the blotchiness and bruise with a coat of primer and liquid foundation before sneaking back into my room and going to sleep, hopefully to replace some of those shitty memories with better ones.

♡♡♡

Time had flown by. It had been almost three months since St. Lucia, five days since my run-in with Justin, and only one more hour left of my last shift, and then it was off to Chicago in the morning to start getting ready for Rowan's baby shower.

Thankfully, the mark on my face had faded—enough to easily cover with makeup. All those years of pageants and stage performances and slapping on a smile had taught me not only how to hide mental bruises but physical blemishes as well. My parents were none the wiser. Now, if Rowan or Chloe had found out or seen what Justin had done to me, they'd kill him. I had no doubt.

"What's on your mind over there?" my sweet coworker and friend Andy asked as he threw a plastic medication topper at me, hitting me square in the forehead.

"Jerk," I said, picking it up and tossing it back at him.

"Only your jerk. And your aim sucks. But for real, though, you seem kinda distant. You okay?"

Hell, I didn't know how to answer that question anymore. Things in my life had gotten out of hand lately, and I needed to reel it in. My nerves were shot over what Justin had done to me, and now I would be seeing Warren again soon.

"Yeah, I'm good. Just getting into vacation mode. Thanks for checking on me." I smiled and batted my eyelashes.

He rolled his eyes. "If you say so. Just gotta check on you. You're my favorite girl." He stood, then leaned down and kissed the top of my head. "But as much as I love you, I love my job even more, and I'm so far behind on my charting. Walk you out?"

"You'd better."

Lyndsay Marie

It had been a good shift. No one had inadvertently used the Q word. None of my patients extubated themselves or coded, which was always a nice way to end the day and start time off.

I wrapped up my own work, made one last round on all of my patients, and finally gave the handoff report to the next shift. I grabbed my stuff out of my locker, clocked out, and waited for Andy so we could walk each other out.

"So," he said, nudging my shoulder as we finally made our way outside into the crisp fall air, "what's on the agenda? You gonna see Mr. Panty Dropper?"

I laughed. "I don't know, maybe. I mean, I'm pretty sure I will. His brother's wife *is* getting ready to have a baby. I'm sure I'll see him eventually."

"Well, I hope you do, and I hope he fucks your brains out. You look like you could use some good dick in your life."

"Ohmigod, Andy." I shoved his arm and looked around, checking to make sure no one else had been around to hear his lewd remarks. "You can't just go around saying things like that out loud." I shuddered and pulled my jacket tighter around me as a gust of wind blew around us. I was going to freeze my ass off in Chicago.

"Ma'am, I say whatever I want to. You've known me long enough to know that by now. Just like I promise you if I ever get my hands on that raggedy-ass bitch of an ex of yours, I'm gonna strangle the life out of him."

Ugh. I wished he hadn't brought him up. I wanted to forget that run-in had ever happened, but Andy was the only person I had told. He was the only person I could trust not to say anything to anyone, just let me handle my own business.

That didn't make him any less pissed off, and rightfully so. But I felt like someone needed to know, just in case.

"Well, hopefully you won't get the opportunity. I can't imagine after what he did he would be stupid enough to show his face again."

"Umm-hmm. He'd best not. 'Cause, bitch, I already know orange ain't my color. Just promise me one thing?"

"Anything for you."

"Move on. From what all you've told me about this Warren guy, you've got a solid chance with a decent man. Take a risk for once in your life. A *good* one."

"I promise, I'm trying."

I'd always believed that everything happened for a reason. That had always been my philosophy for life, work, love. Everything. Especially after spending so many years in medicine watching countless lives come and go. Some were spared that I didn't think needed to be; others were taken way too soon for seemingly no reason, no matter what any of us did to try to save them. Neither of those decisions was ultimately my call. This was how I'd tried to see things with Warren, to convince myself that however all of this played out that it wasn't my call.

"Good girl. You're gonna find happiness, I promise," he said as we stopped at the corner, waiting for the light to change so we could cross the street.

My phone dinged with a new text message. I dug it out of my pocket and checked. It was from a number I didn't recognize.

"Good Lord," I said out loud, more to myself than anything.

"What is it?"

"A text from an unknown number."

"You think it's him trying to be slick?"

"I fucking hope not. He needs to move on already."

"Only one way to find out. Light's green, let's go," Andy said as he started to walk.

I quickly glanced both ways before stepping off the curb with Andy by my side. I decided to see who the message was from. If it was from Justin using a burner phone, I'd just go and have my number changed. This was not a game I wanted to play.

As I glanced down at my phone to read the mysterious new message, the first few words of the message came into view. I smiled so big at the recognition of who the text had come from that my cheeks burned.

Then I heard someone scream my name. It was as if I were underwater, my name a muffled echo off in the distance. That was the last thing I remembered before a shock wave of pain ripped through my entire body, and everything around me went dark.

TWENTY
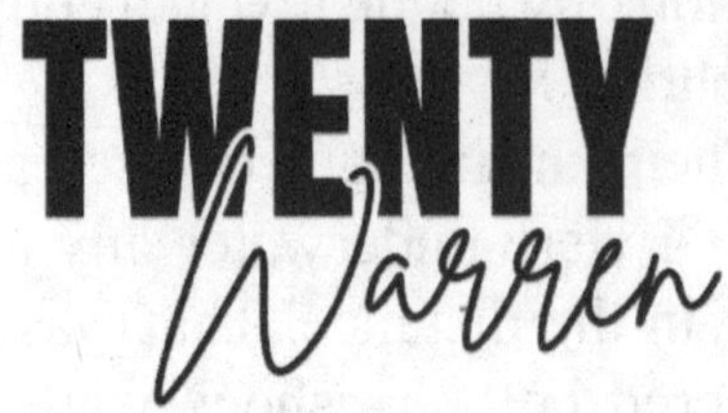

Days had turned into weeks, weeks into months—time meshed together into a boring blur. I'd simultaneously turned into the biggest bitch this side of the Mississippi River. Thoughts of Katie had completely consumed every corner of my mind, nonstop from the moment I'd last seen her.

But tomorrow?

She would be here tomorrow.

I only had one more day before I would be the closest to her that I'd been in months, and I didn't have the slightest fucking clue if she would even want to see me. I mean, shit, we'd gone this long, and not once had she tried to reach out to me, or even ask about anyone me, that I was aware of. Though, I didn't know why I thought she would have. She'd just been holding up her end of the deal. Then again, I hadn't tried any of those things either, so I was just as guilty.

"Dude. You do realize what a douche you're being," Wes said to me in between punches. I held firm to the punching bag as he beat the shit out of it. His wife was expecting their first baby in less than a few weeks, and the closer she got to her due date, the more time he wanted to spend at the gym.

As he prepared to strike again, I swung the bag out of the way, causing him to miss his next throw. "Ugh, you asshole," he grunted.

"I've been called worse. Besides, what's your point? So what if I'm a douche? Katie said she wanted to use this time apart as a cool-off period. We could reevaluate it once she got here. That's exactly what I'm doing." *And going fucking crazy in the meantime.*

"You mean tomorrow? Because that's when she's going to be here. Tomorrow."

"Yeah, I'm well aware. That doesn't mean we'll see each other *tomorrow*."

"Then fucking call her or text her already. Make a plan *before* she gets here. Rowan and I didn't go through all that trouble to get the two of you together for you to act like a little bitch."

"I'll think about it." Hell, I'd been thinking about it since that morning I'd left her asleep in St. Lucia. Sure, I could have just as easily called my brother or sister-in-law at any time and gotten Katie's phone number, and I was sure one of them would have given it to me. But Katie and I had an agreement, and so far, she hadn't broken her end of the deal either.

"Don't think about it too hard. You've already wasted the last three months." He walked over to the bench, picked up a towel, and wiped the sweat off his face and arms.

"That's my towel, dick."

He smiled. "I know." Then he tossed the damp towel at me. "This is also your phone." He picked up my cell, his fingers moving across the screen.

"The fuck are you doing?"

"What you should have done a long time ago."

I spun the towel around in my hands, then whipped it at him with a *snap*, popping his thigh.

"Ouch, motherfucker. Chill out. I'm just putting Katie's number in your phone. When you're done being such a pussy, text her yourself." He tossed my phone back down on my bag. "Now, let's go get some food. I'm starving."

"Sounds like a plan. My place? Yours? Grab-n-go?"

"Rowan is on a tear trying to nest or some shit. I'd rather stay out for just a little bit longer."

"I think the taco truck is out just a few blocks down. We can head there."

"Sounds like a plan."

We packed up our stuff and headed out of the basement gym.

Wes rubbed his hand over his thigh and mumbled, "Prick," under his breath as he walked ahead of me with a slight limp in his stride.

All I did was smile.

An hour later, we were heading back to our building. I'd eaten more calories than I'd burned off at the gym. We got on the elevator, Wes with almost as much to-go food as the two of us combined had eaten—all for Rowan. I wished him luck when I got off on my floor and headed to my condo to finally shower off the day and call it a night.

I'd barely had Katie's phone number a few hours and already had thought of a hundred different opening lines to text her. Not a single one of them seemed good enough to send. Instead, I did the next best thing. I poured myself a glass of scotch and paced back and forth in my living room as I contemplated exactly what I wanted to say.

Drinking and thinking. Thinking and drinking.

How pathetic was I? I could type hundreds, even thousands of pages of documents day in and day out with absolute confidence, never once skipping a beat. Send one text message to Katie? Forget it. Not happening.

"Fuck." I went back into the kitchen and poured myself another drink, hoping this one would help me come up with something creative. Each time I typed a few words, I immediately cleared the screen. When I finally reached the bottom of the glass—each one going down a lot faster than the one before it—I'd finally settled on what to send her. Who knew such a seemingly simple task could turn into such a burden.

I typed out what I wanted to say before I could change my mind, ending this self-induced torture once and for all.

As soon as I hit Send, the message was marked as read.

She'd already seen it.

Despite not having had a relationship in years, I still didn't think I was ready to dive headfirst into anything, not even with Katie. *Yet.*

Sure, she was great, borderline perfect. But between the shit that had gone down with Wes, his ex, and our dad a few years ago, plus working sixty or more hours a week, love was the last thing I had time for, or so I thought.

Almost an hour had passed, and she still hadn't responded. Though I knew she had read my message. Did I dare call her? No. I didn't want to come across any more desperate than I already felt after what I'd said. Instead, I waited.

And waited.

And waited.

I lost track of how much time had passed without a response. The sun had long set, turning the sky as black as ink. The city lights made a tolerable replacement for the lack of visible stars.

I eventually just said fuck it and went to my bedroom, ready to call it a night. The framed picture of us together came into view. The same one that had been sitting on top of my dresser for over a year now.

When Katie hadn't replied to my text, I knew her answer—no response is a response. That was one thing my mother had always taught me.

I walked over to the picture and gave it one last long look before turning it facedown. I didn't know why I'd kept it out this long. Guess I hadn't been quite ready to put it away for good, until now. Because I damned sure didn't want it to be the last thing I looked at every night before I went to sleep anymore.

As I climbed into bed, I checked my phone one more time.

Still nothing. No text, no missed call.

Katie had decided she was done with me.

TWENTY-ONE
Warren

My phone buzzed incessantly, sliding across the top of my nightstand before it eventually fell and landed on the hardwood floor. I pried my sandpaper-feeling eyes open as they fought to adjust to the blue glow of my bedside clock.

Eleven fifteen.

I'd just barely closed my eyes, but damn, the need for sleep had hit me hard. *Must have been the scotch.*

I reached down and picked up my phone, and Wes's name came into focus. This had better be important and not some attempt at trying to pay me back for popping him with the towel earlier.

Then it hit me that he might have been calling about Rowan.

I swiped my finger across the screen to answer his call. "Yeah," I said with a groggy voice. The line went dead. I looked at my phone. Twenty-something missed calls, not one of them from Katie. "What the fuck?"

Before I had the chance to call him back, my doorbell rang. This was bad. I flew out of bed, heading straight for the door, my phone in a death grip.

"I'm coming," I shouted toward the living room as someone, probably my brother, pounded their fists against my door.

"Warren, open up. It's Wes."

"Yeah, no shit it's you." I unlocked and flung the door open. "You wanna tell me—"

He pushed past me, Rowan clinging to his side.

Okay, so not Rowan.

"What the fuck?"

"Listen. We gotta go," he said. "Go get dressed."

"Is this some kind of sick joke? Why are the two of you barging in here in the middle of the night?"

"It's Katie," Rowan said between sobs. Wes wrapped his arms around her, pulling her into his chest.

"Okay, so clearly not a joke. What's wrong with Katie?" My heart sank. It didn't matter what either of them was about to say—something was wrong, and it involved Katie. *My* Katie.

Wes fisted his hair. "Dude, I don't know how to tell you this, but there's been some kind of an accident."

"Accident? Just fucking spill it already." I rushed past them, heading straight for my closet to get ready to go. "Keep up and keep talking."

Wes told Rowan to go sit down on the couch, then followed me into my bedroom.

I reached into my closet and yanked on the first shirt my hand touched. Then I pulled on a pair of jeans, shoving my phone and wallet into my back pockets.

"Warren. Just hear me out first. I need you to try to stay calm. Losing your shit won't do anyone any good, especially not Katie."

"Wes," I said, looking him dead in the eyes, "if you don't hurry the fuck up and tell me what in the hell is going on, I swear to God, I'm going to knock you out, then make your wife tell me." Truth be told, I'd only ever hit my brother one time in my life, and that was when he'd kissed my then girlfriend. We were only in the sixth grade, but he still deserved it.

"She's in the hospital. She was leaving work earlier tonight and got hit—"

"Hit?" I froze. I could feel all of the blood drain from my face. "Hit by what? A patient?"

"A car."

"A ca—what? How is she?"

"We don't know. We don't have a lot of details yet. Rowan got up to pee and checked her phone. Katie's mom had called her."

I braced myself against the bathroom counter.

"Warren, go sit down."

"When? When did this happen? What time?"

Wes's gaze met mine in the mirror, slightly confused. "I—I don't fucking know, probably sometime just after seven when she was getting off work. Why?"

I pulled out my phone and looked at the text that I'd sent her. I'd texted her at 7:24 p.m. She had read it within less than a minute of receiving it, which seemed to fit the timeline of when she would have been hit. *Fuck*. That's why I never received a response. She'd been getting hit by a goddamned car.

"Warren, you look like shit. Please go sit down."

"There's no time to sit down. Is she awake?"

He sucked in a deep breath and blew it out. "No. Not yet. Last we heard, she was in trauma ICU."

"We need to—I need to get to her."

He put his hands on my back. "That's why I'm here. I'll get you there. But Rowan is a damned wreck, and I have to keep her calm, for obvious reasons. Pull yourself together."

I splashed my face with cold water and dried it with a hand towel. I shoved past Wes, threw on a pair of socks and running shoes, grabbed my keys, and headed for the door. "Then let's go."

♡♡♡

The three of us made it to the airport in what I'd consider record time. Wes drove the three of us in his car, no one saying a word the entire ride there.

He pulled up to the curb in the first drop-off zone we came to. I practically jumped out of the car before it came to a complete stop. The kid at the counter outside jumped as I approached him. Before I could say the first word, Wes came up behind me, and in more words or less, told me to shut the fuck up and let him do all of the talking. As it had turned out, that wasn't a bad idea, seeing as I could barely think without my head feeling like it was going to explode.

He talked to the attendant, getting information for every possible flight itinerary from here to Memphis.

"What do you want to do, Warren? They've only got one flight out of here and not for another—" He checked his watch. "—almost six hours."

"I'll wait." I looked at the kid behind the counter, who'd visibly started sweating by this point. It was forty degrees. He paused and waited for one of us to respond. I looked over at him. "That doesn't mean you stop looking. I want on the next plane leaving this airport, arriving to Memphis first. Preferably not six hours from now."

"Yes, sir." He went back to typing on his keyboard as fast as his fingers would allow.

"Warren. We'll get to her soon enough, okay? The reality is there's nothing any of us can do—not here or there."

"This is bullshit. I just don't understand." I couldn't wrap my head around any of it—not what had happened to Katie, or how an international airport running millions of flights a year didn't have a single direct flight to Memphis?

"None of us do." Wes looked back at Rowan sitting in the passenger seat.

"Okay," the kid said. We both turned our attention to him. "The only direct flight I have from here to Memphis leaves at two in the afternoon tomorrow. That's the soonest—"

"That's not good enough. Check again," I said.

"No, don't check again," Wes interrupted, giving me a stern look. "Take the layover, Warren. It'll put you in Little Rock by early morning. You sit there for what? Three hours at best, and you'll get to Memphis before lunch. That's still earlier than any direct flight."

"Fuck." I ran my hands down my face. At this rate, I could get there quicker if I drove, but I was in no condition to drive. "Okay, fine," I caved. "Put me on the flight with the layover."

Rowan finally got out of the car and came up to us. "What's going on? What time are we leaving?"

"We?" Wes asked her. "We are not going anywhere. Warren is leaving. Then we'll see if *we* can catch up with him later on."

"What? Why? I need to be in Memphis more than he does," she argued.

"Yes, but I need to call Dr. Owens first thing in the morning when their office opens and get clearance for you to fly, *then* we leave if she says it's safe."

She started crying again.

"So, just one ticket?" the kid asked nervously.

"Yeah, just one," I told him.

Wes reached out to shake my hand. "Keep us updated as much as possible."

"I will. If either of you hears anything first, call me immediately."

Less than five minutes later, I had a one-way ticket to Memphis in my hand. I said goodbye to Warren and Rowan, then hauled ass to the gate. Not that I didn't have plenty of time, but I wasn't about to risk anything else getting in my way to Katie.

♡♡♡

Thank fuck my flight from O'Hare to Little Rock had been on time—one hour and fifty-two minutes—and entirely uneventful, as promised by the poor guy I'd practically ambushed at the American Airlines counter earlier this morning.

I sat at the gate and waited very impatiently for my next flight. It was all I could do to keep from going crazy. That and check my phone for updates or glance at my watch for the hundredth time since I'd landed. Then I paced around. I still had three whole fucking hours to kill until my flight to Memphis.

Travelers came and went, boarding and exiting around me as the next arriving and departing flights passed through. I walked across the aisle to check flight times on the prompter. It hadn't changed.

Nothing had changed.

If I didn't find something to distract me, I was going to go out of my fucking mind standing around, waiting, pacing, sitting.

I decided to grab a breakfast sandwich and another cup of coffee. I'd been awake since Wes and Rowan first knocked on my door in the middle of the night. I didn't see sleep in my near future anytime soon. As I stood in the aisle, sipping my coffee, finishing off the last of my sandwich, my phone pinged with a new message. I practically dropped everything trying to get the damned thing unlocked.

Lyndsay Marie

Wes: Nothing new. Stable, still not awake.

What the hell did that even mean, stable but not awake? *Fuck.* I'd never forgive myself if something happened to Katie and I didn't get a chance to talk to her, to explain myself. My message had probably come across as my being a major dick, but after the few drinks I'd had, I was feeling extra bold.

Now just look where that got me.

Me: Okay, thanks.

I pocketed my phone and stood back against the wall as travelers rushed past me. The president of the United States could have walked by, and I never would have noticed. Something did catch my attention, a flash of a platinum-colored head of hair at the desk across the terminal.

I tossed my empty coffee cup in the trash as I made my way through the crowd and back to the gate.

"Uh, excuse me, miss?" I leaned against the counter and smiled at the blonde-haired woman as best I could, considering.

"How can I help you?" she asked, looking up from her computer screen with a beaming smile.

"Yeah, I really hope you can. I'm trying to get to Memphis, and fast. Is there any way you can check and see when the next flight is going out?"

"Let me look." Her attention went back to the computer, but she still spoke to me. "I've been watching you pace around this place for the last half hour, Mr....?"

"Miller. Warren Miller."

"Mr. Miller, I can tell you two things: one, you've still got at least two and a half hours left because your next flight is the soonest out. Two, clearly you're in a hurry." She looked back up at me. "Why don't you just drive?"

I stood up tall. "You have my attention."

"Memphis is only two hours from here, fifteen minutes less if you're careful," she said with a wink.

"Really? Just two hours?" So there was still hope.

She nodded. "Yup. Head downstairs towards baggage claim. Rentals are down there. You can probably get a car and be on the road in less than half an hour. That would still put you in the city limits before your plane lands in Memphis. Just a thought."

"You're a lifesaver." I thanked her as I practically ran off, heading toward the exit to the rental car place. Worst case, they couldn't get me anything, and I'd still have to wait to fly out. Best case, I could be at the hospital within the next two hours.

The entire process took all of seventeen minutes.

As soon as my ass hit the seat of my rental car, I was out of Little Rock and headed east on I-40 as fast as I could go. Google showed the drive time to be one hour and fifty-nine minutes.

"Challenge accepted," I said out loud as I punched the gas.

TWENTY-TWO
Warren

Most people—naysayers, skeptics, miserable people—would tell you that love at first sight is complete and utter bullshit. Any other time, they probably would have been right. I mean, how could you lay eyes on someone for the first time ever, someone you'd never seen or talked to in your life, a total stranger, and just know deep within your soul that they were the one? I'm talking *the* one. That person—your person—you wanted to marry, have your children, build a life, and spend all the rest of your days with?

Well, I can speak from personal experience—when you know, you know.

From the moment I'd introduced myself to Katie, taking her hand in mine, it was game over for me. Katie was a flawless creature of human perfection. Everything from her silky, platinum-blonde hair, over each subtle curve from her shoulders to her hips, all the way down to her mile-high tanned legs. The way her soul lit up when she laughed. How she carried herself in public and in private. The way she treated everyone she met.

And from the second my eyes met hers, I didn't even want her to be just someone I fucked. Well, I did, but that wasn't the very first thing that had come to mind. Not even close.

I wanted to marry her.

Just under two hours later, I whipped the car into the first available spot in the visitor parking garage at the hospital. As I climbed out of the car, I was hit with a wave of humidity. I'd never been to Memphis and hoped this would be my last time. It was eerily warm considering it was mid-September. Surely the weather wasn't like this all of the time? If so, I'd decided based on that alone that I would never be able to live here.

I had no idea where to go from here, just that, as per Rowan's instructions, I was to park in the garage and head up the hill to the main entrance. Security would tell me where to go from there.

As I stood on the corner and waited for the light to change, I couldn't help but wonder where Katie had been—which intersection she'd been walking through—when she'd been struck. A chill ran down my spine, and nausea crept up at the thought I was possibly about to cross the street at that very same spot.

The light changed, signaling that it was safe to cross.

I checked both ways, my stomach in knots as I stepped off the curb, and as I began to walk, a car ran the red light, causing me to jump back.

"What the fuck." It was no goddamned wonder she got hit. These people were reckless.

I safely made it to the front desk a minute later and checked in with security. They took my picture and printed out a visitor badge, then gave me directions for how to navigate my way to the step-down unit where Katie had been. She'd already been moved from trauma to step-down. That was somewhat reassuring.

I'd been inside hospitals plenty of times—once for myself, a few times here and there for a friend, but most visits had been family related. Not the day my baby brother died or my own mother losing her battle with cancer, not even when I'd almost lost Wes, not once, but twice—none of those scenarios had felt like this. The thought of almost losing Katie felt different. None of them compared to the feeling I had as I wound my way around this place. Up two flights of stairs, down an escalator, four floors up in an elevator, a right and two lefts, until I reached the area marked Step Down Unit.

I pressed the button on the wall, and doors swung open. I stopped the first person in scrubs as I walked down the hall.

"Excuse me. Could you show me where this room is?" I pointed to the room number on my sticker badge on my chest.

He tilted his head back. "Down on the left, just past the nurses' station. I'd walk you, but I'm needed in another room," he said, lifting his arms full of linen.

"Understood. Thank you."

This was it. I'd wanted so badly to be here, to see Katie; now here I was about to walk into her room, and I was contemplating turning around and going back home.

As I stood outside her door, I took in a deep breath, my closed fist hovering, hesitating to knock.

Just as my knuckles grazed the wood, the door swung open. "Oh! Excuse me. Can I help you?"

"Sorry." I swallowed hard. "Yeah, I, uh, I'm here for Katie. I can come back if now isn't a good time."

"Nope, it's perfect. I'm all done here. Come on in," the woman in navy blue scrubs, who I assumed was Katie's nurse, said as she moved to the side, allowing me to walk past her. "Y'all let me know if I can get you anything else." Then she left and shut the door closed behind her.

She said y'all. That meant someone else was in here too, though I shouldn't have been surprised Katie hadn't been left alone.

Hesitantly, I pulled the curtain back and peeked around it.

The lighting in the room was dim, the blinds shut tight, but I could still see everything as clear as day. A man and woman sat next to the window; the woman had her chair pulled up beside the bed. They both looked up at me. Of course, I didn't have the balls to look at Katie.

The older gentleman was the first to say something as he stood up. "Can we help you?"

He was almost as tall as me.

I walked over to the foot of the bed and offered him my hand. "Warren. I'm, uh, a friend of Katie's."

He shook my hand with a strong, firm grip. "Warren. Nice to meet you. Brantley, Katie's dad. This is her mom, Marcella."

They were her parents. Holy shit. Not exactly how I'd expected our first-time meeting to go. Then again, I hadn't exactly been expecting to meet them at all.

Her mom, Marcella, looked up and forced a smile. She didn't say much, just a soft-spoken hi. Then she went back to looking at her daughter.

"How's she doing?" I asked, hoping for more than the update Wes had given me—*stable but not awake*. I needed more than just that. Having been raised in a household dominated by medicine, and being in medical research myself, on top of everything my family had been through,

I liked to think that I had more than just general knowledge and understanding of the healthcare field.

He blew out a breath, then sat back down, glancing over at his daughter. "Could have been a lot worse."

"That is for sure." I wiped my sweaty palms down my thighs. The walls of the room felt like they were closing in on me the longer I stood there.

"Why don't you grab a chair and come have a seat." He gestured to the only other empty chair in the room. It was directly across from Katie's mom, right beside the bed. I still hadn't brought myself to look at her yet. I didn't know what to expect, how badly she'd been hurt, or what physical damage would be visible.

Hesitantly, and not wanting to be rude, I walked over sat down.

I could see Katie just barely in my peripheral vision. I wanted so badly to reach out and touch her, to run my hand through her hair, hold her hand, anything. But instead, I refrained.

"Has the doctor said anything about her status?"

Her dad leaned back in his chair. "I can't remember what all they've done, exactly, but I know so far everything has been negative except for the CT. It showed a small contusion, but overall brain activity is firing away. Lots of bruising everywhere else too. Nothing broken or lacerated—internal or external—thank the Lord. Doc says she just got knocked the hell around and needs time to rest."

I breathed a sigh of relief. "That's amazing. Has he given her a prognosis?"

"He seems to think she's got a good prognosis as long as she keeps heading the way she's been."

I felt my entire body physically relax. "I'm so glad to hear that."

"Yeah, us too. You said your name's Warren?"

I folded my hands in my lap and sat back. "Yes, sir. I'm Rowan's brother-in-law."

"Ah, so you're Wes's brother? I've heard about you." He grinned ever so slightly.

Oh shit. I had no idea what that meant or what he'd heard, but I wasn't about to ask and find out. "Hopefully all good things."

"Of course."

As we quietly carried on conversation across the bed, about everything and nothing, Brantley watched his daughter. He loved her, there was no denying that. It was visible, and the love he had for her could be felt in his words as he spoke about her. Her mom, on the other hand, still hadn't said two words. I didn't know if she'd even heard any of our conversation. She seemed to be lost in a daze, in her own world.

"I'm surprised to see her here and not still in ICU. She didn't require intubation or anything?"

"Oh, yeah, she did first thing when they brought her in." He let out a soft laugh. "She yanked the tube out sometime during the night. Doc decided to just put her on some oxygen and observe her, watch her vitals, see how she did. So far, she's been holding her own."

"That's impressive. Though, I wouldn't expect anything less of her."

"Yeah, she's stubborn, all right."

"Maybe so. I think she's more of a fighter than anything else." My only hope was that I could one day be the one to give her something else worth fighting for.

"Marcella," Brantley said softly to his wife. "Let's take a break. Give Warren a few minutes alone with our girl."

"No. I'm good," she said without looking at him.

He shifted in his chair, leaning forward. "Well, I'm getting hungry. Katie will be fine for a few minutes without us." Then he stood up and held out his hand to his wife. "Come. We'll run down to the cafeteria real quick. We both need to eat."

Marcella debated for a minute. She finally patted Katie's hand that she'd been holding and told her she'd be right back. Katie's body moved as though she were shifting to get comfortable.

I sat up straight. "Has she been doing that? Moving around like that?"

"Oh yeah," he said. "She comes and goes. She hasn't woken up entirely yet, but I think she knows we're here."

"Holy shit," I mumbled under my breath.

He laughed. "Those were my exact words. She'll come back around. Give it time. We'll be back in a few," he said, ushering his wife out of the room. "You want me to bring you anything back?"

"No, but thank you for the offer. I ate just a little while ago," I lied. I hadn't eaten since breakfast almost four hours ago, but the thought of food didn't sit well at the moment. Right now, I wanted Katie to fully wake up and to be here when she did. I didn't know the exact extent of her head injury, but I had a hell of a lot more hope now than I did before.

Brantley nodded, and they left.

Despite the faint beeping on the heart monitor and the bubbling of the water from the humidified oxygen, the room fell eerily silent when the door clicked shut. I still couldn't look at her. I'd only half-assed seen her silhouette and the shape of her body under the covers.

Never in a million years did I think this would be how we would see each other again.

Yet here we were, just the two of us.

I finally manned up, turning my chair to face her.

She would shit a brick if she knew what she looked like right now or thought others had seen her in such disarray. Her normally straight and perfect hair was completely disheveled and out of place, matted with streaks of dried blood in one spot. It had been pulled up and back in a makeshift ponytail, like someone had tried their best to get it out of her face—her bruised and cut-up face.

I pushed a lock of stray hair out of the way. Her eyelids flickered.

"Katie. It's Warren. I'm right here." I knew she was in there. Maybe she knew I was here too, and she wanted to say something, she just couldn't.

I reached down and grabbed her hand. She didn't grab mine back, but I held on anyway. So many things I wanted to say, to tell her, floated around my head, but I couldn't formulate the words.

We just sat there for a while in silence, my thumb rubbing over the back of her hand.

An unexpected knock at the door startled me. I let go of Katie's hand as someone entered the room.

"Hey, brother," I heard Wes's voice say. "How's she doing?"

I looked up at him in surprise. "What the hell are you doing here? You're the last person I expected to see."

"You didn't think I was going to let you do this on your own. I caught the later flight. I bought the ticket as soon as you went into the airport."

"Nice. Thanks for coming."

"You're welcome. How is she?"

"Like you said, stable, no changes. She does some moving around, so I'm pretty sure she's somewhat aware."

"That's good to know."

I looked behind him. "Where's Rowan? You didn't bring her with you?"

He walked across the room and sat in the chair where Brantley had been sitting. "God no. I left her at home with strict orders to keep her ass in bed. Her doc said no traveling. She cussed me up and down until the very last second I closed and locked the front door."

"Nice. So you can expect to get your ass kicked as soon as you get home."

"No shit. I'm only here until tomorrow, though, since she's due in a couple of weeks. I don't want our child to be born without me or, God forbid, on an airplane thirty thousand feet in the air."

"Fair enough. You think she'll stay put?"

"No. But I've got Chloe and Daniel heading over later to keep an eye on her."

"I appreciate you coming, but you really don't need to be here. I'm fine on my own."

"I know I don't *need* to be here; I want to. At least for this crucial time."

"You'll be happy to know I'm not alone. Katie's parents were just here."

"I figured they would be.'

"Yeah, I feel so bad for them having to sit by and watch their only daughter like this, not knowing when she'll wake up or how she'll be when she does."

"Well, not that it helps, but I've seen people walk away from worse. Hang in there." He checked his phone, mumbling something under his breath. "Un-fucking-believable."

"What's wrong?"

"She's here."

I cocked an eyebrow, trying hard to hide a grin. I knew who, but I asked anyway. "Who?"

"Who do you think?" He shoved his phone deep into his front pocket.

I laughed, a little louder than I'd intended to, but I'd seen that coming a mile away. Not the most ideal situation, but this was the first time I'd felt a moment of happiness since all of this started.

"I'd ask if you're joking, but I already know you aren't."

"I wish to hell I was." He stood up and scrubbed his hands down his face, then popped his neck. "Maybe you shouldn't ever tell Katie how you feel about her. This love shit is going to be the death of me." He huffed and headed for the door. "I'm going to go find her. Keep me updated."

"Will do."

Then there were two.

TWENTY-THREE
Warren

I'd spent the past three months missing Katie something fierce. I should have broken our agreement when I wanted to—the day I had to leave her there. I should have gotten her number and called her or texted sooner—not the day before she was supposed to be in Chicago. God knows I had every chance and opportunity to tell her how I felt. Instead, I kept my word and my feelings to myself, all for what?

Now here she lay in a hospital bed, the future uncertain—neither Katie's nor ours. I knew that I wanted *her* to be my future, and I'd kept my mouth shut. If I'd ever had any doubts or hesitation about how I felt, all of that had vanished when the fear of actually losing her took over. She just needed to wake up so I could tell her myself. Even if she didn't feel the same about me in return, I'd at least have the peace of mind knowing she'd know exactly how I felt about her.

Not long after my brother walked out, there was another knock on the door. I didn't have time to tell whoever it was to come in before the door opened.

An officer stepped out from behind the curtain and removed his hat. "Afternoon. How is she?"

I stood up, reaching over to shake his hand, then sat back down. "I mean, she's about as good as can be expected, I guess. Her dad says she's slowly showing signs of improvement."

"Still not awake yet?"

"No, unfortunately, she's not."

"I'm sorry to hear that. I'm Officer Hudson, by the way. You are?"

"Warren. A friend of Katie's."

He nodded. "Her parents, are they around?"

"They went down to the cafeteria. They should be back any minute."

As soon as I'd said the words, they walked in.

"Officer Hudson," Brantley said, shaking his hand. Clearly, they'd already met.

"Mr. McDonald. I was just stopping by again to see how she was, see if there were any changes."

Brantley and his wife resumed their previous spots in the chairs across from me. "Not much yet. Doc says she just needs time and rest."

"I understand that. Well, I won't take up too much of your time."

"No worries. Have y'all found anything?"

"Actually," the officer said, "we were able to pull video footage from a security camera on the parking garage, this one from a different angle. It, um, so far it appears—" He cleared his throat. "It seems like this may have been intentional."

Marcella's voice cut through the otherwise silent room first. "What? What do you mean *intentional*? You think someone did this on *purpose*?"

Brantley hushed his wife, telling her to keep her voice down. Bold move on his part.

Katie stirred in the bed, and Marcella turned her attention back to her, tears streaming down her face.

"Yes, ma'am," Officer Hudson said. "I'm sorry. It's still very much an open investigation, so we're going to keep looking for anything we can or anyone willing to come forward. Right now, we just don't have much to go on."

"What exactly makes you think this was intentional and not just another hit-and-run?" Brantley asked.

I sat back and listened, absorbing every word they spoke since I had nothing of value to contribute. The more they talked, the more questions I had than answers. My mind reeled back to yesterday afternoon.

"Well, from the new video, it doesn't appear as though the car that struck her hit their brakes."

"So? That doesn't mean anything? Does it?"

"Well, from my experience—"

"What time did this happen?" I cut him off. Fuck it. I couldn't take it anymore.

The two men looked at me.

"Um, approximately…" He flipped through some papers in a manila folder he'd had tucked under his arm.

"Seven twenty-seven," Brantley confirmed. "They rolled her into the unit at seven thirty-two."

I pulled out my phone and scrolled to the text I'd sent Katie.

Jesus Christ. My heart sank.

"Warren. What is it? You're white as a ghost."

I felt like one. My chest squeezed as I stared at the message I'd sent her. "This is my—" I swallowed. "I sent her a text at seven twenty-six."

"One minute before she got—" Brantley rubbed his face.

"I assure y'all," Officer Hudson said, "we are working very hard to find out who did this."

They'd better work extra fucking hard because God knew the cops had better find the piece of shit before I did.

Someone else knocked on the door, then proceeded to walk in. A second officer.

"Sorry to interrupt," he said. "I just need to grab Hudson for a second."

The new guy in the room leaned close to Officer Hudson. They exchanged a few words amongst themselves.

Officer Parker was about to leave when he stopped, doing a double take when he looked at Katie. "I apologize, but I think I recognize her," he said, catching all of us off guard.

This time, everyone looked at him.

"You do?" Brantley and his partner said at the same time.

"Yeah." He stepped forward to the foot of the bed. "Yeah, I do. I ran into her about a week ago. Did she have a boyfriend, or was she seeing anyone?" he asked.

"No," Brantley answered, very matter-of-fact.

I was sure we all had the same confused look on our faces. Her parents especially looked like they had no idea what the hell this guy was getting at.

"You saw her? Where?" her mom asked.

"I ran into her at I Pit BBQ joint. She was getting roughed up by some guy in the parking lot. She, um, took a pretty hard hit. Luckily I walked up on them when I did—who knows what else he would have done."

My blood pressure shot through the roof. Surely this guy had been mistaken.

"What the hell are you talking about? What do you mean she got roughed up? Who hit her?"

Marcella looked at her husband. "Brantley, did you know about this?"

His eyes furrowed, but his facial expression stayed unreadable. "No, of course not."

Marcella looked at the cop. "Did she report it? Did you? Did anyone?"

"Unfortunately, no, ma'am. I ran the guy off and waited for her to get in her car to leave. She said she was fine. But I didn't get any names—his or hers. I was off duty, and she was adamant about going home."

"And you didn't get a statement from her?"

"No, ma'am. She was adamant about leaving. It was her right to refuse. I tried getting her to come back inside the restaurant and let me take a better look at her, but again, she refused."

"This is bullshit," Brantley said, and I agreed. It was bullshit. "We need to know who it was and exactly what happened. She never said a word to us about any of it. What about security cameras? This guy has to be on video somewhere."

I'd wondered that too but didn't want to overstep my boundaries any more than I might have already. Things were tense enough as it was.

"We can try to pull camera footage, but I'm not confident there's gonna be any. This is a small, hole-in-the-wall place. I doubt their inside cameras work if they're even real."

Brantley rubbed the back of his neck. "I'm quite familiar with the Pit. We've known the owners for many years."

"I understand. I got some notes on it in my book in the car—date, time, all that."

Officer Hudson spoke up. "I'll get the info, and we'll look into it."

I took a few deep breaths, debating on speaking at this point. I knew what I was about to suggest would probably cause heads to turn and potentially get myself banned from seeing their daughter, but if Katie had been in a physical altercation with anyone, I had a gut feeling where they needed to look first.

I folded my hands together, tucking my fingers under my chin, staring down at Katie. "Check into her ex."

My words were met with an audible gasp from Marcella. Yup. I knew it.

"Why on Earth would you say that?" she asked.

"Marcella, drop it," Brantley warned his wife. Once again, he had on his poker face. There was something about the way his features hardened when I mentioned her ex. I wasn't sure if it was because my tone had been accusatory or if he agreed.

"It's still very much an open investigation," Officer Hudson reminded us, "but we'll definitely consider all options. I'll dig more into that incident and keep you all updated if anything turns up."

"I would very much appreciate that," Brantley said.

Fuck. I hated this so much. None of this ever would have happened if I'd just kept in touch with her from the beginning. But no. I practically fucking ghosted her in St. Lucia. I'd be damned if I let her go again after all of this.

Both officers said goodbye and left.

I hated the awkward silence that fell over the room, but I didn't know what in the hell to say even say anymore at this point. I figured it best to just leave.

"I appreciate you guys letting me visit," I said as I stood up, "but I think I need to get going. Give you some time alone with your daughter."

Brantley stood up. "You're welcome anytime. Let me walk you out."

I said goodbye to Marcella, and Brantley and I left together.

"Are you staying local for a while or heading back home?"

"Oh, I'll be around. I'm not going anywhere until Katie wakes up, at least."

"We sure appreciate that, and I'm sure Katie would too. You don't have work to get back to?"

"Most of my work can be done remotely on a laptop. Anything else will just have to wait."

"I see. Where are you staying, you know yet?"

"Um, no, actually, I haven't quite gotten that far." I stopped and looked around, realizing I'd been walking aimlessly, not really knowing how the hell to get out of the hospital. "Right now, I'm just trying to remember how to get out of this place."

He laughed. "I see. Come on, I'll walk you to the main door."

We rode the elevator and worked our way around the maze of hallways and stairs and escalators until we were outside.

"Listen," he said. "Why don't you come stay at our place. We got a brand-new camper parked on the side of the house that we were planning on taking cross-country next month. That's obviously been put on hold. You can save yourself time and money staying there."

"Uh, yeah, I don't know about that. I appreciate the offer but—"

"It's got electricity and running water. I'm just saying, you should at least consider it. I'd offer you a place inside the house, but the two extra rooms are spoken for, the guest room is crammed full of God only knows what, and, well, the couch would probably only be comfortable for a day or two."

It was a generous offer, but the thought of staying that close to her parents felt weird. It was bad enough I was clear on the other side of the country with, once again, absolutely no personal belongings, but invading someone else's personal space too?

"Thank you, really. I'll consider it. I need to get to a store and pick up a few things."

"Tell you what, take my number down, and you just let me know. We'll be ready for you if you change your mind."

"Thank you again."

We exchanged numbers, shook hands, and said goodbye.

I got in my car, and as I drove around looking for someplace to buy the things I needed—clothes, toothbrush, and a laptop—I weighed heavily on Brantley's offer.

No sooner had I found a Target and parked my rental than a text came through with a picture attached.

Wes: She's here, and she's perfect.

TWENTY-FOUR
Katie

"Katie. Can you hear me? Squeeze my hand."

My head pounded as light infiltrated in, blurring my vision. I didn't know what day it was, or the time, but this was the most awake I'd felt in I didn't know how long.

"Kit-Kat, I'm here. Come on, wake up."

I rubbed my forehead and felt around my face. Tubes. Everywhere. *Damn it*. I'd lost count of how many times I'd woken up and fell back under—none of which I could hold my eyes open or form words to speak or even tell who was around me.

"Holy shit," I managed to mumble through my cotton-dry mouth.

"There you are. Come on, wake up," coaxed a familiar voice.

"Warren?" No way was that Warren. First, I wasn't entirely sure where I was, other than thinking I was in a hospital, but second, how did *he* know? I didn't remember him being here the last few times I had woken up.

"That's right, it's me. I'm here."

I shifted and turned over onto my side toward his voice. When I finally forced my eyes open to a squint, his shadowy outline came into view and then his face.

He smiled as big as ever, but that was about all that I could make out of him. "Hey, Kit-Kat," he said in a soft tone as he brushed his hand through my hair.

I closed my eyes again, smiling. "Hey."

I responded as best I could, considering. My throat was hoarse, mouth dry, and I had a feeding tube shoved up my nose. I could feel it in the back of my throat every time I swallowed, and it made me want to gag.

He grabbed my hand. "Shh. Don't try to talk, just nod."

I nodded to signal that I understood, then mouthed the words "Mom and Dad."

"They just stepped out into the hall. I'll go get them."

I nodded again as he bent down and kissed my forehead. A rogue tear slid down my cheek.

"Don't go back to sleep," he said, wiping away the tear, then left.

Not ten seconds later, the overhead lights came on, blinding me, as the room filled with people. Mom and Dad ran up to my bed and hugged me. More people whose faces I didn't recognize. Everyone talked in the background, giving orders for this and that.

A few hours went by, and after several sets of vital signs, a slew of blood work, some more diagnostic tests, and much begging and pleading with the doctor, he finally let my nurse pull my NG tube. I told him it was either that or I'd yank it out myself. Since we had worked together in the past, he didn't doubt me for a second. Apparently, I'd already extubated myself. He told me the Foley needed to wait until at least tomorrow. No worries there. That was one thing I would not be pulling out on my own.

After what felt like for-damned-ever, the chaos had finally settled. My nurse had kicked everyone out of the room except for Warren and my parents. The four of us sat around my tiny hospital room. I'd never been a patient before, but it was nice to know I was in my own hospital, where I knew people and had been well taken care of.

I sat up and sipped on a cup of tasteless, lukewarm broth they'd so graciously allowed me to have. "I feel like I've been hit by a truck."

"Close," Dad said. "Do you remember anything?"

I shrugged. "About what? I mean, I've been in and out of it for six days, apparently. Everything is still kind of a blur at this point."

"About your accident. Officer Hudson is going to come back at some point, probably tomorrow, and ask you a ton of questions. He's been waiting for you to wake up. We'd like to know everything we can before he gets back."

I closed my eyes and tried to remember. I thought back to that day. How had it only been six days, but it felt like an entire lifetime ago? Images faded in and out as I tried to recall what had happened.

"I was here at work, I know that, and then I was outside. It was already getting dark out, but not quite. I was on my way to my car." I took another sip of broth to soothe my scratchy throat. "Andy, he was there with me. Where is he now? He was there."

"He's at home today. Still a little traumatized, but he'll live."

"Oh no! Did he get hit too?"

"No," Mom said quietly. "Just you. Tell us what all you remember; did you feel anything?"

"I'm trying, and no, I don't think I felt it." Honestly, I didn't want to remember, didn't want to think about being plowed down by a moving vehicle or even want to think about what I'd been through for the past week. But I kept going anyway. "I started to walk; Andy told me to come on. So I did. I was looking down at my phone." I squeezed Warren's hand. I couldn't believe he hadn't left my side. Not since I'd woken up, and according to my dad, he'd been here almost every day, except for when Dad made him leave to go shower, since day one.

Then I remembered something. "It was you," I said to Warren.

His head shot up. "Me?"

"Yeah, you."

My mom slapped her hand over her mouth. "*You* hit her?"

"What? No! I didn't—"

I rolled my eyes. This time I didn't care if my mother saw me do it or not. "No, Mother. He didn't hit me."

I glanced at Warren beside me. Poor man— he looked like he hadn't slept the entire time he'd been in Memphis. His hair was well overdue to be cut, and I knew he hadn't shaved this entire week.

"You texted me. I was trying to read your text when I stepped out in front of the car or whatever. I was looking down at my phone, not watching where I was walking."

"Oh, thank the Lord," my mother said, sounding relieved, as if she thought Warren had seriously been the one who'd run me over.

"Where is my phone, anyway?"

"It's with the police," Warren said. "You'll eventually get it back, but right now, they are working on figuring out who did do this."

"And so far no one has a clue?"

His head hung low. "No, not yet."

"Police have the video," Dad said.

The thought of my accident being on video for people to watch over and over again made my stomach roll. I set my cup down on the bedside table in front of me.

"You might need to watch it and see if you—"

"Are you crazy? I don't want to see that video. I'm *not* going to watch it. I just want them to figure out what happened. That's all."

The last thing I wanted was the mental image of my near-death experience stuck in my head on replay. I didn't remember the impact or a whole lot thereafter, and I was perfectly okay with that.

"Police said Andy never crossed the street. He was looking at his phone too, but he actually stopped and reached out to pull you back. It was too late. You were already halfway out into the road by the time he realized the car wasn't going to stop."

"Then who did walk? Someone was in front of me. I thought it was Andy."

Dad came over and sat down on the edge of the bed near my feet. "No, it was just another employee who you probably didn't notice. They were ahead of you when the car rounded the corner and came down the hill."

"I don't get it. Why wouldn't they stop?" I ran my hands through my hair. It felt so gross. It was tangled and greasy and had something dry stuck in it. I picked a piece of whatever it was out—dried blood. I almost puked at the sight of it. I needed desperately to take a shower.

"We don't know why, Katie."

"So it was a hit-and-run? But you said you have it all on camera? Did they get a driver or license plate? Anything?"

The room fell silent. Everyone just sat there exchanging glances back and forth. Somebody—all of them—knew something, and they weren't talking. It pissed me off. I was the one who had been almost fucking killed. I deserved to know more than anyone what was going on.

I leaned forward, bracing my head in my hands.

Warren reached out to me, his hand landing on my bare back. "What's wrong? Are you okay?"

"I'm fine. My head hurts."

Dad stood up. "I'll get the nurse to bring you something. Plus, I think it's time for us to leave for the night. You need the rest."

"Rest? I've been asleep for damned near a week. What I need to know is what in the fuck is going on here." My words came out almost as a shout, making my head pound even harder. "Just tell me," I pleaded, sitting back against the bed.

Warren cleared his throat. "We're not entirely sure yet; it's still all under investigation. It appears as though the car that hit you actually sped up. They didn't—" He paused, taking a breath.

"Whoever was driving the car never slowed down. They didn't even tap the brakes."

My eyes burned with tears. "You think it was on purpose? That this wasn't an accident?"

"It seems so."

I was so confused. Nothing made sense. "Why? Who would do this to me?"

"That's what the cops are trying to find out," my dad said, reaching for my mom's hand to pull her up. "I told them to come back tomorrow. You should be up for questioning then. But the longer this takes, the more likely whoever did this is gonna get away with it."

"I—I don't know." Tears that I felt forming finally fell…hard. "I really don't know who would do this to me."

Warren came up and wrapped his arms around me. Dad was right; I needed to be left the hell alone for a while. All the questions—mine included—would just have to wait.

♡♡♡

I woke up, and it was daylight out. I didn't know what time of day it was, but that didn't matter—it felt like morning, and I was finally fully awake and felt well rested for once. That was all that mattered at the moment.

I rolled over to my side so I could see *him*. He'd stayed with me all night as promised. Once my mom and dad had left, Warren made his makeshift bed in the recliner beside me.

"Good morning," I said quietly.

Warren stretched as he faced me. "Good morning. How are you feeling?"

"Much better, I think. I hope they let me get up and walk today."

"Easy, killer. One thing at a time. How's your head?"

"Still a little achy but manageable. Hopefully I'm awake now for good and can get back on some kind of schedule."

"Take all the time you need, Kit-Kat. The only thing you need to worry about is healing. I told you, I'm not going anywhere."

"Good to know. How's that chair sleep?"

"It's all right. I've slept in more uncomfortable places." He gave me a sideways glance.

"Referring to a too-small couch?"

"Hmm."

"Hey, don't blame me. I offered to share the bed. Have you been sleeping there this whole time? I know people have done it for longer, but wow."

"No. Not the whole week. I've been switching off and on with your dad."

That made me wonder where they were. It surprised me that they weren't already here.

"That's good. Y'all need the break. Are you staying at a hotel or someplace close by, then?"

"Not exactly. I've been camped out in your backyard."

I held in a laugh since my throat still burned when I talked. "You what? Are you serious? Like in a tent?"

"Yes, I'm serious, and no, not in a tent. I've been staying in your parents' camper. I wasn't going to do it at first when your dad offered it up, but the more I thought about it, the better it sounded."

I couldn't believe it. Warren had been sleeping in my mom and dad's camper, and in my backyard. Never thought I'd see the day.

"How is it?"

"It's not terrible, actually. I've started to consider getting one for myself, eventually. We lost power to it the other night, though. Not sure what happened there. Your dad's going to have it fixed at some point. So I've actually been sleeping on the couch, except for last night since I was here."

He put the recliner into a sitting position, stood up, then leaned over and kissed the top of my head before sitting back down.

I closed my eyes for a brief moment, appreciating and soaking in his gesture. I didn't know how much longer I had with him now that I was awake. I figured he'd be gone again soon, since there was no need for him to stay and hang out.

"Thank you."

"For what?"

I shrugged. "Everything, I suppose. Being here. Keeping my parents company. Whatever else you've been doing that I'm sure I don't know about yet."

I yawned, stretching my own arms up over my head. Amazing how a person could sleep off and on for almost an entire week and still wake up feeling tired. I was just grateful to still have full movement of all of my extremities and not have any major physical or long-lasting injuries, that I knew of, anyway.

"It's nothing, really. I'd do it all again if I had to. I just hope I never do."

"Me either, but I appreciate it. I wonder where my parents are. I figured they'd already be here. What time is it, anyway?"

"It's just after eight, so my guess is they're still home. They usually get here pretty early, though. So I'd expect them soon. I'll text your dad. He's going to be thrilled that you're finally returning to normal and feeling better. Hopefully for good this time."

"Wait. You're going to *text* my dad? When did you start texting my dad?" Not that I should be surprised, given the circumstances. It was just a weird concept to grasp—Warren text messaging my dad.

He stared down at this phone, typing out a text. "I started texting your dad when some jackass thought it was a good idea to run you over with a car."

My body shuddered at his words. I already knew I'd been hit by a car, but to hear it said out loud gave me the creeps.

I found my remote and turned on the TV.

"So what else did I miss?" I asked, changing the subject.

"Well, let's see." He rubbed the scruff of his new beard. "Your beloved Tigers Football team beat Tulane."

"They're a crap team anyway."

"From the looks of it, the Tigers aren't much better."

"Whatever. Anything else?"

"I learned your dad makes amazing chocolate chip cookies."

"Indeed he does, and I can't wait to eat another one. Maybe you can text him to bring me some."

"I'll relay the message."

"Thank you. Now, tell me something I don't know, something good."

"Hmm, let's see. Oh! I know. Rowan had her baby last—"

"She *what*? You're joking! When?"

"Last week. The day after your accident. Here, actually. They just got discharged from here two days ago. So they're back home and adjusting to their new life."

"Here? Where here? Like here-here?" What the hell? Rowan had her baby in Memphis?"

"The women's center. Warren hopped the next flight after mine and came down to check on you and me. No sooner had he got here than she was texting him that she was here in the lobby and on her way up. Apparently she snuck out on that same flight, and as soon as he reached her downstairs, she went into labor."

"I can't believe it. Wait, yes I can. So what'd she have?" I sat up and crossed my legs. "And she's okay? Her and the baby?"

"Oh yeah. They're both doing great. Baby's healthy as can be expected, even considering Rowan delivered two weeks early."

"Okay, so come on, spill it already. What'd she have?"

He smiled so big. I missed seeing that— seeing him—so much. Even before all of this. Not that I wanted anything else bad to happen to me, but I really could get used to having him around. Seeing him just confirmed that the feelings I thought I'd had weren't all in my head; they were real, and so was he.

"You really want to know?"

"Yes!" I tossed a pillow at him. He caught it and laid it across his lap.

"She had a beautiful baby girl." He handed me his phone. A picture of a tiny baby in a pink-and-blue cap, swaddled up tight in a pink blanket, lying in a hospital bassinet, filled the screen.

"Ohmigod!" I squealed, my voice cracking. "Shit." I reached for a cup on my bedside table and took a sip of room-temperature water. "Wow, that's gross. What did they name her? Rowan never would tell me the names they had picked out."

I handed him back his phone.

"Avery Claire."

"Avery Claire. That's perfect." I smiled to myself at the thought of my best friend and her new baby girl.

"Anything else you'd like to know?"

I shrugged at the only question that came to mind first. Even though, the more time that had passed, I had a sinking suspicion I already knew.

"Who did this to me?"

TWENTY-FIVE
Katie

Somehow, I'd allowed my entire life to be consumed by nothing but work. Work and unnecessary strict routine, which in turn had done nothing but suck the life out of me the entire time.

I wanted more. I wanted more than just working nonstop and paying bills. Not because I thought what I had wasn't good enough or that I didn't appreciate what I had, but I knew there was so much more out there…I just had to take a risk if I wanted more.

At one point, it seemed like everyone around me had jumped carelessly off the deep end, when in reality all they'd done was come to their own realization that there was more to life than monotony.

All it took was a near death experience for me to figure this out.

"Is there anything I can do for you? Get you?"

I giggled at Warren, who had been waiting on me hand and foot since I walked through the front door.

"No, I'm fine. Promise." There was no better feeling than finally being back home. Except this time I had Warren with me.

Once the doctors were convinced I'd completely woken up for good and was well on my way to a full recovery, I spent the next four days in the hospital participating in aggressive physical therapy. My last scan had come back almost completely clear. So between that and my renewed ability to walk and use the bathroom entirely on my own, I'd finally convinced the doctors and everyone else that I'd be fine if they'd just let me go home. In return, I agreed to more physical therapy at home, and at least for another month…and I couldn't return to work for at least another six weeks. That last one pained me just a little, but I conceded because the doc was right. Then again, there wasn't much I wasn't willing to agree to do to get the hell out of there and back to using my own shampoo and bodywash or wearing my own clothes.

Twelve days without a real shower had me feeling like absolute trash. I'd only been able to wash up here and there a few days before getting discharged as part of my therapy, but it just wasn't the same. All I wanted to do was take a scalding hot shower, brush my teeth with real toothpaste, and sleep in my own bed.

"Okay," Warren said. "You know where to find me if you need me."

I walked forward into his embrace. My parents were outside in the yard, and I wanted to take full advantage of what few minutes of alone time we had. His arms wrapped around my waist without hesitation. It was the first time I'd been in his arms since we were last together in St. Lucia. Being wrapped up in him was a feeling I did not want to let go of anytime soon.

"Thank you, again, for everything."

He stared down at me, his hazel-green eyes locking on mine. "I've told you, Kit-Kat, it's nothing. I'm not missing out on anything by being here with you. And I'll be there until you don't need me anymore."

Funny thing was, I felt like I would always need him, want him. The thought of him not being here pained me.

"What if that day never comes?"

"We'll figure it out." He bent down and softly pressed his lips to mine. My body went limp from head to toe as I practically melted in his arms. *Thank the Lord I brushed my teeth before I got discharged this morning.*

He let out a low moan the second our tongues touched, and I almost lost it. I felt his dick jump between us as he lowered his hands to my ass, giving it a squeeze, pulling me tighter against the front of him.

Reluctantly, I broke our kiss out of fear that one of my parents would walk in and catch us together, or we'd go so far we wouldn't be able to stop.

He rested his forehead against mine, almost out of breath just from that one kiss. We were both fighting off a strong, overwhelming, hormone-driven urge. "How much activity did the doctor clear you to do?"

"Not enough for that; not yet. And it's PT that has to clear me. She'll be here tomorrow. I'll ask her then."

"Please do."

I raised up on my tiptoes and gave him a kiss on the cheek. As much as I wanted to climb him like a tree, have him press me up against the wall, and take me right then and there, it was too risky. I didn't want to take any chances while still recovering from a head injury.

I slid down his front, grazing along his steely erection that I missed so much, and backed out of his hold.

"You're killing me," he whispered gruffly.

"Only in the best way possible," I replied, then turned and headed to the bathroom, closing the door, locking him and the rest of the world out for a while.

Almost an hour later, I had scrubbed everything from head to toe, shaven for the first time in almost two weeks. By the time I'd gotten out of the bathroom and dressed in my pajamas—

leggings and an oversized Memphis Tigers sweatshirt—I felt like a whole new person.

I made my way out to the main part of the house; Warren had fallen asleep on the couch, and Mom was standing at the stove cooking dinner. I walked up behind her, stuck my finger in the spaghetti sauce, and sucked it off. I couldn't wait to eat a real, home-cooked meal.

"Delicious, as always. You need any help?"

She stirred a wooden spoon around the pot. "No. You need to be sitting down." She gave me a pointed look.

I walked over to one of the barstools at the island and did as I was told. "You know, I spent twelve days in a bed. I think I'm okay to walk around for a little while."

"Katie. You almost died. At least give me this much, okay?" She turned around, spoon in hand, sauce dripping down the handle as she pointed it at me. "You've barely been home a few hours." She went back to stirring. "You want garlic bread?"

"Of course. Where's Dad?"

"He's still outside fussing with that camper. We can't for the life of us figure out what is wrong with it. He refuses to take it somewhere just yet. He's been waiting for you to get home and make sure you're safe."

I glanced over at the back of the couch, knowing Warren was sound asleep on the other side of it. "I think I'll be fine for a little while if y'all want to go drop it off and have it looked at. Maybe tomorrow? I won't be alone. I've got someone coming over for physical therapy in the morning, and Warren will be here."

She shuffled around the kitchen, pulling plates, glasses, and silverware out of the cabinets and drawers. I'm sure at one point she eyed the cabinet above the stove. Hell, even I'd looked at it myself a few times already.

"I'll mention it to him."

As she said the words, he walked in. He came over and kissed me on the top of my head. "Hey, princess."

"Hey, Dad."

"How you feelin'?"

"Much better now that I've scrubbed the last of the remnants of the hospital off of my skin and hopefully out of my hair." I used my fingers to comb through my damp hair, examining the split ends. I had been long overdue for a trim before I ever went into the hospital. Parts of my head were still tender from the laceration I had on my scalp, which, thankfully, hadn't needed any stitches, just some Dermabond.

"Brantley," Mom ordered. "Go wash up and help me set up this table. I'll fill up everyone's drinking glasses if you take these plates."

"Yes, dear."

Dad did as he was told. He always did and almost always without hesitation or complaint. My mom, on the other hand, drove me fucking nuts with her demands and overbearing tendencies. I always wondered if she did the same to him. If so, he'd never admitted to it.

While the two of them finished getting dinner ready and setting the table, I snuck into the living room to check on Warren. I peeked over the back of the couch. He was still sound asleep. As much as I wanted to curl up next to him, I resisted the urge. Instead, I leaned down, reaching out, and brushed my hand across his warm bearded cheek.

He woke with a slight startle, then nuzzled his face into my hand and smiled up at me. "Hey, Kit-Kat. It smells amazing in here."

I smiled back. "Hey, babe. Sorry to wake you up. Dinner's ready."

"Okay. Damn, I slept hard."

He hopped up off the couch and stretched, and his hands practically reached the ceiling. My mouth watered at the sight of him, the way the front of his shirt rode slightly up, exposing a sliver of skin across his abdomen.

He was the only man I'd ever seen who could take a thrown-together, disheveled look of a wrinkled T-shirt, faded jeans, and what looked like a ten-day-old beard and make it look delicious.

He rounded the couch and wrapped his arm around me, pulling me into his side for a friendly hug. He leaned down to my ear. "Did you just call me babe?"

My face flushed with heat. It was the first time I think I'd ever referred to him as babe or anything other than his actual name. "Probably. That okay?"

"Anytime." He quickly kissed my temple before letting me go and moving into the kitchen. "Mrs. McDonald, it smells delicious. Do you need help with anything?"

I propped against the back of the couch and watched him move around the kitchen, attempting to help my mom and dad finish setting things up. She had her own way of doing things and very rarely asked for help, unless it was from either me or my dad. But she handed him the huge pot of spaghetti off the stove, telling him not to drop it or she'd tan his hide. I held in a giggle on that one.

Everything about him and the way he interacted with my parents seemed comfortable, like that's what he was meant to do all along. The thought that he would need to eventually go home gave me an empty feeling.

"Katie," my mom called out. "Come in here and eat."

"Coming." *Not soon enough*.

♡♡♡

"I think I'm going to take the camper to Dave in the morning, have him take a look at it," Dad said as he loaded up his plate with a second helping of spaghetti.

"I was just telling mom earlier that you should. Now that I'm home and things seem to have settled down a little bit."

"This isn't over, yet Katie," Mom reminded me.

"No, it's not, but I think I'll be okay alone for a few hours if you just want to drop the camper off with Dave."

Dad looked at Mom. "Well, I don't see why not? She has Warren here, and it won't take long. I'd like to get it fixed sooner than later."

"What's the rush?" Mom asked him.

"There's no rush, Marcella. That thing's just been sitting there for a week now, useless. Warren can't sleep on our couch forever. I'm sure he'd like his own space back. Won't you?"

Warren took a drink of his water and cleared his throat. "Um. Yes, sir. That would be fine, or I can get a hotel. It's not a bother either way. I appreciate your hospitality."

I nudged him under the table, and he gave me a look like *what*? I didn't want him out in the camper, much less in a hotel across town.

"So, what are your plans for your trip now?" I asked. They were supposed to be leaving soon, possibly in the next couple of weeks. That was their original plan, anyway.

"It's on hold for now, obviously. Don't you think that's a good idea?"

I shrugged. "I mean, that's up to y'all." I didn't exactly feel safe and secure, knowing whoever did hit me was still out there driving around, but I also didn't want my parents to put their life on hold for me any longer than they already had.

"We're going to stay around until whoever did this is caught."

I set my fork down. "And what if he or she isn't? Then what? Y'all change your entire life around for me? We all just go around living in fear?"

"Don't be silly," Mom said. "They'll catch whoever did this, and things will get back to normal."

She had a lot of faith in an already overwhelmed police department in a city that dealt with at least two murders per day. I couldn't imagine my case was high on their priority list.

"Have y'all heard anything else about the investigation?" I'd already talked to the police several times—twice in person at the hospital and once on the phone. My story never changed. They asked me for details about my relationship with Justin and anyone else before him. That list was short. Then they asked about what had happened at the BBQ restaurant. I gave police every detail I could about us and about him—where he liked to go, where he worked, lived, played, who his friends were—the few that I'd known.

"Well, they still have only one person of interest, and they haven't been able to find him yet," Dad said, never making eye contact with any of us as he spoke.

"Figures."

Justin's name had been mentioned more than once throughout my case. At one point, I'd learned that Dad had even pulled one of the officers to the side and told him they'd needed to look at him. That surprised me. Up until recently, he'd always just quietly sat back, watching, letting me do my own thing. I wondered why he never said anything to me about him before.

My mom, on the other hand? She was in complete denial about Justin. Even still, she "just couldn't believe it." This after learning that he was the one who'd attacked me not long ago. If I heard her say it one more time, I was going to lose my shit.

I picked up my fork pushed the food around my plate, willing my appetite to come back. My stomach dropped as I tried eating my favorite homemade meal but couldn't.

Warren reached over, grabbing my free hand, giving it a reassuring squeeze. "Come hell or high water, they'll catch him, and he will pay. One way or the other."

"Well," my mom chimed in after taking a sip of her tea, which I was fully convinced she'd spiked, "Warren is right. They'll find the right person who did this, and they'll pay. Then we can all go on with our lives not living in fear."

"Not soon enough," I mumbled.

"I just can't believe the police are looking for that ex-boyfriend of yours. I always thought he was—"

"He was a piece of shit, Mom. Stop trying to gloss over it, okay? He was an abusive piece of shit, whether you want to believe it or not. Period."

She threw her hand over her mouth. "Katie! You'd better watch the way you talk to me!"

She leaned over and mumbled something to my dad, who came to my defense and told her to give it a rest.

Poor Warren sat in silence across from them, stunned.

"I'm done here," I said as I grabbed my plate and glass and carried them to the sink.

I already felt ashamed for the things I'd confessed to police, things I'd been in denial about for the duration of almost our entire relationship, even though I knew better. I should have said or done something about it then. Instead, I stayed quiet, keeping all the bad shit to myself, covering things up, sweeping them under the rug. The last thing needed was my own mother actively voicing her denial about everything. All I wanted was to forget everything about our time together, pretend like none of it had ever happened, just like before, except this time with zero chance of reconciliation. I wanted to forget him and everything about him.

Except now here he was at the forefront of an active investigation. All eyes were on him, and investigators didn't have a clue where the hell he'd gone.

Justin had basically ghosted the city of Memphis.

TWENTY-SIX

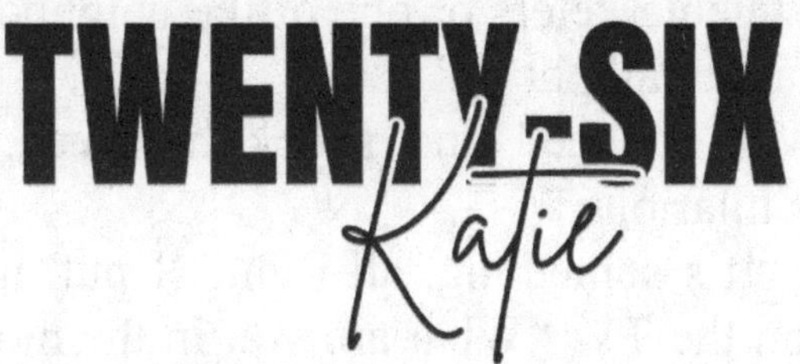

Things had finally calmed down after I'd gotten snippy with my mom—her words, not mine—at dinner. What she didn't seem to want to understand was how sick and tired I'd grown of not taking up for myself or having to listen to other people taking up for the bad guy. Specifically her.

Warren and I had settled on the couch to watch TV—anything to get my mind off everything. Mom busied herself in the kitchen, and Dad disappeared into his makeshift office/storage room.

The house phone rang.

"You guys have a house phone?" Warren asked with amusement in his voice.

"Yup. They sure do."

"Like, an actual phone that plugs into the wall?"

I clicked through the TV guide, trying to find a movie. "It even has a cord. I tried for years to get them to get rid of it. We all have cell phones. Hardly anyone calls on that thing anymore. It's either telemarketers or one of the neighbors, who also has a wall phone."

He laughed and shook his head. "Man. That's hilarious."

"It's something, all right." I put my focus back on the TV. "What are you in the mood for? Scary? Rom-com? Shoot-'em-up?"

I could feel his stare burning a hole in the side of my head. I cut my eyes to him and caught him licking his lips, looking at me like he was about to pounce. We both knew he wasn't going to, but he sure was ready.

He leaned over closer to me, the warmth of his body radiating against mine. "You already *know* what I'm in the mood for. Something I can't have."

His low, husky voice sent chills down my spine, straight between my legs. I closed my eyes for a split second and held my breath, imagining him there.

"Fuck. You can't say something like that to me or look at me like I'm dessert, knowing damn well you and I both know we aren't going to do *anything* until PT clears me."

I turned to face him. He sat up straight, adjusting himself through the front of his jeans. "You are absolutely right. I need to behave. What time's PT coming tomorrow?"

I rolled my eyes and went back to looking for a movie to watch. Anything to get the dirty thoughts of us together off my mind. "Not soon enough. Someone is supposed to be here around nine."

"I can wait."

Good for you. I didn't want to. "Makes one of us, you tease."

No sooner had we distanced ourselves than my mom walked in. "That was Shirley across the street. She wants me and your father to come over and play cards. Will y'all be okay if we head over for about an hour?"

I perked up at the thought of some true alone time with Warren, even if we'd just agreed to no touching. With them gone, I might be able to convince him otherwise, even just a little bit.

"Of course we'll be fine. We were just about to watch a movie, weren't we?"

"Yes, ma'am, we were."

She smiled at him like he'd hung the moon. Lord have mercy. If he kept that shit up, I might end up having to fight her for him. As much as she voiced her adoration for Justin, I think Warren was wearing her down. Then again, maybe he was just what she needed to stop bringing up my ex.

"Okay then. I'll go check with Brantley. See if he wants to go." She walked off.

I smacked Warren on the shoulder. "See. Now's our chance. They'll be gone, and we can—"

"Behave ourselves." He reached out and grabbed my hand, pulling it to his mouth, and kissed the back. "I just can't, not yet. As much as I desperately need to get you naked, the last thing I want is for you to have any setbacks and it fall on me. I already feel bad enough for all that's going on. Please."

"Okay, fine," I huffed. "We'll behave."

Warren got up, abandoning me on the couch, and went straight to the kitchen. My parents came down the hall and joined him.

"Warren, oh honey, you don't have to do any of that," I heard my mom tell him. And *honey*? Did she just call him honey? What the hell had gotten into her? My mom never used pet names. Ever.

"I'll finish with that when we get back," she said as he stood at the sink scrubbing the spaghetti pot.

I was in no kind of hurry to clean up, especially to my mother's standards, so I went and sat down at my seat at the bar.

"It's the least I can do for all of your generous hospitality," he told her with a blazing smile, the kind that if he'd shot my way would have had me dropping to my knees in front of him.

I swear her face turned red. "That—that's very kind of you. Thank you."

"Come on, Marcella. We haven't got all night." My dad grabbed Mom by the shoulders and pointed her toward the kitchen door. "We're just going to play a few hands of Rummy, and we'll be back. If y'all need anything, we'll be right across the street."

"Okay. Love y'all."

"We love you too, princess."

They finally left, my dad locking the door behind them.

"I love my parents, but holy shit, I need a break."

Warren rinsed off a few more dishes, then dried his hands on a towel. "And I'm fairly certain they do too."

"Right, but you just don't know my mother. All of this," I said with a wave of my hand, "is her putting on a show. It only gets more theatrical the more she drinks."

He flung the towel over his shoulder and walked over to me. He spun my chair around to face him. He leaned down, placing his hands on either side of me on the counter behind me, caging me in while wedged between my legs.

"They love you. Even I can see that."

"I know they do. But you're not the one who's spent most of your life dealing with my mother's overbearing need to control me and every aspect of my life as much as possible, just so she can live vicariously through you."

He kissed my forehead. "You're right, and I'm sorry, Kit-Kat. Let's reserve this conversation for another time."

I smiled up at him, his hazel-green eyes seemingly darker tonight, almost a light shade of brown. There was no doubt in my mind what he wanted, but he'd made it very clear that neither of us was going to get it tonight.

We held each other's gaze, just taking each other in. I wanted to memorize, to burn, every little feature about him into memory.

My heart suddenly felt heavy as my thoughts had shifted from one of desire to almost dread.

"What's on your mind?"

I wanted him here, wanted him to stay—and not just tonight or tomorrow night. I didn't want him to go home at all. I knew he had a life of his own that he had just up and abandoned at the drop of a pin, and for me, of all people. Everything about that felt wrong. The guilt ate at me every day extra that he stayed and didn't need to.

"How long do you think you're going to stay here?" I asked, not sure I wanted to know the real answer because I knew he'd be gone too soon.

Just then, we heard keys at the door.

"Fuck," he mumbled under his breath. It took him all of two seconds to put as much distance as he could between us before the door flung open.

"Sorry, y'all," my mom said, half stumbling into the kitchen. "I forgot my…something." She giggled, then sashayed down the hallway to her bedroom. A minute later, she was back and out the door.

"What the hell was that about?" Warren asked, looking almost pale.

I laughed. "That's my mother in true fashion. Probably checking to make sure you didn't have me bent over her designer couch."

He raised an eyebrow as he walked back over to me. He placed his finger under my chin, tilting my head to look up at him. "You'd like that, wouldn't you?"

I bit into my bottom lip. "More than you know." The thought alone sent a chill down my spine.

He worked his way back to his original position, standing between my legs. "Now, where were we?"

"Something about you bending me over the couch."

He grinned. "No, before that. You asked me how long I'd be here?"

"Oh, yeah, that."

He took in a deep breath and blew it out. "Honestly, I don't know. I'd really like to stay until the police figure out who did this, but who knows how long that'll take, considering the crime and murder rate in this city. I'd imagine it won't be solved before I do eventually have to leave out of sheer obligation." He brushed my hair back from my face. "Why? Are you trying to get rid of me?"

I leaned back and looked at him. "No, not at all. I just know you've been gone from home for almost a month, and you have a life that isn't, well, here. I'm sure you're ready to get back home." Not to mention, Lord only knew how many work deadlines he had looming over him and a very sick father who was nearing the end of his own life.

"Kit-Kat, I assure you, there is nothing more important back home than what I have sitting right here in front of me. I'll go back when I need to. Right now, I need something else."

"What's that—"

He cut me off when he pressed his soft, full lips to mine. *That's one way to get me to stop talking.* I was hesitant at first. Not because I didn't want to kiss him but because I didn't know if I had the self-control to stop before trying to go too far.

I reached up and cradled each side of his neck in my hands, making sure that he couldn't easily back away. Damn it, I wanted him. I wanted more. It had been way too long since I'd had him or felt him like this.

I parted my lips, inviting him inside. He let out a low growl as his tongue swept through my mouth. His hands caressed up my thighs, creeping higher and higher until he slid one hand gently between my legs. His thumb grazed up and down over the fabric on my legs. At one point, he grazed over my clit. My heart raced so fast it made my head spin. I wrapped my legs around his waist and tried to pull him closer into me.

He broke our kiss. "Fuck, Kit-Kat," he said out of breath. "We can't. Not yet, and most definitely not here."

I kissed up the side of his neck to his ear, tugging his earlobe between my teeth. "Sure we can. My parents are going to be gone for at least an hour. I don't need even half that time for what I want to do."

This was the first time Warren and I had been left completely alone, despite my mother's recent intrusion. I didn't give two shits anymore about being cleared at this point.

He laughed, grabbing my ankles, essentially unknotting me from him, and backed away. "First of all, you don't know when they'll come home. Your mom has already been by once because she *forgot* something. Second, you haven't been medically cleared. Third…I don't have a third."

I slumped back into the bar chair with a huff. "Fine. Whatever you want." I know I sounded like a brat, but damn it, I wanted him, bad.

"Trust me, it's not for lack of wanting to, clearly." He glanced down between his legs.

Damn. That thing was impressive, even against his jeans. My mouth watered at the sight of him.

"Then what is it?"

"It's here. Regardless of what my mind and, apparently, my dick wants, I can't bring myself to defile you in your mom and dad's home. Especially at the risk of them walking through the door again any minute. They've been really good to me and more than generous in letting me stay here. I can't risk that."

"Fair enough." I had to respect his decision, regardless of what my vagina or I wanted. He wasn't going to cave.

Something crashed outside. Both of our heads shot up toward the side door.

"What was that?" Warren jumped back, distancing himself from me again.

I spun in the chair to face forward, my back to the door, and picked at my fingernail just in case. "I don't know. Probably my drunk-ass mother. I swear. If I'd known she was going to be this annoying, I would've just told them to stay home."

When the door to the kitchen didn't immediately open, an irrational feeling of dread settled in the pit of my stomach. *Stop it*, I told myself. *This is all in your head*.

Warren's body stilled from head to toe as he listened intently, waiting.

Nothing happened.

"It's probably one of the neighbors' cats," I finally spoke up. "Or a raccoon."

He didn't look like he believed me, and I wasn't confident of those options myself. "I'll go check," he said. "Just in case. Stay here."

Surely it had been nothing. All the lights were on outside. Someone would have to have been really fucking stupid to try to sneak around our house at this time of night.

He opened the door. A few moments passed before it closed, and the lock clicked in place.

Warren hadn't said a word, but his warm hand splayed across my back. Relief washed over me, and then a long-stemmed white rose appeared in front of me as he dropped it on the counter.

"This mean anything to you?"

My breath caught in my chest. "Wh— where did that come from?"

"It was lying on the top step. Whoever left it also knocked over one of your mom's flowerpots."

"He's coming after me, isn't he?"

He wrapped his arms around me and pulled me into his chest. "It's okay, Kit-Kat. I'm here, it's me. He's not going to get to you. I promise you that."

No fucking way Justin had been here. He was not that stupid, was he? Surely not.

I wiped my face of the rebellious tears that fell. "It's him. He was here."

Warren reached up and wiped away more tears with his thumbs. "Who, Katie? Your ex? If you know for a fact and can prove it was him, you need to tell me so I can relay it to the police. Please."

There was only one person who had ever given me white roses. One person who once thought they were my favorite but had no idea at the time that when he'd asked what kind of flower I liked when we first started dating, Chloe had jokingly told him white long-stemmed roses. She knew my favorite was pink, and I thought white roses were the ugliest of them all because of the way they easily turned brown. We never corrected him because he'd been so happy to shower me with them. I didn't want to be the bad guy and tell him I thought they were ugly, so I let him continue to give them to me.

Knowing he'd been here meant that he'd never left town and was even more of a threat now. Because police had been looking for him, but he was nowhere to be found, which meant he was hiding. He was still close and wanted me to know.

"Kit-Kat. Talk to me."

I nodded. "I'm sure. It's him."

TWENTY-SEVEN

"Good morning, y'all," I called out as I walked into the kitchen. My mom was at the stove, and Warren was already at the dining table. I missed the smell of my mother's breakfast waking me up in the morning. Sure she was a pain in the ass, and we argued like cats and dogs, but one thing was for sure, the woman could cook. She'd never let anyone in her house go hungry, and that was one thing I'd always tried not to take for granted.

"Good morning, Katie. Have a seat. Breakfast will be ready in just a few minutes."

Mom had her back to us, so I quickly bent down and gave Warren a kiss on the cheek before she caught me. "Good morning," I whispered, then nipped at his earlobe.

He cleared his throat, giving me a *what the hell* look with a grin. "Morning, Kit-Kat. How'd you sleep?"

He pulled out the chair beside him, and I sat down, curling my legs and feet underneath me. "Not terrible, considering."

Lyndsay Marie

I'd gone to bed nervous as hell. The only thing that had given me any comfort was knowing Warren had been asleep on the couch in the next room over. He was just a yell away.

"Good morning, princess," Dad said, joining us at the table.

The table had already been set in perfect order—plates, silverware, napkins, drinks, condiments—everything except for food.

He took a sip of his orange juice. "You two have a good night?"

"Um, yeah, sure. Uneventful," I lied. "How was the card game?"

Mom set down a plate of pancakes and a bowl of scrambled eggs. "It was just lovely. Your father and I really needed that, you know, since your…since everything that has been going on. You know?"

She couldn't even say out loud the words to describe what had happened to me. She kept wanting to refer to it as an *accident*. I stabbed two pancakes with my fork and slapped them on my plate before smothering them in butter and maple syrup.

"Believe me, I do know. We all could use a break from this. What time did y'all end up getting home?" After the flower incident, Warren and I decided to call it a night. He sat on the floor beside my bed until I'd fallen asleep, then took himself to the couch for the rest of the night.

"Sometime around midnight. A little later than expected, but we figured things were okay here, or y'all would have told us."

Warren and I had decided that the flowerpot incident would remain between us. It wouldn't do either of my parents any good to know, and we'd just let the police handle things their way.

"Of course," Warren chimed in before I could. "Everything here was just fine."

I gave him a soft smile and mouthed *thank you*.

"Do either of you know what happened to one of my flowerpots out front?" Mom asked.

I almost choked on my bacon.

"There was dirt all over the driveway. I was out there in the middle of the night sweeping dirt."

I spoke up first. "Nope."

"Not a clue," Warren said.

I shrugged. "Must have been a stray."

"Raccoon?" Warren chimed in.

"Or that. We get those too."

Dad eyed us with suspicion as we fired off answers back and forth.

"Well, whatever it was," my mother said, oblivious to our fumbling, "it destroyed my mums."

Dad patted her on the hand. "We'll get you some more, dear. In the meantime, we need to wrap up here. I've gotta have the camper over to Dave by ten. He's supposed to take a look at it this morning. He's really doing us a favor squeezing me in last-minute."

"Right. And what about you two?" Mom asked. "What are your plans for the day?"

I leaned back in my chair, stuffed as a pig. "I have physical therapy today. Someone's supposed to be here within the hour."

"We shouldn't be too long. I'm going to let Dave take a look at it, and if he thinks he'll need to keep it overnight, I might need you to come pick us up."

"Of course. Just let me know." Then I realized I still didn't have a phone. "Well, let Warren know. I still don't have my phone back yet."

It was still weird to think that Warren and my dad had exchanged phone numbers and text messages.

We wrapped up with breakfast and helped clean up. I walked my parents to the door and watched them out the window as they eventually pulled away with the camper in tow.

No sooner had they'd disappeared down the street than another car pulled up to the curb out front.

"What did you do with the flower?" I asked Warren, who stood behind me with his arms wrapped around my chest, his chin resting on the top of my head.

"Shoved it down the disposal after you went to sleep."

"Good. Did you report it yet?"

"I did. I sent Officer Parker a text last night, then called him this morning before everyone woke up and left him a message. He's already texted me back that they're going to look into it."

I turned in his arms and kissed him without warning. Our kiss quickly fell into a steady rhythm. One that had me wet on the spot. He rocked his hips, pressing his steely erection into me, confirming that our kiss gave him the same thoughts I'd had about him.

There was a knock at the door behind us. We both jumped.

"Shit. I'm not ready," I told Warren, pressing my forehead to his.

"I am. Let her in; I'll go sit out on the back porch and wait."

He smacked me on the ass and disappeared out the back door. I turned to let in my physical therapist. When I opened the door, a familiar face came into view.

"Shayla?" I reached out, grabbed her arm, and yanked her into the house, pulling her in for a tight hug. "This is such a surprise. I haven't seen you in forever."

"I know," she said, returning my embrace. "It's been a while. I saw your name on our list and snatched it up."

"Good. I'm so glad they let you come."

"Me too. I read over your notes." She scanned me up and down. "They better find that motherfucker who hit you."

"Yeah, I know. They're working on it." Little did she know, we were already almost positive we knew who we were looking for, just not where to find him.

"Ooh, shit, sorry, is Mrs. McDonald here?" She glanced over my shoulder, looking for my mother.

"Nope. It's just me and Warren. He's out back."

"Shoo. That's good. Last time I was around her, I dropped the f-bomb and thought she was gonna slap me upside my head."

"Trust me, she was probably thinking about it. Come on, let's go to the living room. There's more room to work in there."

I led her into the house, though she knew where we were going; she'd been here before.

"I thought you transferred to a different department. What are you doing out here making house calls? I didn't know you left the hospital altogether?"

"I did transfer once, and I hated it there too. Then this gig came open, and I jumped on it." She set her duffle bag down and pulled out various items—some weights, a band, a few weighted balls, and a roller.

"Good for you. How's this job going so far? You like it?"

"I love it. It's great. Just regular business hours, no weekends, no holidays. I'm home for dinner every night." She spread some sheets out on the coffee table and picked one up. "Let's do this one first. You don't look like you need a whole lot of therapy to me."

"Other than spending almost two weeks in a bed, I think I'm doing okay so far. And that's incredible about work. I hope this works out for you."

"Thanks, me too. What about you? You going back to the ER once you're cleared?"

"I don't know yet. I haven't thought about not going back. It's all I've known for my entire career." Weird thing was, the longer I'd spent off work and away from the hospital, the more comfortable I'd become not being there and working myself to the bone. The problem was I had zero clue what else I'd do and even fewer skills to do it.

I picked up one of the bands and followed the directions on the sheet.

"I hear you there. I never thought I'd leave the hospital, but here I am."

"I hear ya there. Speaking of being cleared for work, how's about putting in your notes somewhere that I'm okay for more *physical activity*." I nudged her in the side.

She looked at me, then around the room.

"Don't worry, we're alone."

"You talkin' about hottie with a body? 'Cause child, that man is fine. I caught a glimpse of him before you let me in, and word on the street at Regional is he is *fine*."

I laughed. "Yeah, I am talking about him, and I am *sooo* ready to rip his clothes off."

"Oh, I know. I wouldn't wait for clearance for that. I don't know why Doc even has me out here doing this. You were doing fine when you got discharged."

"Tell me about it."

She looked toward the back door. "He got a brother?"

I laughed again, this time louder. "Actually, he does, but he's married to Rowan."

"Oh, that's him?" She rolled her eyes. "Figures. Well, if she or you ever wanna give one of them up or a free pass, you know where to find me. I'll clear you for light duty. That should cover you. Just tell him to go easy. Deal?"

"Good enough. He'll be happy to know this."

Damned near two hours later and performing moves my body hadn't done since I was a cheerleader in high school, we wrapped up our session, and I walked Shayla out. I'd been officially cleared for action, and not just the okay to help out around the house either.

Just as I turned to walk back inside, lo and behold, my parents pulled up with the camper.

"Son of a bitch," I mumbled under my breath. They didn't even give me a chance to sneak in a quickie. Nothing.

"Hey, Dad," I called out as he climbed out of his truck. "How'd it go?"

"It was a quick fix, apparently. Some wires had been cut way up underneath that I couldn't see, but thankfully, Dave got us in and out of there in less than an hour."

"That's good, but—" I swallowed hard. "—someone cut wires?"

My dad kept his head held high, like it was no big deal. However, I knew better. I could see the concern written all over his face.

"It's fine. He said it was a clean cut. Everything's back in working order."

"Mr. McDonald," Warren cut in as he walked up beside me, "have you guys thought about getting some kind of security system installed?"

Dad rubbed the back of his neck. "Well, not really. We haven't had the need for one until recently."

"It might be worth looking into. I'm willing to help if you'd like."

"I appreciate it. I know a few people. We can try to get something installed this week. I know it would make me feel better too."

"So," I said, changing the subject, "I can't believe y'all didn't stay a little longer and shoot the breeze."

"We did a little. I wanted to get back here with you. I'm still not comfortable with leaving you by yourself."

"Dad, I'm not by myself." I pointed at Warren. "See?"

Warren gave me a look like *do not bring me into this*.

Dad gave us both a look that said something totally different. I knew that look all too well. Since he already knew that Warren and I had been on vacation together, there was no doubt in my mind he also knew there had been something between us, and he didn't want any of it happening under his roof.

"Keep it PG. We'll talk about the security system later." He patted Warren on the shoulder as he walked away.

"Yes, sir," I said, biting into my lip to keep from smiling.

"What was that all about? Keep it PG?" Warren asked when we got back inside. "Do you know something I don't? Because if you do, I'm not comfortable being left in the dark."

I held in a laugh. "Fair enough. My dad knows about us. Well, some of it."

"He *what*? Did you tell him?" Warren rubbed his hands down his face. "Fuck. He is going to kill me, Kit-Kat."

"No, he's not, or he would have done it already." I placed my hands on his chest. "Just relax. Besides, I didn't tell him anything…Rowan did."

"Rowan? What the hell does she know?"

"About our vacation? Almost everything. But she's the one who called my dad that they'd set me up and reassured him I was safe because you'd be there. He was worried sick about me vacationing alone."

"Jesus Christ. So he's known this whole time?"

I shrugged. "Guess so. He hasn't said a whole lot about it, so I guess he's okay with it."

"Good to know, I guess. And speaking of the devil herself, she text you this morning." He dug his phone out of his pocket and handed it to me.

"Mind if I call her? I haven't talked to her in a few days."

"Actually, I got you something."

"Me?"

"I stopped by the store on the way here from the hospital. I'll be right back." He took off into the living room and came back a moment later with a white box. "Here," he said, holding it out to me. "This is for you."

"What's this?" I asked, reaching for the box.

"You'll see."

Reluctantly, I pulled the top off. I had a strong feeling I knew what it was. "A phone? You got me a new phone? Warren, you didn't—"

"Yeah, I know, I didn't have to. I already know what you're going to say."

"But—"

"Shh. I don't want to hear it. You need a phone since the police still have yours, and there's no telling when or if you'll get the old one back. I'm sorry it's a new number, but at least it's the latest version of the one you had."

"Thank you. This is—okay, you really shouldn't have. It's too sweet of you. I promise I'll pay you back. You know I could have just got my parents to add me to their plan, though."

"And you still can. Just have to have it transferred over whenever you're ready. But you're not paying me back. I wanted you to be able to get in touch with me or your mom and dad or your friends, whoever, anytime you want, and after talking to the police, it didn't sound like you'd be getting yours back anytime soon. Not to mention, your parents haven't been in the right frame of mind to think about it."

I handed him back his own phone.

"Take a look at it. See if you like it."

"Oh, I'm sure I will." I swiped open the one in front of me and damn near dropped the thing. Instantly, my eyes filled with tears at the sight of the wallpaper. "It's us."

He'd changed the background to a picture of us from Rowan's wedding, the one of just me and him.

"Yes, it is. Me and you. It was the only one I have of us together."

"You know, someone offered to send you a more recent pic of us, but *someone* refused."

He ran his hand through his hair. "Yeah, I— look, I know I've been a hard-ass at times, and I sincerely apologize. Consider it a defense mechanism."

Woah, now we were getting somewhere. Warren, the man who kept himself locked up like Fort Knox, was going to open up to me. I placed my hand on his chest. "A defense mechanism for what?"

He stepped into my touch, wrapping an arm around my waist. "A lot of things, but mostly because at the time, I didn't want to get too attached to you. I knew it would be easier to walk away from you if I kept my distance. My only goal was to do everything in my power to uphold my end of our bargain but still do just enough to push you away so you wouldn't think of me as anything more than just a temporary companion with a mutual end goal."

My heart sank. Warren had been deliberately trying to push me away? I'd always thought it deep down. Hearing it out loud stung. "That explains so much."

"I'm sorry, Kit-Kat. I really am. I wish I'd had more time to think things through, but you caught me off guard."

He lightly brushed his hand through my hair.

"I wasn't expecting you to be there or ever be such a major part of my life. It was a back-and-forth battle on what I wanted to do and what I felt needed to be done for you. Regardless, you're here now, in my arms, and I don't want to let you go."

I leaned into his embrace. "Do you feel that way about me now? Conflicted?"

"Absolutely not. Quite the opposite. I've never been so sure of someone in my life."

"I guess you don't know this, but it wouldn't have mattered what you did, it was already too late for me."

He tipped my chin up to face him. "Kit-Kat, you have no idea." His gaze locked in on mine. "I have no doubt in my mind it's entirely too soon for this—for us—but I—" He paused and cleared his throat. "I just cannot risk losing you or letting you go again."

I nodded. "I understand. I do." Because I didn't want to lose him either. Lord knew we had a lot to sort out in the meantime, like where to go from here.

He bent down and gently placed his lips on mine. My entire body felt like it was about to combust with just that one simple connection. His tongue swept into my mouth, causing me to let out a moan. I closed my eyes, melting into him, a motion that had become all too easy to do.

As difficult as it was to pull away from him, I just knew one of my folks was going to come waltzing in the house any minute. "Hmm. Not here, not now."

He backed up, putting some space between us. "I hate when you're right. Oh, by the way, if you don't like that background, you can change it to something else if you want to," he said with a cocky smirk.

"Are you crazy? I'm not changing it. It's perfect. Thank you, so much…for everything."

He pulled me back into his chest and kissed the top of my head. "You're welcome. Anything I can do for you, I will. Now, go sit down. Call Rowan. She already has your new number."

With my new phone in hand, I went into the living room and settled on the couch. I tried calling Rowan, but she didn't answer. She was probably busy with their new baby, so I sent her a text instead. I never did get the chance to see her or the baby while I was in the hospital. They'd left before I woke up.

Warren joined me a minute later and sat down beside me. "No answer?"

"Nah. I just texted her. She'll get back whenever she can. Thank you, again. Seriously, you don't know how much this means to me."

"You're very welcome."

"I haven't had a new phone in so long, I don't know if I can remember any of my passwords." There were so many accounts and apps I hadn't seen or logged in to in over two weeks. A part of me felt like I'd missed everything, then some part of me felt like I'd missed nothing. Everything I wanted was right beside me.

"Actually, the police advised not logging in to anything. They have full access to your phone and are using it for their investigation. Just use this one to make necessary phone calls and texts. Chloe's and your dad's numbers are already in there too."

"You're probably right, but what about yours? I still don't know your phone number." Seeing as the one and only time I'd ever seen his was when he'd texted me right before…I hated even thinking about it.

He grinned. "It's there too."

I opened the contact app and laughed.

Yup. There it was. His name, well, what I assumed was his name at the very top of the contact list. He'd put his number in as My Babe with a pink heart at the front and end of the nickname he'd given himself.

"That's creative."

He shrugged. "It was the best I could come up with. I figured Mr. Personality was too obvious."

I gave his arm a shove. "Hey, speaking of texts, what did that text say that you sent me?"

He looked at me, confused. "Which one?"

"I think you know which one. The first and only one you ever sent me."

"I thought you read it? That's why I thought you didn't respond."

"No. I didn't get the chance. I barely glanced at the first few words before I was hit."

"Well, shit, Katie. I didn't know. Here, you can read it now." He handed me his phone with the message pulled up. "I've got nothing to hide."

I started to read it out loud, and then my voice faded as I finished reading it silently to myself.

Warren: I'm sorry to bother you, I know we had an agreement, but I couldn't wait until I saw you again.

Warren: I knew the monument I walked in on you in the bathtub, you were it for me. My end game. I actually knew that the first time we met.

Warren: It's not easy telling someone you just met that you want them to be your forever. Okay, it's creepy. But I'm not sorry.

Warren: If you don't respond, then I'll know how you feel about me, and it's not the same way I feel about you. I'll never bother you again. Otherwise, let's not wait anymore than we already have.

I handed Warren back his phone. "Um, wow. I don't know what to say." Warren had all but professed his love, or at least very strong like for me in a string of text messages.

"Keep in mind," he said, as I finished reading, "that I'd had a few drinks…some liquid courage, if you will, before I sent it."

"So you drunk texted me? That explains the typos. Did you mean any of it?"

His head jerked back. "Are you serious? Of course I did. I meant every word. But I know me, and sober, sensible me never would have had the balls to tell you any of that, not yet. Even with the liquid courage, it took everything I had to hit Send. So when you didn't respond…" He paused and stared down at his phone. "Naturally, I assumed you were done with me."

"Oh. I'm sorry…" My voice trailed off. Now I felt like the asshole. Not that there was anything I could have even done about it.

"I—I just want—" He reached over and grabbed my hand, giving it a squeeze. *Spit it out already. Damn it, you just what?* The suspense killed me.

"Katie? Are y'all in here?" My mother's voice rang out as she busted through the back door.

Warren withdrew his hand and stood up, distancing himself from me.

I wanted to scream. "We're kind of—"

"Yes, ma'am. We're in here."

She rounded the corner with a plate full of cookies in her arms and a huge smile on her face. "My dear, I know how much you loved Brantley's cookies, and I wish we had time to make you more, but I swiped these up from Dave's wife, Mel. She made them this morning. It's the next best thing."

He reached for a cookie, and she shoved the whole tray at him. "Oh, um, thank you?"

"You're welcome." She patted him on his stomach. "You could stand to gain a few pounds."

"Mom!" I begged to differ. I was quite fond of his well-defined abs that he'd clearly worked hard to maintain.

"Hush, Katie. Now come." She grabbed Warren by the arm. "Let's get you a nice big glass of milk to wash a few of those down."

He looked back at me over his shoulder, mouthing the word *sorry* as my mom practically dragged him away from me.

My phone rang just in time, Rowan's name popping up on the screen. "Saved by the bell."

"I hope you like your phone," he called out.

"I love it. I really do," I shouted back to him. And I swear if I didn't know any better, I'd started falling for him too.

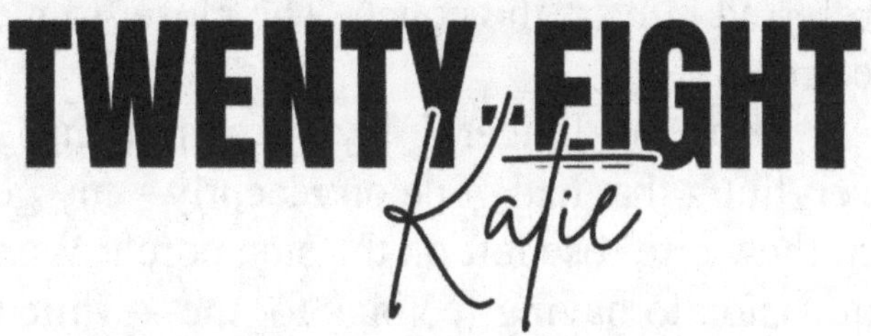

TWENTY-EIGHT
Katie

Later that night, I tossed and turned in my bed—a bed that I'd had since friggin' high school. Somehow the mattress had held up well through the years, not that it had ever seen a whole lot of action, or any, but it was still soft and plush and flat-out comfortable. It felt like home.

But tonight? Tonight everything was off, and my bed just wasn't working for me at all. I'd been lying here for…I checked the time on my new phone. *Two hours*? I moaned into my pillow out of pent-up frustration. It was long after everyone else had called it a night, and I was still wide-awake.

My parents were, I assumed, sound asleep in their bedroom next door; Warren was asleep on the couch, acting as our personal security system. Mom had agreed to let him sleep on the couch one more night, but that was mainly because she wanted to finish cleaning up the camper to her standards and refill it with fresh water before she would let him move back out there for the duration of his stay—however long that was. Fine by me. I

215

preferred him on the couch. The closer to me, the better.

But the longer I lay here thinking about everything that had gone on recently—my getting hit, the white rose left on the side porch, Warren's admission to having feelings for me—while all of that had my mind reeling, I was beginning to wonder that maybe Warren's constant presence might be part of my problem too. Every time I was around him, all I wanted to do was rip his clothes off him.

It had been way too long.

I let out a huff and threw back the covers. "Just go out there, you big chickenshit," I said quietly to myself. It was the best pep talk I could come up with at the moment, seeing as it was after two in the morning, and my mind and body were restless. The unrelenting throbbing between my legs only got worse the more time that passed that I'd spent thinking of him.

I sent up a silent *thank you* to Shayla for clearing me during PT.

Trying not to make my old metal bed frame squeak, I slowly rolled out of bed and quietly tiptoed to my bedroom door. I turned the knob, then held my breath and listened.

Silence.

Convinced it was safe, I cracked the door and peeked out. The house was dark and quiet; the coast seemed clear. I slunk out the door, closing it behind me. That way, if either of my parents did get up, they'd think I was still in my room asleep.

I padded down the hallway toward the living room, grateful my mom had picked out sound-muffling carpet when they'd renovated the house a few years ago. When I made it to the couch, I peeked over the back. Warren was sound asleep. *So much for security—ha!* He looked so peaceful, though, with his eyes closed, arm thrown over his head. Lord knew he needed the rest. But that didn't stop me from making my move to wake him up.

I slowly made my way around the couch and end table until I was just a few inches away and knelt down beside him. His breathing was soft and even between his barely parted lips. He had at least a week's worth of stubble growing on his face.

I reached out and placed my hand on his exposed bare chest.

"Warren," I whispered. I started to feel bad for trying to wake him up, but deep down, I needed him—for a lot of different reasons. I'd find out soon enough which need he was willing to fill.

I shoved down the butterflies that fluttered in my stomach as he stirred awake.

"Warren, wake up."

His eyes shot open, and he jerked back, causing me to almost lose my balance. He reached out and caught me. "K-Katie, shit. What's going on? What's wrong?" He propped himself up on his elbow, ready to spring into action.

"Shh." I placed my finger over his mouth. "Nothing's wrong. Everything's fine," I whispered, trying not to laugh.

He lay back and rubbed his hands down his face. "You scared the ever-loving shit out of me." His voice was soft, sleepy, seductive, and instantly had me wet.

I smiled at him in the dark. "Sorry. I can't sleep. Mind if I join you?"

"You serious?"

"Well, yeah. Can I just lie here with you for a while?"

"What about your parents?"

"They're asleep. Please?"

He thought for a minute before caving in. "Of course." He lifted the blanket and scooted to the back of the couch, turning on his side, making room and inviting me to lie beside him.

I stood up to join him.

"Katie, where are all of your clothes?"

"What?" I looked down at myself. I had on a thin cotton tank top and a pair of panties. I thought that was enough, at least for sleeping. Like he even had room to talk. He was shirtless, himself, wearing only a pair of gray sweatpants that left absolutely nothing to the imagination.

"People aren't supposed to sleep in *clothes*. I don't usually wear this much, but seeing as I live with my parents *and* there's a strange man sleeping on the couch, this was the best I could do." I pointed at him. "You're one to talk."

He huffed. "Fine. Hurry up and get in here already. I'm losing heat. Your dad has the thermostat set on arctic for some reason."

"He always does."

I crawled up on the couch and stretched out beside him. He tucked one arm under my head and pulled the blanket down over both of us while I snuggled into him, my back pressing against his front. He draped his other arm over me and pulled me close.

"Thank you," I said to him, snuggling into him.

"You're very welcome. Now go to sleep."

Famous. Last. Words.

TWENTY-NINE
Warren

Fighting Katie off fully clothed was one thing; now here she was, pressed firmly against my body from head to toe with hardly a stitch of fabric as a barrier between us. It took every ounce of energy I had in my soul and a whole lot of thoughts about baseball to fight off the voice in my other head, telling me all the dirty things I wanted to do to her right then and there.

This battle was about to turn into a full-on war.

She'd come to me because she couldn't sleep. Now, she was settled between my arms, dead weight leaned back against me. My eyes were wide open.

I wrapped my arm around her on top of the blanket because I knew if I held her underneath of it, it was game-fucking-over.

I let out a long, held-in breath. Katie stirred, readjusting herself. *Fuck. Stop moving*, I wanted to tell her. Then I felt her hand on my hip, just above the elastic waistband of my pants. "Katie,"

I said, my voice low, as a warning. "What are you doing?"

She inched back even further as if that were even possible, nestling her ass into my crotch. "Just trying to get comfortable. That's all."

Oh, the hell that's all this is. I squeezed my arm around her, resisting the urge to grind my hips into her ass but hoping she'd catch my hint all the same—or at least sense my resistance as I fought to control myself. There was no way in hell she didn't feel what she'd done to me. My dick was as hard as granite, as I did everything in my power to keep myself from drilling into her.

"Katie…you're playing with fire."

She slipped her hand down the front of my pants, grabbed my rock-hard dick, and gave it a firm squeeze.

Fuck. I'd never been more grateful to not be wearing boxers at the moment. It was one less layer between us, even though every ounce of common sense told me I needed to stop her. We did not need to do this right here, right now.

"What if I want to get burned?"

Annnd down came my defenses. I was sunk. Finished. Motherfucking done.

I kissed her shoulder, then her neck, licking first, then lightly sucking her skin before and after each kiss and swipe of my tongue. She moaned softly, holding back her own sounds of pleasure, trying not to be heard. As I kissed her neck, I slid my hand under the covers, down the back of her cotton panties, and splayed my hand across her bare ass cheek. Her hand pumped up and down my dick agonizingly slowly from base to tip.

My breath caught in the back of my throat with her every move. "Stop me, Katie," I said as I pressed my cock into her hand.

"I—I can't."

I inched my hand further down her ass, the tips of my fingers touching between her scorching hot thighs. "Tell me," I said, sucking on her earlobe, then kissing her behind her ear. "Tell me you don't want this—that we really need to stop."

She breathed softly. "I can't tell you that. I want you, Warren. I want this." Then she pushed back into my hand, and my finger grazed her dripping wet pussy from behind.

"Fucking A," I hissed. She clutched my dick in a death grip as her thumb rolled across the head, glossing it over with precum. My fingers slid easily over her wetness before I slipped my middle finger inside of her and then another, pushing both of them all the way in.

"God damn it, Katie. We should stop," I said, rolling my hips back and forth into her hand that was steadily jacking me off.

"No, Warren. Please keep going. I need you so much."

That was all she needed to say. There was no way I was going to waste another second.

"God, you're so fucking wet." I retreated my fingers and tugged her shorts down. "Hold on," I whispered in her ear. "And be quiet."

She nodded.

I removed her hand from around my dick and placed it on the couch in front of her. Then I pulled my own pants down around my thighs, grabbed myself, and teased between her legs, covering my length with her wetness. She was soaked. I gripped the back of her thigh, urging her leg forward to spread her apart, opening her up to me. Then I pressed the head of my dick against her slick entrance, and as she arched her back, I lunged forward. "Jesus Christ."

"Warren. Fuck. Me."

"Gladly." I lifted her thighs apart even more and sunk as far and deep inside of her as I could from the side. Sliding in and out, at a leisurely pace, teasing her—and myself. It was agonizing and the hottest fucking sex I had ever had.

She grabbed my hand and dragged it under her shirt to cup her breast. I squeezed and rolled her nipple between my fingers, gently pulling and tugging on it.

"Imagine," I said into her ear, "if that was my mouth wrapped around this tight nipple."

"Hmm. Yes." She moaned, rocking her hips into me as I gave a strong push forward into her, careful not to knock her off the edge of the couch.

Lyndsay Marie

As we slow-fucked on her parents' couch, right there in their living room, I heard the creaking of a door opening. "Shit, someone's up."

"What? No! Shit! We're going to get caught."

"Shh. No we're not. Relax," I reassured her.

She straightened her body out, flush with mine, and ducked her head underneath the covers as I pulled the blanket up around my neck.

"Don't move," I whispered in her ear.

A soft light came on in the kitchen, illuminating the living room. Thankfully, the couch faced away, and we were blocked by the back of the couch. I was still rock hard, firmly anchored inside of Katie's tight pussy. It had been way too fucking long, and I was not about to stop now.

My next move wasn't the smartest thing I'd ever done, but we were already in too deep to stop now. I slid my hand down her stomach and grazed my fingertips over her clit. She squirmed as I pressed against her, moving in firm, tiny circles. My dick twitched inside of her. Then I started moving again, slowly, dragging myself almost all of the way out, then pushing in as far as I could, all while massaging her clit.

Running water sounded and then stopped. A few moments later, the light went off, and a door closed in the distance with a soft click.

Katie stuck her head out from under the covers. "Ohmigod. That was so close. *I'm* so close."

"We're about to change that." Gripping both of her hips, I flipped her onto her stomach, planting her facedown into the couch, never pulling out of her. I grabbed the arm of the couch with one hand for support and held on to her hip with my other hand for leverage, slightly raising her ass into the air. With one foot on the floor, my other on the couch, I sunk my dick down into her as far as I could until her ass touched my thighs. Even that wasn't enough for her, apparently. She arched her back, raising her hips even higher; it felt like an invitation to go deeper.

Yes, ma'am. RSVP accepted.

I rocked back on my knees and pulled her ass into the air, giving me full, unrestricted access to every inch of her. We started at a slow pace, and the only sounds in the room were her soft moans as she released them into the couch cushion, her wetness on my dick as I slid in and out of her.

"I'm sorry, Katie. I can't take it anymore." Our pace had been slow and steady for long enough. "I need to come."

My tempo quickened as I began pounding into her relentlessly, my hips crashing into her ass cheeks with every thrust. It didn't matter at that point who was around or if her dad walked in and caught me in the act of drilling my cock into his baby girl from behind.

I held her by the hips firmly, putting her on full display. Her pussy felt like heaven and fire. I couldn't help thinking of what it would have felt like to be buried balls-deep in her tight ass. That thought alone had me moving faster and harder, sending me over the edge.

"You have a beautiful ass," I said with a ragged breath. "Maybe one day I'll fuck it too, but I need you to come, Kit-Kat. Like *now*."

I leaned down and reached between her legs, rubbing her clit hard and fast. She felt fucking amazing, and nothing would stop me now. Her muffled cries and moans were music to my ears as her pussy clamped down around me. I slammed into her one more time, holding myself upright as my dick pulsated inside of her. The room spun. I held my breath while spilling my long-withheld release into her.

Eventually, Katie's body slumped as she relaxed, taking me down with her. I cradled her in my arms and held her in the same position we'd started when she had first woken me up. As she lay nestled in my arms, I brushed her long, disheveled hair to the side and softly kissed her neck. Our time together this go round felt surreal. That this had all been a dream, and I would wake up at any minute, alone. The more time I spent with her, the less and less I ever wanted to be without her. But at this very moment, it wasn't worth one of her parents walking in on us together, not yet, and definitely not like this.

"Warren?"

"Hmm?"

"Can I ask you a question?"

I gently massaged the back of her neck and tops of her shoulders. "Of course, anything."

She softly moaned while my hand explored her body, from her neck to her shoulder, down her back to her hip, this time over her clothes. "Think we could go for round two?"

I let out a soft laugh and nuzzled into her neck. "As much as I would love that, I think it's time for you to go back to bed."

As the next few days went by, we all kind of fell into a comfortable and easy routine. It were as if Warren belonged here.

Every morning, Mom woke up first and made everyone breakfast. I was next. Once I'd gotten myself somewhat presentable, I'd go outside to the camper to grab Warren, if he hadn't already made his way inside—because Mom had finally made him go sleep out there. *Bummer.* Otherwise, he was already awake and ready for the day, sitting at the small dining table, working on his laptop. Dad was usually last to the table but not necessarily the last one awake. If he did get up early, sometimes before the rest of us, he'd lock himself in his office until it was time to eat.

Once we wrapped up breakfast, Dad either disappeared into his office or out in the shed, aka his man cave. I caught up on some reading— sometimes a magazine, sometimes the news. I even worked in a few chapters from one of my favorite romance novels here and there. My favorite part of all of it had been my time with

Warren. Sometimes he stayed out in the camper for a few hours working remotely. Other times he came inside with me, and we watched a movie or caught up on the local news. When the weather allowed, we walked around the park where Rowan and I had conditioned ourselves for the half marathon we ran in Vegas.

At one point, Warren and my dad worked together to install a temporary security system. The guy my dad had originally wanted to install the camera system had been booked up solid for at least the next two weeks. In the meantime, he'd given us these little motion alarms to put on the windows and doors. It wasn't very high-tech, but without Warren sleeping on the couch anymore, something had been better than nothing.

I thoroughly enjoyed having Warren around day in and day out, watching him interact with my parents, our neighbors on occasion, all of his futile efforts to help my mom with various chores around the house, in addition to us being able to relax on the couch until my mom kicked him back out to the camper. That was my least favorite part of our day. But he didn't argue with her about it; he just went.

"Katie? Warren? I'm calling it an early night. I've got to meet up with Mona for brunch tomorrow morning and do some planning with the garden club," my mom called out as she entered the living room. She stopped in the doorway. "What on earth are you two watching?"

"*Yellowstone*. It's a—"

"It's graphic and lewd is what it is. My word, I don't know how you can watch such filth."

I cut my eyes to Warren, who'd been sitting across from me on the other end of the sectional. He glanced back at me and subtly shook his head, mouthing the word *shh*.

I paused the show and turned off the TV. "Fine. We'll finish it tomorrow after you leave." Though, in her defense, she had walked in on Rip and Beth going at it pretty hot and heavy. The whole scene had me riled up and ready to go, that was for sure.

Warren stood up first. He smoothed his hand down the front of his pants. Apparently, that scene had done the same thing to him.

"You're right, Mrs. McDonald. It is rather *lewd*." He looked back at me with a smirk.

I stuck my tongue out at him. *Suck-up*.

"Now," she continued, "if you need anything at all, just text Katie, let her know. She can bring it to you."

"Yes, ma'am, she can. I think I'll be okay for the night. Thank you for everything."

I got up and stood beside Warren. "I'm sure he'll be fine, Mother." I grabbed his arm and pushed him toward the door.

Mom pulled her robe tighter around her, staring at us, waiting. She wasn't going to leave us alone until he went outside and the house had been locked up tight.

"Good night, Warren," I said, attempting to hide my disappointment.

He gave a curt nod. No hug, no kiss, no subtle graze of his hand against mine. Then he opened the door and disappeared into the night. I locked the door and set the alarm.

"I've really enjoyed having your friend around here. He's been really helpful."

"Yes he has," I said in agreeance. Her reference to Warren as my *friend* made me cringe a little. Maybe she didn't notice him the way I did. Then again, we'd tried our best to try to hide any overly friendly actions toward each other. My best guess was once she found out about us, then that would be the end of that. She'd make him stay somewhere else.

"And seems to be a true gentleman."

"Yup, that too." My chest burned as I held in a laugh that threatened to bust out. Yes, Warren was a gentleman, but she wouldn't be saying that if she knew what he'd done to me on her precious, custom high-end sofa the other night.

"Well, I'm calling it a night. It's been quite the day. Good night."

"Night, Mom." I followed behind her down the hall, veering off into my own room, locking myself inside.

I clicked off the bedside lamp and crawled into bed.

As soon as I tucked myself in, I pulled up Warren's and my text conversation. The bright glow of my phone screen lit up my bedroom in the dark. Seeing his name, along with all of our text messages, had me grinning from ear to ear. One of the most recent ones being pics from our vacation that I'd sent to him, specifically the one of us together.

How was it I could miss someone already, someone who was barely a hundred feet away and hadn't been out of sight more than ten minutes?

Insanity. That had to be it. Surely it hadn't been because I lo—no way, not that fast. I did not love Warren Miller. Did I? I mean, *could I*? Shit.

The thought had crossed my mind over the last few days to tell him how I felt about him, tell him that my feelings for him were strong. Even more so than before. But love? He absolutely would have agreed that I was insane if I told him that.

As much as I'd wanted to have that talk with him, another part of me—that voice of doubt that clung to the back of my mind—told me to just keep my mouth shut. *Don't scare him off. It's too soon.* Regardless of what he'd already told me about how he felt. *Don't get your heart stepped on again, Katie. It's not ready.* He was just here to help out for a while, keep me safe, then we'd return to our old, normal, and boring lives when the time was right.

Damn it, I missed him—a lot. Okay, his dick too. Especially now, just thinking about him and our time together. Something about tonight had felt different. Maybe it was watching Rip and Beth, or the memory of our own romp on the couch, but I wanted him, like, yesterday.

I tapped out a quick text.

Me: Come inside. I'm ready for a repeat.

His reply was instant.

My Babe: The house or you?

Me: Both. That show has me worked up. I need you.

My Babe: Me too, but is that a good idea? Your mom just went to bed.

I rolled my eyes. Of course it was a terrible idea. That didn't stop me from wanting him.

Me: Fine. I'll touch myself, instead.

My Babe: Naughty. You wouldn't…would you?

Me: If necessary. I'd rather it be you, but it wouldn't be the first time I've had to take care of business without you.

My Babe: You drive a hard bargain, Kit-Kat…and make it very, very hard…to say no.

Me: Prove it.

My Babe: Pics?

Me: In person. I'll disable the alarm system.

I quickly snuck out of my room, practically ran down the hall, and disabled the alarm on the back door. I bolted back to my bedroom and jumped back into bed.

My Babe: We almost got caught last time. You need the alarm on. Come out here.

I would have considered his offer, but I knew if we did anything in that camper, we'd rock it right off its wheels. Then the whole damned neighborhood would know Daddy's little girl was getting banged by the stranger from out of town.

Me: Ever sent a one-handed text? I'm about to.

I slipped my hand under the covers, then beneath my pajama shorts. I bit into my bottom lip as my finger grazed over my clit, sliding across my wetness and further between my legs.

Three little dots danced on the screen.

My Babe: You wouldn't.

Me: Finger number two. Hmm.

Fuck. Okay, enough games. I really needed Warren to get his ass in the house. Like yesterday. I rubbed myself up and down, in and out, slowly, as I waited for him to cave. I even debated on just using my toy I had stashed away.

Pressure built up fast at the thought of my hand being his.

My Babe: God damn it. Disable the alarm.

My hand with the phone in it trembled as I responded with my thumb using the swipe text feature.

Me: Already off. I'm so close.

Lyndsay Marie

I knew my parents were asleep. I'd heard my dad snoring when I snuck out to turn off the alarm.

My Babe: Give me two minutes. I need to wrap up this email. Do not finish without me.

Me: No promises.

I set my phone on my nightstand and debated hard on finishing myself off. It wouldn't take more than the two minutes it was going to take him to sneak in, but I needed to be out there waiting for Warren. Deciding to stop where I was, I cleaned myself up, snapped a quick tit pic and sent it to him, and told him I'd meet him on the couch.

A few minutes passed before I slipped quietly out of my bedroom, heading toward our meeting spot to anxiously wait for Warren.

The house was dead silent, except for the neighbor's dog, who barked in the distance, probably at Warren sneaking around out back. My heart raced with anticipation. It was like we were teenagers trying not to get caught doing something wrong.

"Stupid-ass dog," I whispered to myself in the dark.

Note to self: buy dog treats to toss over the fence next time.

I sat down on the couch, sinking just low enough where I could see the hallway and have a clear shot of the back door but could easily duck down if need be.

A shuffling in the kitchen caught my attention. I shot straight up, peeking over the back. At first, I didn't see anyone as I glanced around, my eyes still adjusting to the darkness. It was damned near as pitch-black inside as it was outside, except for a slight bit of moonlight coming through the small window above the kitchen sink.

A tall, stocky figure appeared from the shadows. "Daddy?" I said softly. "Dad, what are you—"

He was pressed against the wall on the far side of the dining room, across from the back door. "Shh." He waved his arm in a *get out of here* motion. "Go back to your room," he whisper-yelled.

"Wha—why?" My eyes darted between my dad and a tall, dark figure approaching the back door. I looked back at my dad. That's when I saw it—the gun in his hand, held up close to his chest.

He'd taken years of gun and safety classes—we all had. So he knew when, how, and where to shoot in self-defense.

The doorknob turned, and the back door slowly swung open.

Lyndsay Marie

I started to launch myself over the back of the couch, screaming at the top of my lungs for him to stop. *No! No, no, no, no, no.*

But it was too late.

A single shot rang out as the man stepped over the threshold. His body fell forward, dropping to the floor.

THIRTY-ONE

Katie

I held my hands over my head and cried uncontrollably.

I didn't know if the words that left my mouth even made any sense, I couldn't hear them over the deafening sound of the gun firing still ringing in my ears.

A man had been shot in my parents' kitchen. Thankfully, it was a single gunshot wound to the shoulder—a warning shot. Or as my dad would have referred to it, just a flesh wound.

Justin was going to be okay, eventually, but it was gut-wrenching to watch unfold, regardless.

Warren wrapped his arms tightly around me and pulled me into his lap. He held on to me, as paramedics loaded Justin onto a gurney and wheeled him out the kitchen door.

"It's going to be okay, Kit-Kat. I've got you."

I sniffled and choked back more tears. "I— I thought that was y—you. Ohmigod, I thought— I really thought my dad killed you."

More tears sprang free as the dam busted wide open at just how close Warren could have been to losing his life tonight. He knew it, I knew it, we all knew it.

All in the name of getting laid.

I felt like such an asshole. But how could we have known? We couldn't.

There was no way to know that Justin had been lurking around the backyard waiting for just the right moment to make his next move—whatever that was.

"I know. I know," Warren reassured me. "That was really fucking close. So close I don't even want to think about it. But I'm still here, unharmed, and you're safe. It's over." He pulled me back and wiped the tears from my cheeks as more fell in their place. "We need to leave. We all do. Let's at least get your mom and go somewhere. Police are going to want to keep your dad for a while questioning. I'll get us a hotel, but we don't to stay here while the police finish doing their job."

I nodded in agreeance. "Okay…okay. Let's go."

He stood up from the couch, leaving me temporarily cold and empty at his absence, to go find one of my parents.

With my back to the room, I listened intently to all of the commotion, trying to hear what was going on behind me. I could barely make heads or tails of any of it as conversations ran together. One sound that had stuck out as it got closer was Warren's deep voice over all the noise.

I angled my ear to hear better what he was saying. The only words I made out were "dad" and "died."

I covered my mouth. *His dad died*? When?

After what had felt like forever, he returned. "She's not coming with us."

"What? Why not?" I went to stand up in defense but quickly sat back down, remembering what was going on behind me. The thought alone had my stomach rolling. "What did she say? And what did you say about your dad?"

He sucked in a deep breath through his nose and blew it out. "Your mom is going to stay in their RV tonight, and for me to take you away from here. Just let her know where we end up."

"Okay, but you didn't answer my question, Warren."

"We'll talk later."

He knew I needed peace and quiet; we both did. We needed to be far and away from anyone who might provoke conversation neither of us wanted to have.

"Fine. Let's just go wait outside. Please."

He helped me to my feet. "We'll go out through the front door. That way, you don't have to see anything else. I think you've already seen enough."

"What about a statement? Aren't they going to want one from me?"

"Eventually." He tucked me under his arm, shielding my face from our surroundings. Every light in the house had been turned on, on top of the massive floodlights the detectives had brought into the kitchen, dining, and living room.

He held me close as we made our way out into the front yard. The entire neighborhood had been taken over by fire trucks, EMS, law enforcement—houses, trees, and cars were washed in red and blue flashing lights. Both ends of the street had been blocked off with police cars and crime scene tape. Every neighbor on the block stood outside in their pajamas, curiously watching, talking amongst each other to get the latest scoop, probably coming up with their own theories about what had just happened.

We were all eventually taken downtown to the police station to give our statements. I'd never been, personally, much less in the back of a cop car, but I'd driven by the place a million times.

After hours of statements and questioning, a written statement, and me repeating my story at least five more times, they'd finally let me go.

I found Warren half asleep in a chair in the lobby, arms folded over his chest, feet kicked out in front of him crossed at the ankles.

"Have you seen my mom yet?" I asked as I approached.

"No. I think she's waiting to see what happens with your dad."

I didn't want to leave her, but I knew she wouldn't leave without him. Hanging around any longer than I already had did me no good. "I'll just text her then. You ready?"

"More than you know." He stood up and wrapped his arm around me. "Let's get the fuck out of here. This place is like a zoo."

We made our way outside and to his rental car parked in the visitor lot. The sun had already started to rise over downtown.

He helped me into the car, then collapsed into the driver's seat. "Any particular place you want to go?"

"As far away from here as possible."

"Say less." He put the car in drive, and we were out of there.

Life as I'd known it slowly faded into the sunrise behind me—behind us.

Warren reached over and took my hand in his. "I promised you, Katie, that I wouldn't let anything happen to you ever again, and I meant it. I would have taken that bullet myself if I knew it meant you were safe."

I reclined the heated leather seat and turned toward him, curling my legs underneath me. "I'm glad you didn't. I hope you never have to either. And Warren?"

"Yes, Kit-Kat?"

Lyndsay Marie

"I don't want you to go home."

He kissed the back of my hand as we stopped at a red light. "Something else I'm going to promise you right here, right now: I'm not going anywhere without you, not now, not ever again."

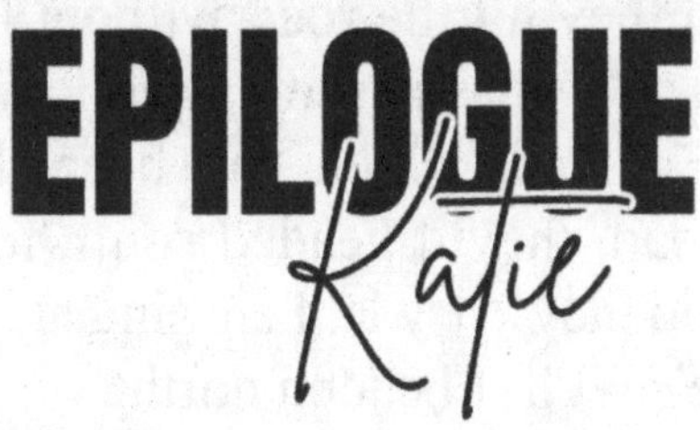

EPILOGUE
Katie

Case closed.

Two simple words. I'd never felt so much relief as I did when I heard them.

After that night my father did what he had to do to defend his family, we never looked back.

None of us did. We didn't have to.

When Warren vowed to protect me at all costs, and when he'd said he wasn't going anywhere without me then or in the future? He'd meant it.

I left behind my parents' house, the house and hometown I'd grown up in—the only life I'd ever known—all in the rearview mirror.

My dad was eventually let go and found innocent on grounds of self-defense, as we knew he would be. My parents soon thereafter hired a moving company to pack up everything they and I owned within those four walls and loaded it into two different storage containers and had my stuff shipped to me.

Once the investigation came to an official close, Dad hooked the trailer up to the back of his truck, and they hit the road without looking back either. They'd missed seeing the leaves changing in New England, which had been their original plan. Instead, they'd headed south for the rest of winter, said they'd try leaf chasing again next year.

Me? Well, I headed north.

Far north.

After Warren and I left the jail that morning, he drove us until sleep took over and he couldn't drive anymore, which had landed us just on the north side of St. Louis. In a bold and brazen move, he called my mom at almost seven in the morning and told her he was taking me home with him, in more words or less, and that she and my dad were welcome to visit anytime they wanted to. I almost passed out when he told her that. I'd later found out Warren had already talked to both of my parents about it before we had ever left town.

Warren had finally opened up about his father's situation. While Van Buren hadn't passed on that night that I'd overheard Warren talking about him—I'd misunderstood—he did clarify that Wes had called him just before he was on his way to sneak inside. Their dad had taken his last turn in life just before transitioning over, according to the hospice nurse. She advised any family that wanted to be present to get home ASAP. Warren wanted to get there in time, and he did.

As far as me, there was no court, no ruling. Nothing else had needed to be done on my end, according to the lead investigator. Justin would be released from the hospital and straight to 201 Poplar to serve time.

I did learn that during the initial investigation, police had pulled camera footage from a Ring doorbell on the neighbor's house across the street. While they couldn't without a doubt identify the person on the camera, they did have a man lurking around the house on several different occasions, a few times trying to get into the camper. He could be seen crawling underneath of it, which we all knew was when the wires had been cut. The other time, he was the one who'd not only been caught peering through the window into the kitchen but had done it several times before. He'd also left that ugly white rose on the porch step. Then he tripped over my mother's flowerpot while running away. I'd never been more grateful for having a neighbor who video recorded his flowerbeds to catch plant thieves.

Another person had eventually come forward from the day I'd been hit. She had a dash cam and had caught my accident on her camera. They were able to compare her video with others they'd had from different angles, as well as the ones my neighbor had collected, and without a doubt verify it was all the same person.

Lyndsay Marie

My ex.

The police eventually offered to return my phone, but I told them to keep it, trash it, whatever. I'd already moved on with my new one and had gotten used to my new number. They did advise I change all of my passwords, which I'd already started doing after the shooting. Officer Parker told me next time I fell in love, keep my passwords to myself. Little did he know, I'd already done one of those things.

I'd had no idea that for years, at the very least three, Justin had been remotely accessing my phone and everything on it, just by having my passwords—every app, text message, email. All. Of. It. They'd said Justin had been escalating with his stalking, because apparently, he'd been following me around for a while. He knew my next move before I even had a chance to pull out of the driveway. Not to mention, every private text I'd ever exchanged between Rowan or Chloe and myself, or the three of us in group chat—all our girl talk about Warren, our vacation, the sex? Justin could read every damned bit of it. Then he used it against me for his own sick pleasure.

He'd once told me while we were together, *If I can't have you, nobody else will either.*

Apparently he'd meant it.

As for everything else that had gone on in my life over the past year? Well, let's just say,

Katie Michelle Miller has a really nice ring to it, similar to the one on my left hand.

I would equate my love life to the predictive text of a Magic 8 Ball. "Reply hazy, try again". "Don't count on it". "Outlook not so good". Unfortunately, Magic 8 Balls didn't predict the future. And neither did I. Which was why I never could have guessed in a million years just how accurately my life would end up relating to those fortune-telling phrases. I only wished that Magic 8 Ball could have told me a few months ago that what I thought was going to be a very sweet and heart-felt birthday speech given by my ex, Derrick, as he stood front and center of my favorite restaurant, surround by our closest friends, would turn out to be a dumping of epic proportions. And that he was going to lovingly follow up his speech with one big fat but—and not the kind of butt that Sir Mix-a-Lot rapped about. 'Cause at that moment, I would have gladly taken him putting on an impromptu karaoke session to "Baby Got Back" over what he did to me any day.

My head spun and my ears rang with the highest-pitched noise I'd ever heard as he spoke into the mic. The only important thing I remembered from his entire spewing of bullshit was "Sorry Chlo, this just isn't working for me anymore. I need to find myself." I didn't even have time to react—I like launch myself across the table and beat his ass down.

But, boy, did that asshole find himself, all right. Smack-dab in between the legs of Jensen, my best friend's cousin. Okay, so I didn't have hard proof of that, but given her track record, and apparently his, dinner wasn't the only thing he ate that night.

Such is life, I guess. As pissed off as I was at myself for not seeing his red flags sooner, after all the years of my life I'd wasted with him, I knew I still had time to find *the one*. Eventually. Maybe. But not today. And definitely not by the morning. Nope. What was left of my alone time was going to be about rest and relaxation and scouting out a one and done. Mama needed to be given a big O by a big C.

No sooner had I closed my eyes and lain back on the lounge chair, adult beverage in hand, trying to block out the thoughts about my piece of dog shit ex, than the double doors across the room busted wide open with an explosive echo. My eyes flew open as a huge group of people with at least eight kids and counting came barreling in—all yelling and running in circles, some jumping straight into the pool.

Fan-fucking-tastic. So much for rest and relaxation.

Time to move on to plan B—the spa, which was fine by me. I needed a massage, and I'd already planned on getting one at some point anyway. This just pushed things ahead of schedule. So, I pulled up the hotel's website up on my phone, and the first damned thing on their homepage was a notice in bold red letters that they were "Temporarily closed for maintenance. Sorry for the inconvenience."

"Of fucking course," I mumbled quietly to myself. It looked more and more like my time would be spent in the suite…alone. Just me, Netflix on the big screen, and room service dropping off enough fried food for two. One plate for me, another for my feelings—not because I was literally eating for two people.

In the meantime, I popped in my earbuds and set my music playlist to something upbeat. The first song that played was CeeLo's, "Fuck You." How appropriate. A soft *ding* interrupted the song, alerting me of a new text message. I checked my phone. It was Tanner asking me how my day was going and if I was still enjoying my trip.

Ah, Tanner. We'd only been out on our first date prior to my leaving for Vegas, but he seemed like an okay guy. Sweet, gentleman-like, and completely dumbfounded by who he'd agreed to go on a date with. Me. He'd agreed to a blind date through a mutual friend and probably regretted it but didn't wanna piss off the crazy lady, so he'd kept in touch since then. I had to hand it to him, he'd been a trooper during my *slight* breakdown when I witnessed Derrick out with Jensen while we he and I were out on our date. We did make it through the rest of dinner, but then he'd dropped me off at home without so much as a hug or a handshake.

I sighed as more folks steadily trickled in, filling up the pool area—families with kids of all ages and a group of young girls who appeared barely old enough to drink and entirely too mature for their age. A crowd from the local senior citizens' center filed in behind them. *Who opened the flood gates?* Any thoughts I'd had of having the pool somewhat to myself went up in smoke.

A woman with her hair in a disheveled ponytail and dark circles under her eyes headed straight toward me. She had beach bag stuffed to the brim hanging off one shoulder with pool noodles sticking out of the top, a small child in her other arm, propped up on her hip, a second kid clinging to her leg, and a third one running literal circles around her.

I paused my music as she approached because I just knew she was going to talk to me.

"Hi," she said, all smiles and positive attitude as she glared at my cup, probably dreaming of her kid-free days. Personally, I couldn't imagine having that many kids and not staying completely shit faced. "Sorry to bug you, because you look really comfortable, but do you mind if we sit here?" She tipped her chin towards the table and chairs just on the other side of the empty lounge chair beside me acting as a barricade between me and the war zone.

Lyndsay Marie

"There's no more open tables. We kind of have a big group and need the space."

Clearly, I was not going to catch a fucking break today. "No, of course not," I said with a slightly forced smile, mostly out of pity because I felt sorry for her. "Not at all. Be my guest." As if I were really going to tell her to take her circus and go sit somewhere else. I wasn't *that* mean. I thought it, I didn't say it.

"Thank you," she mouthed as she peeled kids off her limbs and plunked herself and her pool paraphernalia down on the table.

I pulled my bottle of pink champagne out of my bag and refilled my cup practically to the brim, then gulped too much of it in one sitting, way too fast. If there'd been fewer people around, I would have just drunk it straight from the bottle. Then again, all these people were my reason for wanting to get a little tipsy.

Unpausing and turning the volume up on my music, I scanned the room, and—*helllloo, hottie. Where did you come from?* Just when I'd thought there was no hope, the afternoon showed a sign of improving. Not that it was going bad, but my goal of getting laid and having every stupid and ridiculous thought of Derrick fucked out of me started looking more and more promising.

I watched the sexy man across the pool, with dirty-blond hair, tanned, muscular arms bulging out of his white T-shirt sleeves, and brightly colored Hawaiian swimming trunks, as he peeled his shirt off over his head, exposing hell of a lot more tanned skin and muscle that flexed with his every move. My face flushed with heat. It could've been the champagne, but I wanted to give all credit to the stud himself.

One hundred percent, without a doubt, he was the man I wanted to sink my teeth into later…because that was exactly my mission tonight.

Then, as if right on cue—because story of my life—interrupting my inappropriate and wandering thoughts, the music faded out as my earbud dinged again with another text notification.

Keep reading book three here—
https://www.amazon.com /dp/B0CJ4F34LR

www.AuthorLyndsayMarie.com

Visit me on Amazon —
https://www.amazon.com/author/lyndsaymarie

www.ingramcontent.com/pod-product-compliance
Lightning Source LLC
Chambersburg PA
CBHW011144100726

47899CB00010B/3161